BRAY

LIGHTHOUSE SECURITY INVESTIGATION

MARYANN JORDAN

Maryann Jordan

USA TODAY BESTSELLING AUTHOR

Cover: Graphics by Stacy

ISBN ebook: 978-1-947214-88-0

ISBN print: 978-1-947214-89-7

❀ Created with Vellum

"Are you kidding me? You must be because there's no way you're serious about this, Cory!"

Marie Brighton drummed her fingers on her kitchen counter, livid, and had no problem letting her brother know it.

"Look, sis, I—"

"You just have to stick your nose into what I'm doing? Think you can manage me like you do your agents?"

"No, that's not it at all. I just think—"

"You think what? That I can't get on a train by myself? That I can't travel by myself? Good God, Cory! I'm a thirty-two-year-old professional woman. I hardly think that I need you to make that kind of decision for me!"

"If you'd let me finish, Marie, I'll tell you why I did what I did."

She pinched her lips together and closed her eyes. She loved her brother, but at this moment, he was seriously overstepping his bounds. Standing in her furnished, short-lease apartment in Seattle, she'd sent the movers on their way with her personal belongings, heading back to the east coast for her next job in Boston. Tomorrow, she and another doctor from the practice she'd been interning with were driving to Vancouver for a week-long conference. Then she was traveling on a luxury train from Vancouver to Montreal before driving to Boston.

An exclusive train trip through the Canadian Rocky Mountains was a dream vacation she'd saved for, and she wasn't about to pass up the opportunity. And her overprotective brother was going to ruin it all. "Fine, talk, Cory, but I can assure you that I'm still going to be angry with you when you're done!"

"The Carboni case."

Marie's chin jerked back slightly. "Huh?" Plopping down on the sofa, she flopped back onto the cushions and stared at the ceiling. "Okay... I'm listening."

"The Carboni case that you testified in last year when you were in Philly. He made threats against anyone involved in the case."

"Oh, good grief, Cory. He was a petty criminal who had visions of being a big mob guy. I only testified about the abuse to his daughter when he grabbed her and broke her arm, and I was one of three doctors that testified. That's it. He was tossing around threats just to sound big and bad. But that was months ago, so don't pretend that's the reason you want me *accompanied* now."

"Okay, maybe so, but I don't want to take a chance. So, just deal with it, sis. Someone will contact you."

"Cory, I don't want my vacation ruined by some no-neck man in an ill-fitting suit hovering over me. I've paid a fortune for the luxury rail trip so that I can relax, take in the sights, and just enjoy my own company for a week. Is that too much to ask?"

"What about your latest condition?" he pushed.

"I'm a doctor, or have you forgotten? I think I can be trusted to take my medication."

"Marie, you'll be traveling through the Canadian Rocky Mountains, and you've never been very adventurous."

"I'll be on a train, not hiking or camping!"

"Mom, Dad, and I just worry," he said, pulling out the big guns to make her capitulate.

Sitting up, she sucked in a deep breath, willing her irritation to slow. *He is my brother, after all. He cares... he's just maybe a bit overprotective.* She rubbed her forehead. "Look, Cory, it's not that I don't appreciate everything you've done for me, but seriously, I've got this. I'll be fine. It'll be a boring trip by myself, but I'm used to my own company. I'll take lots of pictures to show you when I get back east."

"Marie..." This time, his growl held a warning tone.

"Tell you what, brother dear... you find a bodyguard that is movie-star gorgeous, smart, well-read, fills out a pair of jeans in a way that makes me do a double take, and can kiss in a way that'll make me weak in the knees. Then I'll agree."

Disconnecting before he said anything else, she

stood and walked to the window overlooking Seattle. Living there had been fun, and she'd learned a lot at the children's clinic where she worked. But she was ready for her next adventure and didn't mind taking it alone. Ready to say goodbye to Seattle, she turned from the window and smiled. *For once, I got the last word in with Cory.* Her smile slowly dropped from her face. There was no way Cory could find someone to fit her description. *Pity, though. I'd have loved to have someone like that to share my adventure. Someone like that in my life.*

*A dollhouse and a military bunker. Together. Fuckin'
brilliant.*

Allan Bray had watched the sun rise over the coast
of Maine as he drove down the lane and parked to the
side of the older house. He sat for a moment, staring up
at the monstrosity in front of him. His perusal
concluded with one part awe and one part disbelief—
and a huge grin.

The large, pale blue Victorian house nestled in the
tall pines sitting back from the rocky coast resembled a
dollhouse his sister used to have when they were kids. A
wraparound porch on one side. A three-story turret on
the other. A circular window was in the attic room on
the front. Staggered rectangular windows moved up the
side. The heavy, ornate wooden double front doors
didn't fit with the rest of the house, looking as though
the previous owners had purloined them from an old
church before fitting them into the space.

It hadn't surprised him to find out the house had sat

on the market for a long time before a buyer came along. It also didn't surprise him who the buyer was.

Climbing down from his truck, he jogged around the house through the dewy grass that needed mowing and down the concrete stairs at the back of the property. The area resembled a small outdoor amphitheater with sprigs of tall grass gone to seed rising from some of the cracks in the concrete. Overgrown shrubs and vines crept over the top and along the sides.

Moving down the final steps and around to the side, he came to a door located in what would have been the back of the 'stage', and while it retained the appearance of age, he knew it was new reinforced steel.

Finding the keypad, he waited until the door swung open and then entered the lit concrete hall. Turning at the end, he stepped into one of the rooms that had been restored. His gaze scanned the concrete room now containing several desks and tables, all loaded with computer equipment. "Damn, man, you know this is fuckin' crazy, right?"

Josh looked up from his computer screen and grinned like a kid in a candy shop with his whole allowance to spend. "It is, isn't it?"

"And Mace wants to use it at times?"

"Hell, yeah. He gave me full access to add what I need here as a backup for the Lighthouse compound."

The two men were sitting in one of the abandoned World War II concrete bunkers that dotted the coast of Maine. And Josh, their security firm's computer guru, had bought a house with one in his backyard. He'd slowly been cleaning the space and reinforcing it with the help of the others who worked at Lighthouse Security Investigations, known as Keepers.

"Well, as much as I'd like to stay, we've got to get going," Bray reminded Josh. "Mace may let you use the bunker for an expansion of LSI, but he'll want us on time for the morning meeting."

It only took another moment for Josh to set the security for the computers and the room. Then, as they walked out of the bunker, Bray watched as Josh engaged the overall security system. They climbed into Bray's truck, and with a three-point turn, headed back out of the driveway.

Five minutes later, they turned into the entrance of Lighthouse Security Investigations' headquarters, located in one of the many decommissioned lighthouses that dotted the coast. In truth, Josh's house was just around the peninsula coastline from the LSI compound, easily within running distance. But since Mace had hinted that Bray would have a new assignment today, he preferred to have his truck close by.

He'd woken that morning with a strange foreboding, wondering if it had anything to do with work. *Work? More like a dream job.* For a has-been Special Forces medic, he considered himself lucky to have received the call several years ago from Mason Hanover.

Mace had been in the Special Forces before becoming a CIA operative, working with a multi-task force. Recreating that experience when he got out, he offered invitations to ten others he'd considered worthy to start his security business, nine men and one woman. Bray was humbled to be considered one of the best of the best that Mace gathered around him. Now that Mace had established the business he'd wanted, he was in the process of expanding.

Like Josh's new bunker computer enclave, the LSI compound was fucking amazing. The gorgeous view from the whitewashed, red-roofed house located at the base of the lighthouse with caverns located deep underneath sure as hell beat going into an office every day.

He preferred to get to work early, but with Josh's SUV not starting, he'd agreed to pick up his fellow Keeper, knowing full well that Josh would have lost track of time. *And now that he had a bunker to play in, Josh really had an excuse to be late.*

Stepping inside the LSI house, Bray moved through the large kitchen, surprised that Marge and Horace Tiddle, the two caretakers for the compound, were not in their usual early morning positions. Unless Horace had an early duty to perform, he was found sitting at the kitchen table, a cup of coffee and the newspaper laid out in front of him while Marge fixed huge biscuit sandwiches for someone to take downstairs for the Keepers. But this morning, the kitchen was empty.

Glancing behind at Josh, who merely shrugged, he led the way through the multilayered security systems that Mace had incorporated, taking the elevator down to the cavernous main room of the compound.

As he took the first step into the room, he was assaulted with cries of 'Happy Birthday!' and rocked back a foot, blinking in surprise. Birthdays were usually celebrated with a trip to Moose's bar, plus, his birthday was not for several days. Josh clapped him on the back and moved ahead of him into the room, a shit-eating grin on his face.

"You fucker." Bray shook his head. "Your truck is fine, isn't it?"

"Had to make you late somehow," Josh laughed.

He looked toward the others grinning at him and once again shook his head. From the mouthwatering scents coming from the counter on the side where the industrial-sized coffee maker always sat, it appeared that Marge had outdone herself with breakfast.

Babs bounced over, her dark hair with neon blue tips gliding about her shoulders. "Happy birthday early, Bray." She lifted on her toes and kissed his cheek before being snagged about the waist and pulled back by Drew, who leaned over, kissed his wife's neck, then grinned at Bray.

Sylvie, Mace's wife and LSI office manager, squeezed his arm as she walked by. "Since it's your birthday celebration, you'd better get to the front of the line, or Marge's breakfast treats will soon be decimated."

Knowing she was right, he figured his fellow Keepers would only give him a few seconds to make up his mind to get to the food first, and considering he'd only had a piece of toast for breakfast at his house before going to get Josh, he definitely wanted some of Marge's treats.

It didn't take long for everyone to be seated around the large table that sat in the middle of the room.

"We'll buy you a drink at Moose's," Rank called out. "You know the women don't want to be left out."

He nodded, and it was not lost on him that so many of his friends and coworkers had found love, each one of them through various missions. And every one of them fit in well with being the mate to a Keeper, including the desire to see everyone as happy as themselves. Even Mace, their taciturn leader, had met Sylvie when he protected her and her son.

"So, what do I owe this early birthday surprise to?" he finally asked, pushing his empty plate back.

"Got a mission for you that'll take about a week. When Sylvie was making arrangements, she realized you'd miss your birthday here, so she wanted to make sure you had a chance to celebrate."

Walker, sitting next to him, clapped him on the back. "Plus, we didn't want to turn down Marge's breakfast."

Pretending to stare at Walker's stomach, he asked, "Man, how does Julie feel about that gut of yours?"

"Fu— Shut up, Bray." Walker patted his middle. "Abs of steel, man. Julie loves my abs of steel."

The others laughed, and the good-natured ribbing continued. Finally, Marge and Horace walked over, wished him a happy early birthday as well, then left the main compound room to go back upstairs, leaving the rest of the group to their meeting.

"So, what do you have for me?" he asked, turning his attention back to Mace.

He was intrigued when he saw Mace hesitate, the inaction something he'd never seen from their boss before.

"Had a conversation with Cory Brighton, currently the Executive Assistant Director of the FBI's Criminal and Services Branch. Former Special Forces. We served together at one time. Good guy, best there is. And he's a friend of mine. He's got a request; actually, a *personal* special request."

Curious, Bray turned slightly in his chair, his head cocked to the side. LSI took missions that included basic security and investigations and often government contracts. It would not be that much of a stretch to imagine a high-up at the FBI had a request.

"His sister, Dr. Marie Brighton, is attending a week-long conference in Vancouver, Canada. She's been living in Seattle for the past six months and drove to the conference with another doctor. She's moving to Boston and is taking a charter train back through Canada to enjoy the trip more."

"Okay…" He drew the word out, still not understanding the mission.

Mace continued, "She doesn't fly. Ever." Mace scrubbed his hand over his face. "Marie was in a helicopter accident many years ago as it was landing. Damn blade broke, flipped the bird over. She was injured. The pilot was killed. She was only fourteen at the time. So, according to Cory, she never flies."

Nodding, he asked, "Is there a specific threat to Dr. Brighton?"

"This is where the personal request comes in. There's no specific threat although, when she was practicing in Philadelphia, she had to testify in the child abuse trial of a low-level mob boss. At the time, he made threats against anyone who testified. Nothing came of it, but because of Cory's high-profile job with the FBI, he's come under some threats due to the investigations of the same mob. There have been no more threats toward her, but this is where the special request comes in. He'd prefer she be accompanied by someone trained in security while on this trip. He feels sure that it will probably turn out to be a vacation more than a security job but asked if anyone on my team has medical experience. That falls to you, Bray."

His gaze hit Mace's, and he tilted his head to the side. "Medical?"

"She was recently diagnosed with a medical condition. He admits the family is overly nervous where she's concerned but has asked for our assistance, and while a security escort with no imminent threat isn't normally a job we would take on—"

"No, no," Bray waved away his boss' concerns. "It's fine. Just accompany the doctor on a train ride through Canada, making sure she gets to Boston. Hell, I'm ready for a simple mission."

Mace squeezed the back of his neck, hesitation in his manner.

"Is there more, boss?"

Mace cast his gaze through the gathering before nodding slowly. "We used to call Cory 'The Psychic.' Sounds like voodoo shit, but he'd get a sixth sense about things. We learned quickly to listen to him."

"And you're saying that he has a bad feeling about his sister's trip?" As Mace continued to nod, Bray said, "Well, all right. I go and make sure to neutralize any problems."

"Plus, you haven't had a vacation in a while," Sylvie

added with a smile. "While this isn't a vacation per se, at least it should be relaxing. I've already looked at the luxury charter train. It's first-class all the way."

"Damn, sounds great. So, I leave tomorrow?"

Mace nodded. "All the info is on your tablet. We are investigating the small passenger roster as well as the employees although they change often. We'll continue to update you on what we find."

"Sounds good."

"You can make preparations today and fly to Vancouver tomorrow." He hesitated again before continuing. "Oh, and one more thing. Cory warned us that while he's told her what he's doing, she's not happy with having someone watching her. He admitted that he and their parents were always overprotective, and she chafes at the idea of someone tagging along. I told him that you'd be just a fellow traveler to everyone else."

He nodded, wondering what cover he'd need to use for anyone else on the trip who might ask. Grinning, he figured he could pull out the ubiquitous 'businessman.' *Hell, that'll cover just about anything.*

He zoned out of the rest of the meeting, including what plans Mace and Josh had for the WWII bunker, more interested in his vacation mission. Clicking on his tablet, he stared at the travel itinerary. A five-day train trip across Canada with first-class accommodations… hell, this could be a dream mission.

Continuing to scan through the file on his tablet, he came to Marie Brighton's photograph. Dark hair pulled back severely away from her face. Bright purple glasses surrounding green eyes. Average height and petite build. Pretty smile. Attractive, but not his type. *That's not true... I don't really have a type.* It was easy while in the Army to not look for relationships, so his *type* was less discriminating as long as they were looking for the same thing he was, which was physical, fun, and all emotions checked at the door. Now that he was out of the military, he wasn't opposed to a relationship based on friendship and mutual need, but unlike his friends who became involved with someone while on a mission, he wasn't seeking a life partner. He liked his freedom. He liked going where he wanted when he wanted. He liked waking up by himself... *especially if woken by the fuckin' dreams of my last operation.*

Shaking off that last thought, he shot his gaze around as though the others could hear what was inside his head. He breathed easier seeing everyone busy with their own assignments.

Sylvie looked over and smiled. "I've got you booked into the Pinnacle Downtown Hotel, king room, city view. And it will be next to Dr. Brighton's room."

He laughed, knowing someone just got their room reservations bumped so that he'd be that close.

"And she's traveling on an overnight rail. The five-day trip from Vancouver to Toronto is on a private rail reserved for charters. It consists of a couple of sleeper cars, a lounge car, an observation car, and a private dining car. Only a few other people had reservations, and guess what? You do, too!" She offered him a mock expression of surprise, complete with full, wide eyes and a big grin.

"Sylvie, you're amazing." Bray winked, loving the

idea of a private, first-class, chartered rail trip. Looking back down, he continued perusing Marie's information.

Cory and Marie's father had been a state senator of Pennsylvania at the time of the accident, therefore newspaper articles documented the helicopter crash. She had been traveling back from a political event by herself, her family coming later. The helicopter was landing at the airport when a mechanical malfunction sent it crashing the last twenty feet to the ground.

Marie had been in a coma and then endured multiple surgeries and a long rehabilitation that lasted most of her adolescence for a shattered leg. *Damn. Her nightmares might rival my own.* Her father retired from politics soon after, settling back into his law career.

A brilliant student, Marie managed to graduate from high school on time despite long hospital stays. Finished her undergraduate program in only three years, then four years of medical school in Philadelphia. Then she switched to a Doctorate Program in Physiotherapy. And the past five years, she'd worked in a large pediatric medical center in Philadelphia although she'd spent the past six months working in Seattle under a nationally acclaimed orthopedist. *Physical Therapist?* He could imagine the amount of physical therapy she'd had while recuperating.

According to her brother, she was moving back east. Her belongings had been shipped to Boston and the train would be her vacation before starting at a new clinic. Continuing further, he read her brother's notes about her health. Hyperthyroidism disease. He knew it was an immune disorder... *Thyroid*. But other than that, he needed to do some research.

Standing, he walked over to the bank of computers where Josh had set up his station, the newest Keeper, John, sitting with him. John was still learning the ropes and this week was tasked with familiarizing himself with Josh's security systems.

Taking a seat at one of the stations, he began scouring what he could find out about Hyperthyroidism. *Predominantly affects women. Onset is usually under the age of forty. Tremor. Heat sensitivity. Weight loss. Rapid heart rate. Fatigue. Might be in concert with other autoimmune diseases. Medication is necessary. Surgery is a possible outcome.*

According to her brother, she was only on medication. So, as long as she didn't become stressed, took her medication regularly, ate well, and slept well, it looked like Marie Brighton would have a safe train trip across Canada. *And I'll have an easy mission.*

3

The lights of Vancouver greeted Bray as he landed the next evening with the use of a private chartered airplane that only made two stops. As the taxi arrived at the Pinnacle Hotel, he glanced up at the glass and chrome skyscraper. Once inside the hotel, he welcomed entering his room. The king-size bed faced a wall of windows overlooking the Vancouver skyline. After taking in the scenery, he stretched out on his back on top of the bed, allowing the thick comforter to cradle his body as he attempted to relax the travel kinks from his back.

After years in the Special Forces where he'd slept on the floor, on the ground, on rocks, he found that all it took was a firm mattress covered with a thick comforter and it was a battle to keep his eyes open. Like right now.

Lifting his arm, he looked at his watch and knew the conference attendees would have finished their last session and probably be at dinner. According to her brother's notes, Marie wouldn't plan on shutting down the bar. In fact, she rarely drank alcohol. *So, she'll probably return to her room after dinner.*

He climbed from the bed and called LSI. "Hey, John, sounds like you got hit with the new-guy evening shift."

"Yeah, me and Rick are hanging here. Part of the newbie routine. Everything okay there?"

"Yep. I need you to check into the hotel's restaurant security cameras and see if you can find Dr. Brighton."

"Already done. We clocked her from the time she left the conference. She went back to her room, then down to the restaurant about an hour ago."

"Good. I'm ordering room service. Ping me when she leaves the restaurant and is on her way back up."

"Got it. In fact, Josh showed us how to send the security feed to your phone."

"Perfect. Do that, and I'll buy you a beer when I'm back."

Disconnecting, he settled at the table near the windows and pulled up the security feed on his phone, grinning at Josh's ingenuity. He could see Marie sitting at a table with several others in the hotel restaurant.

A knock on the door indicated his dinner had arrived. Tipping well, he opened the tray lid, sniffing appreciatively. He'd ordered his steak rare, knowing the sitting time would make it more medium-rare. *Perfect.* Fully loaded baked potato. Broccoli. And a slice of chocolate cake.

His father always liked the rich, complicated food that his stepmother insisted on having prepared, but Bray was happy with basic meat and potatoes. Sitting down at the table near the expanse of windows, he dug in with gusto. Not the best he'd ever had, but then, for room service, it was good. That was another thing that he enjoyed after his time in the service: a decent meal.

While eating, he kept his eye on the phone screen. Marie ate her dinner, appearing to enjoy conversation with her dinner companions. The others had wine and dessert but she declined. He watched her sign her receipt and offer her goodbyes. As she walked out, he stood and moved to his door. It only took a few minutes until the sound of the elevator reaching the floor met his ears. Opening his door, he stepped out, giving her plenty of time to see him at a distance so that she wouldn't feel crowded, but her head was down as she walked along the hall. *She's oblivious to her surroundings!*

Her dark hair was no longer pulled back severely but floated in waves that hung just below her shoulders. Under the lights in the hallway, the tresses glistened. Dressed simply in dark slacks with dark flats, it was now evident that she walked with a faint limp. Her royal-blue blouse showed her porcelain complexion off to perfection, and just as he suspected, her height put her almost a head shorter than him.

"Dr. Brighton?" he said to draw her attention before she ran right into him.

She jumped backward, wobbling before regaining her balance. Her green-eyed gaze shot upward to his face, and her hand landed over her chest before she smiled widely. "Oh, my, I'm sorry. I wasn't looking where I was going. Not that I'd be able to run you down or anything. I'm more likely to have bounced off you and landed on my ass in the middle of the floor."

He blinked at her response. Instead of registering suspicion, her smile was open and friendly. A sense of déjà vu slammed into him, and he jolted at a long-forgotten memory. When he was a little boy, his grand-mother used to read Italian fairy tales to him from a large picture book with a pretty, green-eyed, dark-haired princess on the cover. While his grandmother read, he would stare at the front cover until his eyes grew heavy.

Cocking her head to the side, she said, "I'm sorry, I can't remember your name. There were so many people at the conference."

Shaking his head slightly to dislodge the childhood remembrance, he affixed a smile on his face. Getting back to business, he lifted his hand, offering his identifi-cation. "I'm Allan Bray. I'm from Lighthouse Security. I believe your brother told you that I would be traveling with you on your way across Canada."

A small gasp left her lungs, and her eyes widened as they moved over him from head to toe then back, seeming to halt on his lips. Female perusal wasn't unusual, and while a blush hit her cheeks, he had no idea of her thoughts. Her smile faltered as she cocked her head to the side, her gaze penetrating as she studied his identification before moving back up to his face. Expecting purple glasses, he was surprised to see her in bright blue glasses that matched her blouse. So focused on her eyes, he almost missed when she began to speak.

"You're kidding, right? No way are you what you say you are."

His body jerked, uncertain of her meaning. "Dr. Brighton, I assure you, I am with Lighthouse Security. But please, call your brother for confirmation."

Reaching into her small purse, she whipped out her phone, punching only one button, indicating she had Cory on speed dial. "Cory, I've just met the person you hired. Very funny! I didn't know you had it in you to play a practical joke!"

He watched as she listened to her brother, her brow lowering as their conversation continued.

"Allan Bray from Lighthouse Security. Yes, he's standing right here. Oh… okay." She turned her green eyes toward him and said, "I need to take your picture."

Nodding, he smiled. "No problem."

She snapped his picture and then hit a few more buttons, continually shifting her gaze between her phone and him. Dialing again, she said, "Did you get the picture, Cory? That's him? The person you hired to protect me from the imaginary threat?" She glanced up at Bray again and then turned slightly, lowering her voice. "Really? I swear, only you, brother dear, could come up with someone like this. Fine, fine. I'll play nice. Love you, too."

Shoving her phone into her pocket, she faced him squarely. "Well, Mr. Bray, it seems you are exactly who you say you are. I thought you might have attended the conference." She pursed her lips together, her nose wrinkling slightly. "My brother had told me someone would be coming along, even though I let him know that I don't need a babysitter."

"I'm not here to babysit, Dr. Brighton—"

She threw her hands up and turned, pacing to the other side of the hall before turning and coming back, stopping right in front of him and peering up once again. "I'm perfectly capable of traveling by myself. Cory worries too much. I swear, if he and my parents could put me in bubble wrap, they would." Her eyes flashed, appearing even greener if possible. "I fear, Mr. Bray, that I have no intention of having someone hover when I'm trying to experience the beauty of Canada. So far, all I've seen is this hotel, and while nice, I can't say that I've experienced much. I'm so hoping the train ride will fulfill those desires." Her lips now curved slightly as she closed her eyes. "Snow-capped mountains. Green valleys. Bridges over rivers. Deer. Elk. Eagles. Maybe even a bear." She appeared lost in her imaginings when suddenly she popped her eyes open. Shaking her head, she said, "Good night, Mr. Bray," then stepped to the side, starting to walk around him.

He whirled around to keep her close. "Dr. Brighton, your brother has concerns that stem from many angles and just wants to ensure your safe travels."

Her shoulders snapped back as she jerked to a halt, her attention snapping up to his face. "Many angles? Is this about him? Is Cory in danger?"

Bray carefully observed the change in her demeanor, evidence she was concerned for her brother, and he hastened to offer assurances. "As far as I know, he's in no more danger than any person in a position of national authority."

She remained in place, her perusal steady, her gaze holding as she appeared to weigh his words. Lifting her chin slightly, it hit him that even if she was looking upward toward him, he had the feeling she was used to being in charge. It was a bit disconcerting, but he was hit with embarrassment, realizing that most women he met gave in quickly, wanting him to be in charge, whether clients needing security or women he dated.

"You seem distracted."

Her words cut through his thoughts and he blinked, realizing this was twice after just meeting her that his mind had wandered. He jerked back to the matter at hand: getting Dr. Brighton to work with him and not against him in his mission to provide a security escort. "No, Dr. Brighton, I assure you, I am fully aware of what I need to be doing." As the words left his mouth, he prayed the tips of his ears didn't turn red. There was something about her already *reading* him that reminded him of the nuns at the elementary school he attended. Although, she looked nothing like the Sisters.

Her hand lifted to smooth her already-in-place hair. "I know none of this is your fault." A heavy sigh left her lips. "I did tell my brother that I wanted a leisurely trip. A vacation before starting at the Boston clinic. And, please, call me Marie. The doctor label feels stuffy, especially after the conference. Doctor, doctor, doctor." She rolled her eyes.

Without skipping a beat, he jumped into the tiny breach she opened. "Then, Marie, let's consider ourselves traveling companions. I haven't had a vacation in a long time, and this can be enjoyable for both of us. I'd like to see Canada by train, also."

Still standing in the hall, her lips tightened as she appeared to ponder his words. "I suppose that would work. And I'm sorry you haven't had a vacation recently. Everyone needs to relax and do something different sometimes. Experience something new. But, please, Allan, understand... this isn't personal against you. I'm sure you're very good at your job or my brother wouldn't have hired you, but I really want to just enjoy the trip. I don't want to feel like you're hovering constantly."

"Understood." His ready acquiescence appeared to surprise her as her eyes narrowed slightly as though trying to figure him out. He fought the desire to grin, knowing she was still making up her mind about how she felt with this new twist to her travel plans. "And, please, call me Bray. Allan makes me want to look over my shoulder to see if my father is approaching."

Her lips quirked upward, and he battled the desire to pump his fist in the air. He'd never had to work so hard to get a woman to want to spend time with him. On an assignment, they were glad to have the security. On a date, he ensured they had a good time, even if the *date* was more of a pickup. But winning a small lip twitch from Marie felt like a win. "My room is next to yours. I'll say good night and look forward to seeing you in the morning."

If she was surprised that he occupied the room next to hers, she gave no outward evidence. She simply nodded, murmured 'good night,' and pulled out her key card to enter. As her door closed with the resounding click, he then heard the deadbolt turn. Nodding his approval, he walked into his room, breathing a sigh of relief. *Made contact. Came to a tentative understanding.*

The sun had set behind the other skyscrapers, and many of them were dark with only a few lights dotting the sides facing him. He pulled the wall of room-darkening curtains closed, leaving only the light next to the bed illuminating the room before heading into the bathroom for a shower. The water pounded his muscles, but instead of relaxing, his mind turned over the mission.

Marie Brighton was not what he expected, and he was rarely surprised. He knew she was intelligent but had made the assumption she would be more bookish. Instead, he not only survived her analytical gaze but there was also a light-heartedness about her that caught him off guard. She hadn't been security-conscious when walking with her head down in the middle of a hotel hallway, but now that he was on the job, he would watch out for her.

There was a mixture of qualities about her all mingled together. A bit quirky but not coy. A hard-earned smile that made the recipient feel like a winner in a contest they had no idea they'd been in. Of course, the fact that he'd read the dossier on her gave him insight beyond the few minutes spent in her presence in the hall. But those minutes were nothing like he'd expected.

She was much more beautiful in person than her photographs indicated. Her hair glistened in the lights of the hall. She was petite and slender but not excessively thin. Her curves were subtle but not emphasized in her clothing. The color of her eyes had been much more vibrant in person than in her photographs. Green. And considering she stared back at him through glasses, he knew she wasn't wearing contacts so the color was her own. Her eyes were large, but according to her brother, she didn't suffer from Graves' ophthalmopathy. He wondered if she had glasses frames in multiple colors to match her clothes.

She was dressed for comfort. Standing next to him, she was shorter than he expected, and a glance down gave proof that her shoes were flats, not simple ballet slippers or stylish loafers but sturdier shoes. He thought back to the devastating accident she'd had at the age of fourteen. Her leg and ankle had been pinned together, and even though that had been many years ago, he wondered if it still gave her pain.

His chest squeezed at the thought she might still be in pain, and he turned off the water, giving his head a shake, slinging water droplets from his hair. Stepping onto the plush bathmat, he toweled off before sliding on boxers. He faced the mirror but paid no attention to the reflection staring back, his mind still going over what he'd noticed about Marie.

Strong, more of a spitfire than he'd imagined... and yet, there was a fragility about her that called to his protective instinct.

He brushed his teeth then flipped off the light, sliding under the covers. Setting his alarm for early the next morning, he turned off the lamp, plunging the room into darkness. Pushing personal thoughts of Marie aside, he focused purely on the mission. *Spending time getting to know her so that I can ensure she's safe and healthy on the train ride. Easiest mission I've ever been assigned.*

4

The red-brick train station was much smaller than one of the main Vancouver stations. Unassuming from the outside, Bray found its basic decor to be just as utilitarian on the inside. Various kiosks were in the center selling food as well as tourist memorabilia. Plastic and metal chairs were arranged to one side, ticket agents on the other. Resembling the gates at an airport, there were families with their luggage piled onto carts, kids holding onto their toys and snacks, and harried tourists awaiting the call to board. The station was used for several economy touring rails as well as the private charter.

Approached by one of the employees in a bright red jacket, he showed his ticket. "Ah, Mr. Bray, please, follow me."

He walked past the masses and was taken down a hall toward a separate lounge where the noise from the main gates diminished to a faint murmur. Sylvie had told him that on this particular train, unlike most of the touring rails where numerous economy cars would be toward the front with the first-class cars and accommodations near the back, the private charter rail would be traveling by itself. Exclusive—but expensive. The only way the rail company could afford to offer such luxuries to a small handful of customers.

"If you'll wait here, sir, there's coffee and refreshments. I'll take your bags and get them on board where they'll be placed in your sleeper cabin. As soon as we are ready, I'll escort you to the train."

Nodding his thanks, he tipped the man before watching his luggage roll away. Keeping his briefcase with him, he stepped through the doorway, immediately immersed in more luxurious decor. Wood-paneled walls. Leather chairs and sofas. A heavy wooden table along the back wall with a coffee station, complete with china cups and saucers along with croissants on a silver tray.

But none of this mattered as he scanned the room, his gaze landing on the one person he sought. Marie. Finding her, he held his irritation in check as he walked to the back wall, poured a cup of coffee, and then made his way to where she sat, claiming the leather chair next to her.

"Good morning. I hope you rested well." Her smile was wide as she looked up at him through bright red glasses, and she twisted in her seat to set her coffee cup on the small wooden table between their chairs. Her thick hair was pulled back in a low ponytail, but today, a few wavy tendrils framed her face. A lightweight red sweater was paired with navy blue slacks, her shoes the same as last night. Her makeup was applied with a light hand, enough to play up her green eyes, and a swipe of ruby on her lips. A purse and small black carry-on case sat at her feet.

He lifted a brow at her casual greeting. "Yes, thank you, I did. But I admit it was a surprise for me to knock on your door this morning only to discover you'd already left for the station." He kept his voice low, not wanting to draw undue attention to their conversation. And, to be honest, he was furious with himself that he'd allowed his guard to drop, assuming they would travel to the station together, never imagining she'd leave the hotel by herself. A mistake he would not make again.

She opened her mouth, then shut it again quickly, her gaze moving about the room before settling on him. "I didn't realize that we were expected to travel everywhere together. That seems rather restrictive. After all, you did agree not to hover."

His voice dropped an octave. "Marie." At the deep sound of her name growled, she had the good grace to blush slightly. He kept his gaze pinned on her, and she leaned back in her seat, offering a slight huff as her shoulders fell.

Scrunching her nose, she sighed. "God, you sound just like my brother when you say my name like that. All right, Bray. I admit it. I snuck out. Let's just call it my one tiny rebellion before we're stuck on the train for the next five days."

He admired her refreshing honesty. A few security missions assumed the Keeper was there for not only protection but to carry bags and get food as well. That was one of the reasons Mace was now so careful in the contracts they accepted and the terms were clearly spelled out. But even for government contracts, some officials had expectations that were not aligned with true security. Now, looking at her guileless eyes staring up at him, it was obvious there were no expectations from her.

Nodding, he inclined his head. "I suppose we're all entitled to our little rebellions. But let's make sure that was the last one." Leaning closer, he added, "I don't want to interfere with your trip's enjoyment, Marie."

They held gazes for a moment, and he had the feeling he was under her microscope, being carefully analyzed for truthfulness. He tried not to squirm under her intense perusal. Finally, she must have decided he was sincere when she smiled and nodded. "I appreciate that. I promise to be the perfect security mission from now on."

"I don't want you to feel like a mission."

Taking another sip of her coffee, she grinned. "Traveling companion, then."

Relaxing, he took a sip of the rich brew and looked around. He'd clocked the others in the room when he'd entered but now sent his gaze over them again. He'd already researched the passengers and knew the two men at the refreshment table were cousins. So alike in looks they could be mistaken for brothers. They offered a polite nod toward him as one settled onto a leather sofa.

The other caught Marie's gaze, his smile wide. "Madam, may I get you a croissant?"

"That's very kind, but no, thank you."

Bray hid his smile behind his coffee cup as he watched the other man's face fall before walking over to sit with his cousin on the other end of the sofa while managing to keep his attention still on Marie. She ignored the men, leaning instead toward Bray as she sipped her coffee.

Returning his gaze to her, he asked, "Have you eaten this morning?"

"No, I knew they'd serve breakfast on the train this morning, so I didn't even leave my room to go down to eat."

"I'm a fan of room service, myself. I'm afraid I wasn't sure what they might have for us this morning, so I had them deliver something early."

Her mouth formed an 'O' before she smiled. "I saw the dish tray outside your door when I left. I never thought of ordering room service. I admit I was a bit jealous that I hadn't thought of that."

He smiled in return before noting the two men continued to talk but their eyes strayed over to him and Marie often.

She followed his gaze and inclined her head toward them, obviously deciding to cut through the social awkwardness. "I suppose since we're a small group that will be traveling together for the next several days, introductions are in order. I'm Marie Brighton."

The men sitting on the sofa sat up straighter and hastened to introduce themselves. "I'm Anthony Robbins. Pleased to meet you, Ms. Brighton."

The slightly heavier of the two smiled widely. "And

I'm his cousin, Theodore Robbins." They turned their gazes toward Bray.

"Allan Bray."

Without skipping a beat, Anthony's gaze roved over him, lifting a brow. "Mr. Bray, what business are you in?"

Bray immediately recognized the *'my cock is bigger than yours'* question. "I'm not." He almost chuckled at Anthony's blink. He loved offering a vague answer, giving the impression that he was independently wealthy and didn't need to work.

Theodore's head bobbed, and his smile remained in place. "That's what I'm hoping to do one day, too. Until then, we run Robbins Electronics. We're a small but up-and-coming company in Canada and hope to soon expand into the United States. Anthony's in charge of that expansion, and we've got great hopes for the future."

Bray also nodded, and the two cousins turned their attention back to Marie. He noticed they didn't ask what she did for a living, but she provided the information, nonetheless.

"I'm a doctor of pediatric physiotherapy."

"A doctor?" Theodore repeated as his eyes widened, not hiding his surprise. "I'm impressed."

Marie's brow furrowed slightly. "Impressed with what, may I ask? That I'm a doctor?"

Again, Bray had to hide his smile. While somewhat reserved, it was becoming evident Marie was no pushover.

"Forgive my cousin," Anthony said. "I'm sure he

meant no offense."

"None taken," she replied easily, a smile playing about her lips.

"No, no! Absolutely no offense. The only doctor I remember as a child was an old man who I thought was rather crotchety, and I was never sure he liked children." Theodore laughed, attempting to smooth over his social gaffe.

The door opened again, and several more people were led inside the room, receiving the same instructions. Before leaving, the station attendant announced that they would be boarding in five minutes. Another round of introductions was made, the newcomers including Gregory Manitov, an elderly couple, Beth and Maurice Hogue, and a woman elegantly attired for travel, Cherelle Vanders.

Bray's research of the passenger list before he left Maine had everyone except Gregory. Obviously a newcomer, Bray watched him carefully, knowing he would need to have LSI run a check on him. Cherelle was a Canadian actress, having snagged bit parts in a few television series. Before they had a chance to find out more about each other, the attendant came in and announced it was time to board the train. They left through a side door, bypassing the main terminal. Bray walked just behind Marie, noting Theodore immediately moved to her side. Cherelle's lips curved as they landed on him, and she walked with a purpose directly toward him. Not wanting to give the tall, well-heeled blonde a chance to lay claim, he adjusted his pace to allow him to walk next to Beth and Maurice, offering to carry one of her bags for her.

"Oh, thank you, young man. I know I should've let one of the rail workers carry it for me, but this bag has my husband's medicine in it. I wasn't sure how these things work. We don't usually travel this way, so this is all very new to us."

Maurice nodded, his smile as wide as his wife's. "This is our sixtieth wedding anniversary present! Our children and grandchildren got together and surprised us with this trip. We're getting off on the second stop at Banff."

They had walked past the two sleeper cars and the observation car and now came to the lounge car. Assisting Beth up the steps, they stepped into the luxurious lounge where he placed her bag on one of the leather sofa seats. "Congratulations on your anniversary. You should tell the attendant so that we can have a celebratory drink in your honor."

She clapped her hands as she turned and looked at her husband. "Oh, what a lovely idea."

As Beth and Maurice settled together on the sofa, he turned, noting Marie standing nearby, smiling at him. Gregory, Anthony, and Theodore were busy putting their briefcases next to other leather chairs. Theodore's eyes were still mostly on Marie while straying sideways toward Cherelle, who managed to ignore everyone other than Bray. He was reminded why LSI didn't take celebrity security contracts.

He waved to the seat next to his. "Marie? Would you do me the honor of joining me?"

"Thank you." Leaning closer, she whispered, "That was a lovely suggestion about an anniversary celebration for them." She set her case in the seat just before Cherelle managed to maneuver her way over. The glare she sent toward Marie would have singed the doctor if she had noticed. But ever since stepping onto the train, Marie's face had registered delight, much like Beth and Maurice.

He breathed a sigh of relief. It seemed that perhaps Marie's excitement over the train ride through Canada would override her desire to not have a security detail. Seeing the smile on her face, it struck him once again how lovely she was. She glowed, exuding health, another reason for him to feel relief.

"Can you believe how beautiful this is?" she asked, her gaze darting around. "As soon as I found out about the conference coinciding with my move back east, I researched ways to travel here. When I discovered the train, I was enthralled. But to see it in person, it is so much more beautiful."

He followed her example, noting the dark paneling and plush black leather and red velvet seats. Heavy, floral-print brocade curtains were pulled back, framing each window. Brass wall sconces filled the space between windows, and on the walls were framed railway paintings. "I once saw a photograph of my grandmother as a child traveling on one of the elegant, old-world European trains. This reminds me of that."

Grabbing his arm, she nodded, her eyes wide. "Yes! I was just thinking of the old trains that were built for luxury travel, not speed!"

Once everyone had been seated, a man wearing a dark jacket with red accents entered the car, his arms extended, his smile bright. "Welcome all. We are pleased to have you travel with us on one of our exclusive chartered rail excursions. I am Enrique Dupont, your lead service attendant, and will coordinate with each of you to make sure you have a lovely trip. We will be leaving the station soon. All your luggage has been placed in your sleeper cabins, and we are pleased to announce that a light breakfast will be served as soon as we are underway." With that, he moved amongst the small gathering, offering individual welcomes and taking breakfast orders.

"Dr. Brighton, we are honored to have you," Enrique said, stopping at her chair. "What may we get you for breakfast?"

"Your breakfast special looks amazing. I'd like the eggs scrambled and bacon for my protein, please. Oh, and a croissant with butter. And coffee, sweet with cream."

Bray placed his order, then turned to her as the attendant moved on to the Hogues. "I hear they have a wonderful chef on the train. That's one of the advantages of traveling this way."

"I never fly," she replied, her large green eyes holding his gaze as she leaned toward him. "I usually travel by automobile, so this is a treat." Leaning closer, she said, "Since I didn't think to have room service breakfast at the hotel, I'm famished."

He chuckled and winked. "I'll make sure you won't miss any meals while on this part of the trip."

"Just fruit and yogurt," Cherelle ordered, then looked over her shoulder toward Marie, her face set in disdain.

"I can't imagine where you put all that food!" Beth exclaimed, smiling toward Marie. "You're such a tiny thing!"

Marie blushed but simply shrugged. "It must be my metabolism."

Bray knew one of her symptoms was an increased appetite while still losing weight. Wanting to take the attention off her, he drew her into small talk until the service attendants brought in their breakfasts. He had ordered the same as Marie except for his coffee. He sipped the strong, black, flavorful brew, a little moan slipping from his lips met with one from hers at the same time.

His brows lifted at the dual sound of pleasure that immediately had him thinking of other ways to elicit that same response. He darted his gaze over to find her chuckling.

"Wow," she said, placing her cup back onto the saucer. "I gather we both like our rich coffee."

Clearing his throat, he nodded his agreement, deciding to turn his attention back to his breakfast before he embarrassed himself.

Just as they began eating, the train pulled out from the station, and Marie's gaze moved from her plate to the window, an expression of delight crossing her face. Turning to him, she said, "This is what I wanted to experience. Traveling on the ground so that I could see my surroundings but not be stuck in a car!"

Before he had a chance to reply, Beth overheard and

agreed. "Absolutely, my dear. After this experience, I might not ever want to travel any other way."

Maurice laughed. "Well, next time, we'll have to be in coach, not this first-class charter."

With breakfast over and the dishes cleared, Enrique announced that they were free to move about the cars. "If you wish to see your room, our sleeping car attendants will be happy to show you where your cabin is located. The dining room car will serve lunch at one o'clock. Dinner will be at seven o'clock. This lounge is available for your pleasure as well as the observation car with its upper deck."

Cherelle stood, her gaze landing on Bray, a smile curving her lips as she announced, "I will be shown to my cabin."

Ignoring the statuesque blonde, he turned to Marie. "Did you want to see your cabin now?"

She shook her head. "No, I think I'd rather stay and watch the view as we travel toward the mountains."

"I agree. May I suggest the observation car?"

This time, she seemed to notice the searing glare sent her way by Cherelle. "I'd love to." As they stood and walked to the front, she glanced behind them before leaning in, a smirk on her lips. "I think Ms. Vanders would prefer that you escorted her to her cabin."

He kept his gaze on Marie. "I assure you, I'm right where I want to be." With his hand lightly resting on her back, they moved into the next car and climbed the carpet-covered stairs to the observation seats. She gasped at the curved windows that reached toward the ceiling in a dome, giving them a perfect view of the vista all around. They had traveled out of the city and were already moving through thick forests as they began ascending toward the mountains.

She quickly sat, pulling out her phone for pictures, and he slid into the seat next to her. The view out the windows was spectacular, but it was the pure delight on Marie's face that captured his attention. Once again, he was struck with the same thought. *Easiest mission I've ever been assigned.*

5

Marie stared out the window at the multitude of green-hued trees gliding by and sucked in a deep breath before letting it out slowly. She felt a little foolish having just reenacted taking in the cool mountain air when, in fact, she was in an enclosed train, but the full-dome windows surrounding her gave the feel of being able to reach out and touch the scenery. And that was not the only thing she wanted to reach out and touch.

Her body was very aware of Bray sitting on the bench seat next to her. While there were many individual seats in the observation lounge, there were also small settees sprinkled about. With her attention immediately directed to the outside, she hadn't chosen the dual seat settee with the idea that he would sit next to her. But when he sat down, his large body so close, she wasn't immune to his masculine presence. *There wouldn't be a female or many males in the entire population that would be immune to Allan Bray.*

Recalling her conversation with Cory when he told

her he was arranging for someone to accompany her on the train ride for security, she'd nearly bit his head off, focusing on how much she didn't want some stranger hovering over her. She'd endured that enough as a teenager when her parents and brother were afraid she would hurt herself and again recently when she'd had her recent diagnosis. Now, with her brother's career investigating mobs, gangs, and doing his part to make sure he was successful in putting them behind bars, his protective stance increased. Of course, the ridiculous threats against anyone who had testified in the child abuse trial the previous year hadn't helped Cory's concern.

She also remembered what she'd told him at the end of their conversation. *You find one that is movie-star gorgeous, smart, well-read, fills out a pair of jeans in a way that makes me do a double take, and can kiss in a way that'll make me weak in the knees. Then I'll agree.*

Glancing to the side, she swallowed deeply. *Jesus... did Cory have to send someone so blatantly gorgeous?* She tried to remember the last time she'd had such a visceral reaction to a man she'd just met. Certainly, there had been some attractive men at the conference but no one that sent sparks through her. Of course, there were always the doctors who seemed to vie for *who's stethoscope is bigger*, a trait she found wholly unattractive. After all, if a man has to brag about the size of his *stethoscope*, he's probably overcompensating.

She'd assumed whoever Cory hired would meet her at the station and not tick one single box of her ridiculous list. Perhaps a woman in a dark suit and white blouse, the requisite FBI ensemble. One who could handle a weapon, toss a much-larger man onto the floor, and still manage to put her low-heeled black pump on his neck, all while throwing a glare toward Marie because she needed saving. Or maybe it would be the grey-haired, steely-eyed, barrel-chested former agent who reeked of don't-mess-with-me security, keeping anyone seeking interesting conversation from approaching.

Marie had endured both of those in the past. As her brother's career in the FBI had taken on more and more nationally known cases, especially with gangs of all types, threats to him were not uncommon. What unnerved him was the thought that his career could impact her. She'd tried to tell him over and over that a pediatric physical therapist who spent their day with children wouldn't be a target even after the case she testified in. Her life had settled into a routine, and she was fine with that. Not exciting, but sometimes, uneventful was all right.

Seeing Bray in the hotel hall near her door had been a surprise. The kind of surprise that made her stop in her tracks, stare at the tall, muscular gorgeousness, and wish that she could say something witty... or flirty... or direct, like *let's skip the preliminaries and just jump into bed.* When he'd said her name, she instantly assumed he'd been at the conference although, upon hindsight, there was no way she would have missed seeing *him* at the various sessions. She wasn't opposed to a conference fling; she'd had one before but couldn't remember his name... or his face if she was honest. But

Bray? She would have remembered that face for a long time.

Finding out he was there for her and the reason why made everything fly from her mind other than her irritation at Cory. But having laid in bed the previous night, knowing that her *travel companion* was in the next room, had her not only get little sleep but decide to race out to the train station alone. Being around a man like him would make it hard to ignore the person her brother hired.

Now, with Bray next to her, ignoring was the last thing she wanted to do. He was the ultimate gentleman, his leg near hers but not touching. And yet, just having him near was enough of a distraction that she had to force her gaze to stay on the expanse of glass windows.

They sat in companionable silence for several minutes. As the mountains rose before them, the edge of a waterfall was visible in the distance. As she relaxed, she allowed the beauty surrounding them to override all other thoughts. Her hand darted out, her fingers wrapping around his forearm as she pointed out the window closest to her. "Look!"

Their shoulders touched as he leaned over closer. "Magnificent," he said. His breath brushed by her ear, but then he shifted back so that their bodies were no longer touching.

The simple exchange seemed to loosen her tongue as she began to point out other sites of interest, and he did the same. "I love seeing snow-capped mountains."

"It's amazing the view we get from being on the second floor of the train," he said, leaning over again to view a small lake outside the window next to her. "The mountains are calling, and I must go."

She gasped as she whipped her head around. "John Muir? You just quoted John Muir!"

He chuckled, and she could have sworn a blush crept up his face as he admitted, "It's one of the few passages I can remember from one of his essays. I loved his work on naturalism and conservation and recently read more about him in… well, in a book on travel."

She nodded her head with enthusiasm. "Me, too. I actually read that quote a few weeks ago when I was preparing for my trip. I found myself wanting to get into the proper mindset." She smiled, then turned toward the vista again, her mind filled with Bray's ability to offer the perfect quote for the moment. Seeing movement by the water, she leaned closer to the window. "Elk! I can't believe we're seeing them so early in our trip! I know the online info about this charter train talked of the wildlife that could be seen but I thought it might be all advertising hype."

"Maybe the railway puts out fake elk by the lake just so the train riders can get excited."

His words were so serious, she jerked her head around in disbelief. "They wouldn't!" Scrunching her brow, she looked back to see the elk dip its head, drinking from the lake. A soft chuckle came from Bray. Lifting her brow, she tried to appear stern but laughed instead. "That was a mean trick. For a few seconds, I wondered if perhaps they had planted fake wildlife just to keep the passengers happy. Sort of like an amusement park ride."

He laughed fully, and the sight almost made her forget that she was here to see the sights. *The sights of nature outside... not staring at my companion.* Turning back to the window, she forced her gaze to remain on the amazing view. After a few minutes, she relaxed. "I've wanted to do this for a long time." She heard the wistfulness in her voice but was unable to stop the words from slipping out.

"Why haven't you?"

It dawned on her that he was paid to keep an eye on her and wondered if the friendly conversation was part of the deal. Shrugging, she replied, "Life, I suppose." Keeping her answer purposefully short and vague, she assumed it would suffice for their tenuous and short-lived relationship.

"How so?" he prodded.

She turned and saw interest flaring in his eyes. Still hesitating, she was surprised when he nudged her with his elbow.

"Really, Marie. I'm interested."

It struck her that the trip would be nicer with someone to share the experience with even if he was a paid security specialist. Settling deeper in the seat, her lips curved slightly. "For a long time, there was school. And then internships. And then finding a job. And then, once I had the job, it didn't feel right to take a vacation. I was the youngest doctor on the staff and single, so it was easier to just work during the summers when the other doctors wanted vacations. Then, over the holidays, they needed to be with their families, and it was easier to stay in town and continue the therapies for the children that needed continuity of services."

"My father is also in medicine so I know how demanding your field is." A slight grimace crossed his face, and she wondered the reason.

She patted his arm. "What is his specialty?"

A sigh escaped Bray's lips before he replied. "He's a cardiologist... well, cardiac surgeon, to be precise. He likes everyone to know the difference."

Surprised, her eyes widened. "I'd say his specialty is extremely demanding."

Nodding, Bray twisted slightly toward her, his face now fully in her view. "I know it is. He spent his adult years building his medical practice, and while he loves to socialize, he lets his wife arrange the many dinner parties he likes to host."

"His wife?" She blurted out the question, and immediately the heat of blush hit her cheeks. "I'm so sorry. That was an intrusive inquiry—"

"No, it's fine." He chuckled, the sound rumbling from his chest putting her at ease. "My parents divorced when I was twelve. It might sound cliché to say that it was amicable but that's how they describe it and how I remember it. My father and mother were opposites but more the type to clash than attract. He was into science, a career built on precision, and the singular dedication to making sure he's considered the best cardiac surgeon in the state. My mother loves to visit new places and writes travel books. To this day, I can never figure out how they got together."

She nodded. *God knows I've been around people like his*

father... not that they aren't brilliant medical doctors, but their life is all about the career, sometimes more the profession than the patient.

He chuckled again, and she was mesmerized by the sound and the way his dark eyes focused so intently on her face when he spoke. "They stayed together until I was twelve. There were no screaming matches, no knock-down-drag-out arguments, no nastiness. They finally just looked at each other and said, 'this isn't right.' And at the age of twelve, even though I hated the idea of my parents getting a divorce, it seemed to make sense. My father kept the large house. My mother and I moved to a smaller house in a nice neighborhood not too far away. I stayed with my dad when Mom was traveling, but when she was home, I stayed with her. On top of that, I had my two sets of grandparents around."

"I'd love to know more about your mom's travel books. If you give me her name, I can look her up."

"Caroline Bray Vane. She kept her first married name and added her second husband's name since she already had books published under Caroline Bray."

She gasped. "I've read her! I've got one of her books in my cabin right now. She has the most awesome way of adding quotes from others and blending them with her travel narratives."

Bray's smile widened, roping her in like a cowboy with a wayward steer. She leaned forward slightly, her hand landing on his thigh. *Was he for real?* Everything he said pulled her in. Every smile he offered made her long to see if kissing his grinning lips would taste as good as they looked.

Marie shook her head slowly, forcing her thoughts off his lips, still fascinated by his story. She knew many couples who had divorced, and amicable was not the word that would have described them. Plus, the fact that his parents remained involved in his life and with each other as parents was a testament to their love for him. "That's amazing, your parents have worked hard to make even their divorce work. It seems like by the time most people get divorced, they're so angry, and that singular emotion colors everything about the separation."

"My father married a woman he met at a social gathering a couple of years later, and they're much more suited for each other. She loves hosting their events, and he focuses on his practice. My mom married a man that she met on one of her trips, and they share a love of travel. He's a great guy. Actually, he's the one that went to my high school ball games."

"That's nice that you had that. My brother may drive me batty sometimes, but I know he cares. Family can mean everything, something I never want to take for granted."

He smiled, his eyes warm as he nodded.

"Mr. Bray?"

They both turned at the interruption coming from the top of the stairs to the observation deck, seeing Enrique, an ever-present smile on the attendant's face.

"May I beg to interrupt to have a word, please?"

Bray glanced back at Marie. "Excuse me, please."

"Of course."

He stood and walked toward Enrique, her eyes

following for a moment until Enrique's gaze jumped between the approaching Bray and her. Turning back around, she didn't want to appear to be eavesdropping, regardless of how curious she was.

"I'm so sorry to interrupt your enjoyment of the view, but I needed to let you know that Ms. Vanders requested a cabin exchange."

Enrique's voice was low, but Marie was still able to make out what he was saying. Brows lifted at the mention of the actress who'd made it plain with her blatant, sharp-eyed devouring that on this trip, Bray was the only person she was interested in. Marie doubted it was for his conversational skills but could barely blame the woman. Nosy, she no longer minded eavesdropping.

Bray sounded surprised. "Ms. Vanders?"

"Yes, sir. We have two sleeper cars; the last one has Ms. Vanders and passengers that are getting off early, Mr. and Mrs. Hogue. The sleeper car in front of that one is where we placed those of you that will be traveling all the way to Toronto. You, Mr. Manitov, the two Mr. Robbinses, and Ms. Brighton. In fact, when your reservation was made, I was given specific instructions that you and Ms. Brighton were to have cabins next to each other."

Not facing the two men, Marie couldn't see Bray's expression but clearly heard him say, "That's correct."

"I wanted to let you know that Ms. Vanders requested that she and Ms. Brighton exchange cabins. I told her that wasn't possible, but she wanted to insist, saying that Ms. Brighton hadn't seen her cabin yet, therefore would not know there'd been a change—"

"Absolutely not! Change them back immediately."

Marie blinked at the forcefulness of Bray's demand and battled the desire to turn around to see the exchange, having no doubt Bray would get his way.

"Oh, no, sir. We didn't make a change. I simply wanted to inform you of the situation. You and Ms. Brighton are still in the first sleeper car, your cabins next to each other. I want you to continue to enjoy the view, but I can show you to your cabins whenever you would like."

A smile moved across Marie's face but was soon followed by a sigh. As nice as it had been to hear Bray insist that he stay with her, the reason was obvious. It was his job. *I need to get a grip. I'm not a teenager all agog over the new cute guy.* She snorted. *Like I knew what that was like!* She thought of the men she'd met during the conference. Many were nice-looking and single, intelligent and hard-working. But there was no desire for even a conference fling. *Is it so wrong to wish for a spark?* There was no doubt she felt a spark with Bray, and she sighed. *I'm his mission.*

Pushing that thought down, she turned as he approached, plastering what she hoped was a pleasant smile back onto her face. "Is everything all right?"

Whatever irritation he'd expressed, his dark gaze was warm as he looked down. "Yes, no problems at all. Enrique just wanted to know when we'd like to see our cabins. I don't want to interrupt any of your time taking in the view, but I thought you might like to freshen up before lunch."

"Now is as good a time as any." Standing, she ignored his outstretched hands, clutching her purse to keep from reaching toward him. Gliding in front, she walked to the top of the stairs where Enrique waited. Nodding for him to proceed, she followed the attendant downstairs and into the first sleeper car, trying to ignore the presence of the man walking directly behind her but finding it an impossible task.

"Dr. Brighton, this is your cabin," Enrique announced as he stopped by the first door in their sleeper car. He slid open the door and waved his hand to indicate she should enter.

"Thank you, but please, call me Marie."

Bray placed his arm on hers as she was about to step inside, murmuring, "I'll go first." As he entered the room, he scanned the area, opening the bathroom door and closet.

She glanced up toward Enrique, wondering what he thought about their arrangements, but he simply maintained the polite smile on his face. *He must be used to this... people traveling with security... or overzealous boyfriends.* Before she had time to travel down that imaginary path, Bray stepped back out.

"All clear," he announced, his deep voice moving over her, making her feel safe just with his words. "I'll be just next door. We can walk to lunch together."

She heard the order, not suggestion, in his words but nodded. There was no reason to pout like a child just because Cory wanted her safe. If she had to have a companion, she certainly couldn't have picked one more attractive, and if she were honest, he was damn interesting as well.

Enrique walked away to show Bray his cabin, but Marie barely managed to wait until they left before she giggled out loud as she looked around the room. Wood-paneled walls. Plush carpet. Brass wall sconces. A bed with a luxurious brocade bedspread matching the curtains was in one corner, and while it took up much of the room, there was still enough floor space for a dresser and settee. Opening one door, she discovered a bathroom, well-appointed with a sink, toilet, and shower.

Another door opened up to a closet. Her luggage was placed on the luggage rack in the closet, and she dragged it out and was in the process of hefting it onto the bed when it was suddenly lifted from her hands. Gasping, she whirled and watched as Bray set it easily on top of the mattress.

"Oh, you scared me again!" Before she gave him a chance to speak, she bugged her eyes out and tried to whisper her excitement, which proved to be impossible, coming out as more of a squeak. "Can you believe this room? Is yours like it? It's so nice."

He grinned, hands on his hips, and looked around. "Yeah, mine's just like it."

"When I first considered a train trip, I thought I'd be stuck with just a sleeper bed that is nothing more than a couch folded out over the toilet! Did you know they had those? I think they call them sleeperettes or something like that. I watched a video. If you wake up at night and need to go to the bathroom, you have to fold your bed up just to use the toilet and then put your bed back down!"

He opened his mouth then shut it again, and she laughed. "Sorry, my patients would love that story, but I sometimes forget that adults are more discriminating."

"No, it's fine. And you're right, having to constantly move the bed to use the toilet would be a real drag. This is far superior."

Thrilled that he hadn't looked at her as though she were crazy or completely uncouth, she grinned before looking around the room once again, taking in every nuance. "You were right in your earlier description of this train being like the old European luxury cars. It's like we're on the Orient Express. But then, we'd better hope no one gets murdered."

He jerked his head around to her and scowled. "Marie, don't even joke about that!"

She shook her head, her smile widening. "Oh, Bray, no one is going to get murdered!"

6

Bray sat at the table in the dining car looking at the 'light fare' offered and wondered what would be served for dinner if the meal in front of him was considered *light*. Soup, salad, roast chicken, root vegetables, and a variety of desserts. Unable to exercise on the train the way he was used to, it crossed his mind that he might step off the train in five days several pounds heavier than when he began the trip.

Glancing to the side, he noticed Marie eat soup and salad but little else. He wanted to ask if she felt all right, but the dining car had been set up with the tables together, everyone all around, and he didn't want to draw undue attention to her.

His concerns of earlier when Marie had left the hotel without him had now fled. She appeared to not only accept his presence but embraced the idea of a travel companion. To the others, he was sure it appeared as though they were previously acquainted, and neither of them said anything to disavow that notion.

"And what business are you in, Mr. Manitov?" Anthony asked, his gaze on the quiet man sitting across from him.

"A private company," Gregory replied, dabbing at his mouth with a linen napkin. He hefted his shoulders and chuckled. "I'm afraid it's not very exciting. We make parts for microwave ovens."

Anthony opened his mouth, but Beth jumped in. "Isn't it funny how we've gotten so used to things like that? I couldn't last a day without my microwave, but what about all those years before when I did all the cooking with our old-fashioned stove?"

"I'm always telling Beth that she can get the newest gadget for the kitchen as long as she keeps feeding me," Maurice laughed.

"Do you enjoy cooking?" Beth asked Marie, then threw her hands into the air before giving Marie a chance to answer. "I realize that was incredibly sexist! I should ask everyone that question, not just the other women!"

Marie smiled, her mirth shared by the others except for Cherelle, who appeared bored with the conversation entirely.

"I do like to cook," Marie replied, "but get very little time to do so."

"I imagine your job keeps you very busy," Theodore said, leaning forward so that he could peer down the table toward her.

"I can't imagine spending my day with children,"

Cherelle mumbled under her breath, offering a visible shiver for emphasis.

"I'm sure you can't," Beth said, her pointed smile aimed at the other woman. "Thank goodness we all have careers that incorporate what we do well so that society can function. And what is it that you do?"

"I was going to ask the same thing," Marie said, nodding as she looked down the table toward Cherelle.

"I'm... I'm surprised you haven't recognized me, but then, you are American." Her voice dripped with disdain. Sucking in a deep breath as though to cleanse herself from ignorance, she continued. "I'm an actress and an influencer."

A crinkle formed in Marie's brow when she cocked her head to the side and asked, "What do you influence?"

Cherelle lifted her chin, offering her the opportunity to look down her nose at everyone seated. Offering a belittling smile, she replied, "A line of cosmetics and hair care products." When the others remained quiet, she huffed. "I endorse products that I use, such as cosmetics and hair care, post on my video channel, and get paid for those endorsements." She smiled as she looked around the table, her face expectant.

"Oh." The one word was accompanied by the crinkle still present in Marie's brow.

"It must be so rewarding to have a career that means something," Beth said.

Bray looked toward the older woman, then stifled another chuckle to see that Beth was speaking towards Marie.

Maurice added, "There's something so attractive about someone in a selfless job." His words were greeted with a wink from his wife and a chuckle from Theodore.

Cherelle tossed her napkin down and scooted her chair back. "If you'll excuse me."

After watching her stalk out, Marie looked toward Bray and winced. "I didn't mean to offend her. I rarely go to the movies, and I'm not on social media very much."

Unable to hold back, he laughed out loud, but seeing her brow furrow even more, he leaned over and whispered, "No, Marie. It wasn't you. I just think she's used to getting all the attention and isn't used to sharing the spotlight."

Now, Marie's brows hit her hairline. "Me? I can hardly share the spotlight with an actress and an... um... influencer. She walks into a room and people take notice. I'm more likely to be passed over, which is fine with me."

"I'd never pass over you."

Her gaze jumped to Bray's face, and she smiled. Leaning closer, she whispered, "Yes, but you're on a job to notice me."

Before he had a chance to respond, several of the others stood from the table. "Would anyone like to join my cousin and me in the lounge for a game of cards?" Anthony asked.

"Oh, Maurice and I would love to." Beth bobbed her head in agreement, and the four made their way out of the dining car, leaving just Gregory, Marie, and Bray.

He had sent off a message earlier to LSI about Gregory, not believing for a moment that he was who he presented to be, but hadn't had a chance to check on a reply.

"I think I'd like to go back to the observation car," Marie said, her voice soft. "You don't have to come. I'm perfectly fine—"

"I'd love to come," he said, standing.

"Would you like to join us?"

Marie's question to Gregory surprised him, and he looked over at the man whose penetrating gaze was settled on her.

"Thank you, but no," Gregory said, lifting his gaze up to Bray, a slight smile playing about his lips. "I have some work to attend to in my cabin."

Marie said goodbye and followed Bray out of the dining car, past the game table with the others playing cards in the lounge car, and into the observation car, climbing the steps to the top level once again. He led them to the settee they had claimed earlier but stood to the side, waving her in first, letting her be closest to the window.

She smiled then settled into the seat, her face immediately turned to the window as their trip through the mountains continued. She appeared more subdued than earlier, and he kept his attention on her. Finally, unable to stand the silence, he gently nudged her shoulder with his and asked, "Are you okay?"

Nodding, she turned and faced him, her lips sucked in, her expression pensive. Concern speared through him, and he shifted in his seat so his body was angled more toward hers. "Do you not feel well?"

Her eyes widened as she shook her head. "Oh, no. That's not it." She looked down, shaking her head slightly before looking up at him again. "Do you ever feel that you don't quite fit in?"

The question caught him off guard, and he opened and closed his mouth a couple of times, uncertain of her meaning.

She jumped in, not waiting on his response. "No, of course, you probably don't. But then, so many people look like they have it all together on the outside, but on the inside, they're floundering like the rest of us." She shifted in her seat, mirroring his posture so they were now completely facing each other. "But me? It's like I always feel a little off-kilter."

She appeared so perplexed, it was all he could do to not reach over and smooth the lines in her forehead with his thumb. Instead, he twitched his fingers on the back of her seat, forcing them to not touch her shoulder. "What makes you feel off-kilter?"

Rolling her eyes, she chortled. "Cherelle was obviously piqued that I didn't know who she was. I wasn't trying to belittle her career."

"Don't let someone as shallow as Cherelle Vanders make you feel less!"

"Oh, I don't feel *less*. Just... well, different. I could see it was very important to her. And probably to a lot of people if she has a huge following. But how can one person who says, 'Hey, I used this eyeshadow,' make that much difference to what makeup you use?"

A chuckle slipped out. "Well, it wouldn't to me. I don't wear eye shadow."

Her perplexed expression morphed into a wide grin, and she play-slapped his leg. "Okay, jokester! So, not *you*, but it must mean something to someone for her to influence others. I had no idea someone did that for money!" They laughed, then, as her mirth slowly ended, she shook her head. "I was never in the popular crowd growing up, and it seemed like that followed me into adulthood. Now, here I am in my thirties and proud of what I do, but I'm still the nerd trying to figure out what everyone else is talking about."

"There's a lot out there that's not worth knowing about, Marie. What you do with your life makes a difference. You give kids a chance to heal. So what if you don't know what the newest *cool* thing is that's out there? Most of that shit goes by the wayside anyway. What you do has lasting effects."

She sucked in a quick breath while staring into his eyes. The green was so surreal. He'd never had anyone stare at him with that color of jade. It drew him in, kept him mesmerized. She was still wearing the red frames, the color complementing the green.

"That's a really nice thing to say."

So caught in staring at her eyes, it took a few seconds for him to remember what he'd said to her. "Well, it's true. You make a difference in the lives of kids that goes way beyond what hair care products they could spend their money on." He leaned back and said, "Tell me what you love about your career."

She smiled, her shoulders relaxing. "It doesn't matter

if a child has a sports injury, an injury from an accident, or even an injury since birth or from disease, they all need to feel that they have a sense of control. I hope that I give that back to them, even if it is in little steps, little accomplishments."

Settling back in the seat, she turned her gaze back to the full windows but didn't move further away from him. For the next hour, they watched the scenery pass by, pointing out what caught their attention and chatting amicably. When accepting the mission, he'd hoped it would be pleasant and that the train ride would be enjoyable. What he hadn't counted on was enjoying time spent with her as well.

They were joined by the Hogues and the Robbinses, who were just as entranced with the vistas out the observation windows as they had been. Enrique had served tea, including sandwiches and cookies.

Marie groaned as she pushed her saucer away. "I can't believe how much I'm eating, and we haven't had dinner yet. But then, that's the way vacations should be, isn't it? A moral imperative for us to buy tourist crap, do things we'd never normally do, and stuff ourselves until we burst!"

He chuckled at her enthusiasm again but wanted to ask about her condition. He hated to bring up the reminder that her brother would have given him private health information and would rather her tell him herself but had no idea how to bring up the subject.

Deciding to keep their conversation-friendly, he simply laughed. "Eat whatever you want. After all, it's a moral imperative!"

7

She stifled a gasp. Eyes wide, taking in the whole room, Marie stepped into the dining car set for a formal dinner. The tables were covered in thick white table-cloths, crystal water and wine goblets, gold-edged china, and heavy silverware. The table settings alone rivaled any she'd had at the most elegant dinner. Certainly, her parents attended gala events when her father's political career was in full swing, but dinners like this weren't what she was used to.

She and Bray had gone back to their cabins to get ready for dinner. After a shower where she delighted in the scented soaps and shampoos provided by the train, she'd re-applied her makeup and then dressed in black flowing pants and a grey silk blouse. She'd debated her choice of eyeglasses but chose a silver-framed pair.

A knock on her door had caused the butterflies in her stomach to take flight. The reason was on the other side of the thick, wooden door. Bray. A man she'd only known for twenty-four hours, and yet, had enjoyed his company more than any other man she'd actually dated. She'd always found it hard to start a new relationship. So many things to learn about the other person. So many things for them to learn about her. Maybe that's why she felt comfortable with Bray. There was no expectation of a relationship other than he was there at her brother's behest to make sure she was safe, even though there was truly no reason for concern.

Throwing open the door, her smile had faltered as she stared at the man in front of her. She'd seen Bray in jeans. She'd seen him in a casual shirt and slacks. But nothing could have prepared her for seeing him in a tailored black suit and pale gray shirt with a silk tie. His hair, a little long on top and often mussed from his fingers, was now combed neatly although it was apparent he did not use any product. His handsome face still had a five o'clock shadow, giving him a devil-may-care appearance. The whole package of Bray was breathtaking. Somehow, he managed a casual air in formal attire, and she battled the desire to reach up and run her fingers through his hair just to make it messier.

Her gaze had moved from the top of his head down to his shiny shoes and back again, finally settling on his dark eyes, smiling as she noticed his gaze roved over her as well. Now, self-conscious, she wondered what he thought of her efforts.

"Wow."

"Wow."

They'd both spoken at the same time, then burst into laughter. "Well, if I got the same reaction from you that I was offering, I'll take that as a compliment," she said as she leaned to the side and collected her small purse before stepping out into the hall.

"It absolutely was a compliment. You look beautiful."

With his fingers resting lightly on the small of her back, they walked from the sleeper car, through the observation and lounge cars, and into the dining car. Aware of his presence each step of the way, she was struck with how unobtrusive he was. While she'd chafed at the idea of having someone with her, Bray truly felt more like a traveling companion than hired security.

Anthony and Theodore were already seated at one end of the long table but stood when Marie entered the room. She glanced down to see if there was assigned seating, breathing a sigh of relief to see that there was not. She moved forward, glad to sit on the end with Bray next to her and the two cousins across. Gregory came in, taking the seat next to Bray. Beth and Maurice entered next, filling in the two chairs beside Theodore. They all sat for several minutes until the dining car attendant finally announced that the meal would begin.

Leaning to the side, she whispered, "Good. I was afraid we would have to wait for everyone."

Bray grinned. "Me, too. I have a feeling Ms. Vanders prefers to make a grand entrance."

He'd leaned over as well, and with his lips so near her ear, his words brushed over her like a caress. She shivered. Sucking in a quick breath, she glanced around, wondering if anyone was watching her reaction, glad to see everyone else's attention focused on the servers as they brought in the first course.

And when it came to the food, Marie was equally impressed. The appetizer of chicken confit terrine was followed by a delicious artichoke salad. Cherelle finally made her entrance, and each of the men stood slightly as she halted, her face registering surprise, but Marie knew it was not from the lovely table setting or the food but from how the others had already begun their meal. The beautiful woman's eyes flashed irritation, but she sat in the only chair left, barely nodding her acknowledgment to anyone else as the attendant brought her appetizer.

Conversation flowed and Marie relaxed as she enjoyed the food. The meal included a fish course, venison Wellington entrée, and a cheese course with roasted pear.

Gregory asked, "What business are you in, Mr. Bray?"

"Oh, he's a man of leisure," Theodore said, his smile wide. "I told him that was my goal."

Gregory lifted his brow, his gaze speculative.

"I'm involved in various ventures." Bray's voice was hard.

"Do you travel often?" Gregory asked.

Marie looked over, seeing Gregory's gaze on Bray. Dabbing her mouth with her napkin, she swallowed nervously, uncertain how he usually answered when on an assignment.

"I travel extensively when necessary," Bray replied easily.

Gregory's eyes darted between Bray and Marie. "And this trip? Business or pleasure?"

Marie had no idea why she did what she did, but her hand reached over and landed on Bray's hand resting on the table. Turning toward him, she smiled. "When we're together, it's always a pleasure."

"Oh, excellent answer, my dear," Beth called out, her smile wide as she lifted her wine glass in a mock toast. "Traveling with your partner is always so much fun."

"How long have you two been together?" Anthony asked.

Marie assumed he was speaking to Beth, then looked up to see him peering directly at her. She blinked, grateful when Bray answered.

"It seems like we've known each other for years."

Afraid others would try to delve into their relationship, it seemed the conversations tended to jump around.

"The microwave parts business must pay very well," Theodore said, looking at Gregory sitting next to him. "I'm still not sure how we afforded this trip, but I'm glad we have a good accountant! We need it just to keep my cousin in style. He's adopted a decidedly expensive taste in clothes and shoes."

Anthony rolled his eyes, a smile on his lips, but just as Marie looked back down at her plate, she felt the table move slightly as though someone's foot had kicked the table leg. Theodore jerked his head around to his cousin, and she was reminded of her childhood when she and Cory would occasionally squabble. Their parents didn't allow fussing at mealtime, so she and Cory became creative at ways to kick each other underneath the table. She wondered if Theodore had said something that Anthony didn't want him to. She grinned at the memory of her brother's antics, then caught Bray's lifted-brow expression. "Sorry. I just remembered something Cory and I used to do when we were kids."

The dinner was followed by more wine with dessert. By now, she was full and sleepy. At home, she usually ate dinner right after work and then read until it was time for bed. Now, dinner was just over, and the others were chatting about playing cards or having more coffee or wine in the lounge. Knowing she would be poor company, she leaned toward Bray and murmured, "I'm ready for bed, but please, stay if you'd like—"

"Yes, Mr. Bray, we'd love to have you join us for drinks and poker," Anthony invited as he, Theodore, and Gregory stood.

He shook his head quickly. "Thank you, no." Looking down at Marie, he smiled. "Are you ready?"

Not wanting to draw undue attention to themselves, she simply nodded and turned to say good night. Scooting past the other chairs with his fingers once again resting lightly on her back, they walked into the observation car when she stopped suddenly. "Oh, I forgot my purse. I'll be right back."

She hurried past Cherelle, who was exiting the dining car, and moved to her seat. With her bag in hand, she once again offered goodnights and headed into the next car. Cherelle had stepped closer to Bray and her voice, slightly slurred by the copious drinks she'd downed, carried throughout the car.

"I'll be having more wine in the lounge if you'd care

to join me once you've put your little companion to bed," Cherelle purred. She appeared to have gotten over being miffed at the dinner service starting without her grand entrance, and it was evident she hoped to salvage her evening. Dragging her long, red, tapered fingernail along Bray's arm must not have had the desired effect as he stepped back, his expression hard.

"No, Ms. Vanders. I would not care to join you."

Marie's eyes widened at the harsh staccato of each word. Her lips curved slightly at the way he refused to let the other woman commandeer the situation. He stepped to the side, his gaze hitting Marie's. Lifting his hand, he beckoned her, and she swallowed a grin as she passed a now visibly steaming Cherelle and placed her hand in his. Strong fingers wrapped around hers, she relished the warmth.

It only took a moment to walk through the lounge car, entering the first sleeper car. Stopping at her door, he leaned around and opened it with her key card before stepping inside. She moved in behind him and shut the door, waiting as he checked the closet and bathroom. With his hand no longer holding hers, cold reality settled over her. *He's not here with me... he's here for me.* Perhaps an off-duty Bray would love the type of evening that Cherelle could provide. As he turned back to her, she wiped her sweaty palms on her pants and lifted her chin to face him.

"Bray, you and I both know there's no threat against me. I honestly can't imagine why Cory wanted to hire your agency. I know he and my parents are worriers for... well, for various reasons. But I'm perfectly safe on the train. I accept that you have a duty to perform, but there's no reason you have to forgo enjoying this trip yourself."

She held his gaze as he turned and faced her, the floor space of the cabin seeming so much smaller with his larger-than-life presence. Her brother was like that, too. She tried not to think too much about Bray other than the obvious gorgeous factor that made her eyes automatically drawn to him whenever they were together. Or the fact that he seemed completely in control of any situation, whether it was dealing with a sweet older couple like the Hogues, the competitive nature of the businessmen on the trip, or the not-too-subtle attention-seeking from Cherelle.

But now, watching his hands land on his hips, his chest even more expansive, his dark hair raked to the side, she knew he was much more than a typical hired body. His very presence screamed former military. And if her brother's Special Forces career was anything to go by, she did not doubt that Bray had a similar background.

And instead of feeling stifled in the space, she felt a strange combination of being completely safe while being completely turned on. *Movie-star gorgeous... yep. Smart and well-read... yep. Fills out a pair of jeans in a way that makes me do a double take... hell, yeah. And can kiss in a way that'll make me weak in the knees... God, I want to find out.*

"Have I given you a reason to think that I don't want to spend time with you?"

She blinked, her brain taking a few seconds to catch

up from where it had wandered to his words. "Um… no. You haven't. You've been the perfect bodyguard. Present but not hovering. You've been exactly what we said last night… a travel companion."

"So, don't worry about what you think I do or don't want to do. I've played enough cards in my life to kill time so that if I never see another deck of cards again, it won't be a loss. I've been around businessmen who want to shake your hand if they think you can give them a leg up, then jerk their hand back if they figure out you can't. Believe me, again, no loss. I've been around women like Cherelle. Doesn't matter if they hang in bars waiting to bang a Green Beret for bragging rights, or worse, think that banging one was the same as holding on to one. Doesn't matter if they've got money and think their shit doesn't stink while shoving it down your throat. Been around that before and not looking to do it again. So, walking away from the others is no loss to me."

Her brain short-circuited trying to filter through everything he'd just laid out. She opened and closed her mouth a couple of times before finally managing to mumble, "Wow. That's… uh… wow." His face had been closed off while he'd given his speech, and she wondered if he was pissed. As she continued to stare, she watched in utter fascination as his lips curved slightly and he disavowed her of that notion. She grinned in return. "So, I take it from that speech that you're the kind of man who does what he wants, sets his own course, and isn't waylaid by shiny objects that are dangled from the side."

He threw his head back and laughed, his hands dropping from his hips. The sound was beautiful. She'd never thought of a man's laugh as being beautiful. Hardy, maybe. A deep belly laugh, perhaps. But beautiful? Never. Not until that moment. Deciding to push down her thoughts about his laughter, she focused instead on the military. "Green Beret. So was Cory, but then, you probably know that, don't you?"

He nodded his head slowly. "I didn't know him in the service. I've never met him, but he served with my boss. Heard nothing but good things about him."

"I can imagine the same thing was said about you."

His dark-eyed gaze was penetrating, and while she was asking the questions, she wondered what he could see, staring at her.

"I'd like to think it was. But I was ready for a change."

His words were simple, but a dark specter passed over his face, almost like a shadow along his tight jaw. *He's known pain.* No matter what else she might understand about Bray, she was sure of that.

She remained quiet for a moment, the silence swirling about the soft lights and shadows in the room. She pulled her lips in and pressed them between her teeth before making a decision. "Thank you for being you." She wasn't surprised when he startled, and she rushed to add, "I know many servicemen and women don't want someone to thank them for their time in the military and their sacrifices. I know that Cory feels that way. So, I'll thank you for being you and the choices you've made in your life."

Their gazes never strayed, but she had no idea what he was thinking. All the mysteries of the universe could have revealed themselves to him, but from his careful expression, she'd never know what they were. She watched as his body relaxed and his lips curved once again.

"And do you accept the choice that your brother wanted to make sure that your travels were safe? And accept the choice that I made in taking this on?"

Understanding moved through her, and she nodded. Men like Cory and Bray didn't make decisions lightly. They understood honor, duty, strength. She'd only known him for a day, but that's all it took for her to know that he would protect her. *From what?* It didn't matter. She just knew that he'd do whatever it took to keep her safe. "Yes. I accept that you're where you want to be, doing what you want to do, and with who you want to be with."

"Good." He stepped forward, reached his arms out, and placed his hands on her shoulders. She looked up as he bent down, her heart skipping a beat. He veered to the side and whispered, his breath once again brushing warmly past her ear. "I hope you sleep well, Marie. I'll see you in the morning."

His hands fell away as his arms dropped back, and he stepped to the door. She immediately missed his close presence but managed to offer a smile as he looked over his shoulder and said, "Good night." He opened the door and closed it behind him with a quiet click.

She stood in the middle of her cabin, not moving

except for her gaze as it drifted over the room. The bed was turned down, exposing luxurious white sheets with a bar of wrapped chocolate placed precisely in the middle of her pillow. The only light came from the soft glow of the wall sconces, warming the polished wooden walls and brass fixtures.

So far, the luxury train line had given her spectacular views of the Canadian Rocky Mountains and forests, sumptuous food and wine, and a private room that surpassed the best hotels she'd ever stayed in. But it was the man in the next cabin that seemed to fill her thoughts.

Fatigue began to pull at her very core, and shaking off the melancholy that had settled when he walked out of the room, she headed into the bathroom. After preparing for bed, she lined up several pill bottles and began to take her prescriptions. Her hyperthyroidism caused much of her fatigue, and part of her longed to explain to him why she'd sought her bed immediately after dinner. Even her noticeable limp hadn't been mentioned. But both were so personal, and she had to remember that he was not there as her friend or partner, but as a job.

Turning off the light in the bathroom, she climbed underneath the covers, stretching out on the soft mattress. Sleep was generally elusive, but with the gentle rocking of the train, she soon fell into a deep slumber.

8

Bray lay in bed, unable to sleep. Disquieted, he tried to sort through the multitude of thoughts all clamoring for attention. He agreed with Marie's assessment of the minimum threat risk on the train after having talked to LSI about Gregory, the only passenger he hadn't been able to investigate before he arrived in Canada. The Robbins cousins were partners in their own business, exactly as they'd said. He'd wondered about the trip on the luxury train, but it appeared they'd sold some electronic patents recently and intended to live large for a little while.

Gregory did work for a Canadian microwave company that sold parts in both Canada and the U.S., but Josh had difficulty discerning how he was able to afford the level of travel that they were on. Bray and the other Keepers agreed that Gregory was probably an unscrupulous employee, possibly earning money on the side since there was no evidence of any other income, and there was no evidence of a tie-in to Cory's mob investigation. But the man's speculative gaze and interest in Bray had not gone unnoticed. *What's he up to?*

The Hogues were exactly as they portrayed—Canadians, retired grandparents who'd received the money to pay for the trip from family gifts for their anniversary.

And Cherelle Vanders was exactly who she said she was, an actress and blogger. Josh had investigated the railway employees, finding no threat from that direction, either.

So, why not relax and enjoy the trip? That question had no answer that he could discern. But it wasn't just Mace's description of Cory's nickname. The same kind of tickle in the back of his mind had saved his ass many times in the service... *until that last mission in the fucking desert of Afghanistan—*

A knock on the door sounded, and he jerked the covers back, his feet hitting the floor almost immediately. He checked his weapon, tucking it behind him as he unlocked the door and opened it slightly, not knowing if it was Marie or one of the train personnel.

Seeing Cherelle standing so close to the door caught him by surprise. Her gaze dropped from his face down over his bare chest, and the tip of her tongue darted out to slick over her bottom lip before she smiled, cocked her head, and met his eyes again. He knew what she expected him to say, so he did the opposite and said nothing, keeping his expression hard and the door only opened a few inches.

Her smile faltered, and she cleared her throat before forcing her smile to brighten once more. "I couldn't sleep, so I thought if you were having the same problem, we could pass the time together."

Again, he maintained his statue demeanor.

"I know that you and the sweet little doctor are traveling together, but it's obvious you aren't *together*." She straightened her spine, her breasts on display in the deep-V of her dress. "I get off the train tomorrow, so I thought tonight would be the perfect opportunity for us."

"Not interested." With those two words, he slid the door shut and snapped the latch with a loud click. Her gasp was heard through the thick wood. He pushed down his irritation, almost glad that her interruption had given him something to think about besides his former military days. Rechecking his weapon, he placed it on the nightstand and climbed back into bed.

The reality was there was a time when Cherelle's offer would've been welcome. A chance to mindlessly sink himself into a beautiful woman's body with no thought of what happened afterward other than they'd part company forever. But those days were long gone. Even if he hadn't been on a mission, he wouldn't have gone there. Cherelle's offering had drama written all over it.

Now, as he lay in bed, he thought of the woman on the other side of his cabin wall. Marie was nothing like the type of woman he thought he'd be attracted to, and yet, during the past day, he'd laughed and talked more with a stranger than he ever had. He couldn't remember the last time he talked about his parents so much to anyone.

And now that he thought about it, Marie was no longer a stranger. He found himself looking forward to the morning when he'd see her again and get to spend another day in her company. That was another first, one he refused to analyze. *Who wouldn't enjoy interesting and stimulating conversation... and a gorgeous smile?*

He thought of her brother who was unable to come up with a specific threat, and yet, was worried. He couldn't get Mace's opinion out of his mind. *Cory had a sixth sense... we called him The Psychic.* On that last thought, he fell into a fitful sleep.

Carruthers, Marcowitz down. Not moving. Blood pouring from both of their bodies, mingling with the dirt. Falconi, Bingle down but still moving. Where the fuck had the ambush come from? God-fucking-damn! Get Falconi stabilized. Get Bingle splinted. Someone get Carruthers' and Marcowoitz' bodies. Christ, where the fuck is the bird?

Running. Falconi thrown over his shoulder as he's heading toward the bird. Dropping to the ground as more gunfire kicks up the dust around his feet. Arms reaching out, pulling Falconi from his arms. Climbing. Looking at what was in front of him.

Blood. Broken bones. Death.

He woke with a jolt, clawing his way out of his dream while kicking off his sheets. It took a few seconds to identify the rocking motion his body was experiencing as a luxury train and not the military helicopter as it hauled what was left of his team to safety.

Breath ragged, he sat up in bed, willing his heartbeat to slow as he fought the feeling that something bad was coming.

"Wasn't that amazing? I couldn't believe how deeply I slept!"

Marie's enthusiasm was contagious, and Bray nodded as he smiled down at her. He'd given up on sleep after the nightmare and had taken an early shower, allowing the hot water to get rid of the sweat he'd been covered in.

At a reasonable hour, he'd knocked on her door to escort her to breakfast, and she'd flung the door open, her smile and sparkling eyes slamming into him. She was wearing a pair of dark jeans that fit her slim build perfectly. Her rose-colored framed eyeglasses were paired to complement her pink shirt. Today, her feet were encased in athletic shoes.

"Give me just a second, and I'll be ready to go." She turned and walked back into her room, and he stepped just inside the door.

His gaze scanned the room, a professional habit even if there was no evident threat. What caught his attention was that she'd made her bed. "You know, the sleeper car attendants will take care of your bed."

She looked over her shoulder as she shoved her phone into her purse and smiled. "I know, but I can't stand the idea of someone having to go to extra trouble because I was a slob. Plus, I like the look of a neat space." She stood and faced him, her brow crinkled. "Not that I'm a neat freak, but I do like my space to not feel overly messy." She stepped into the bathroom, and his gaze followed. As she pulled her hair back into a ponytail, he noted the black case sitting on the small vanity, several prescription bottles visible from where he stood.

She caught his gaze in the reflection in the mirror and asked, "Do you think we'll be eating fairly soon?"

Surprised by her question, he nodded. "It's my understanding that they will already have a continental breakfast of coffee, juice, and pastries set out, and then will take your order for the full breakfast."

Nodding, she looked down and opened a prescription bottle, then quietly tapped out a pill before popping it into her mouth and swallowing it with water. Before she turned around, he shifted so that he was looking out her window, not wanting her to feel self-conscious.

"Look at what I downloaded last night."

Her words had him turn to see her Kindle in her hands, one of his mother's books opened. Grinning, he took it from her and glanced at the passage she'd highlighted. "Meanwhile the world goes on. Meanwhile the sun and the clear pebbles of the rain are moving across the landscapes, over the prairies and the deep trees, the mountains and the rivers. Meanwhile the wild geese, high in the clean blue air, are heading home again. Whoever you are, no matter how lonely, the world offers itself to your imagination, calls to you like the wild geese, harsh and exciting – over and over announcing your place in the family of things."

"Your mom had a quote from Mary Oliver in here, and all I could think about was the scenes we were watching from the observation car."

Her eyes were bright, drawing him in as he caught her enthusiasm. "I can't wait to tell my mother that you're enjoying her book. She'll want to talk to you for sure."

"Oh, I'd be honored," Marie gushed.

Holding out his hand, he waited, his breath halted in his lungs until she reached out and linked fingers with him. Locking her door behind them, they walked into the lounge car where they found the continental breakfast set up on one side. "Go ahead and get some pastries, and I'll bring you coffee." She appeared grateful, and he assumed the medication she'd just taken needed to be accompanied by food. He prepared her coffee, remembering how she liked it, and by the time he walked over to the table she'd selected, she was munching on a buttered croissant, and he discovered she'd placed another croissant on a saucer at his chair.

They were the only people in the car, but it was still early. She bit into the buttery, flaky pastry, a moan slipping from her closed lips as she chewed. His gaze shot up, but her eyes were closed and the expression on her face screamed ecstasy. Her tongue darted out and licked a stray crumb from her lips, and his blood ran south.

Grimacing, he slammed the lid on those thoughts. The muscles in his jaw ticked as he clamped his teeth together and closed his eyes, mentally running through the exercise of cleaning his gun to keep his thoughts off Marie, her moan, and her lips. *Especially her lips.*

"Are you okay?"

His eyes snapped open to find her staring at him, head tilted to the side, her green-eyed gaze penetrating as a crinkle of concern settled on her face.

"Yeah, yeah. Fine."

"You don't look fine. You look like you're in pain."

"No, no. Just… had a thought… something I needed to put out of my mind."

She nodded while still licking her lips. "I get that. Sometimes, thoughts jump into my head, and it's as though they want to take over my whole being. Sort of like an alien invasion of the mind!"

He chuckled, shaking his head at her description. "You said it perfectly. That's exactly what it's like." Her expression grew pensive, and he asked, "What alien invasion bothers you?"

She shrugged and shook her head. "I think everyone's past is always full of aliens that are willing to take over. But today is too beautiful to think of that."

Beth and Maurice walked into the lounge car, wide smiles on their faces as they greeted Bray and Marie. "Oh, my dear, I'm so envious that you get to continue your journey. We're getting off today but do so with heavy hearts because we have loved this experience!"

"Please, join us," Marie invited, inclining her head to the two chairs adjoining their table.

The Hogues soon had their pastries and coffee, and by the time they'd given their full breakfast order to the attendant, Anthony and Theodore, followed closely by Gregory, came in as well. Soon, their meals arrived, and the conversation lulled slightly as everyone was busy enjoying the excellent cuisine.

"I wonder where Ms. Vanders is this morning?" Beth asked.

Right on cue, the tall blonde walked into the room, her clothes immaculate, her makeup and hair perfect, but the whole effect was marred by the scowl on her face. Sliding into a chair near Gregory at a two-seater table, she glanced over at Bray and her scowl deepened.

"Hmmm, it looks like someone isn't happy this morning," Marie murmured underneath her breath, eliciting chuckles from the Hogues and a blush across Bray's cheeks. Narrowing his eyes at her, she merely winked as she continued to munch on her breakfast.

Most of the passengers joined them on the observation deck, the mountains still rising on each side, giving way to valleys the train snaked through. By lunchtime, they arrived at Banff, pulling into the station.

As they all disembarked, Cherelle stepped off, waving to a man wearing a ski-jacket, making a grand production of air kisses while a nearby photographer snapped pictures. She looped her arm through his but turned to wiggle her fingers at Bray before leaving through the crowd.

"Good riddance," he muttered under his breath.

Marie pressed her fingers to her mouth, but he could hear a giggle slip through. He tossed her a pretend glare but that just made her laugh more.

A moment later, the Hogues came up behind them. Bray stood to the side as Marie hugged Beth. Maurice stepped forward to offer his hand, and Bray clasped it warmly. Maurice leaned in closer. "Don't know what is or isn't going on between you two, but you and Marie make a nice-looking couple."

"We're just friends, sir."

Maurice chuckled. "Well, friends are good to have, but a woman like that doesn't come around very often."

As the older couple walked away with a wave, Marie sidled up next to him. "We've got lunch here in this resort town. Where would you like to go?"

They wandered around the quaint town, finally settling on a small restaurant overlooking one of the main streets. After finishing their meal, they sipped their coffee and enjoyed the view of the Bow River with the snow-capped mountains in the distance.

Marie leaned back in her seat and sighed. "This is incredible."

"It really is," he agreed. "I had no idea what this trip would be like when I started, but it's been an amazing way to travel."

She nodded, her eyes bright. "I was just thinking the same thing. It's one of the reasons I don't like flying. You're above everything but you don't really get to *see* a place."

Her expression was so calm, but it was on the tip of his tongue to ask her why she didn't fly. It didn't matter that he already knew the reason, he just wanted her to open up more to him.

Suddenly, recognizing someone on the street beyond her shoulder, his attention was drawn. Gregory was standing at the side of the street in the shadow of an old building, engaged in what appeared to be a heated conversation with another man. It didn't last long, and finally, Gregory reached inside his pocket and pulled out a large envelope. Handing it to the man, he received a small black case in return. Bray wondered if he had just witnessed a deal that Gregory's microwave company probably didn't know about.

Marie's head was twisted to look over her shoulder, and it hit him that she'd noticed his perusal of Gregory's activities. She looked back around, eyes wide, and asked, "That looked suspicious! What do you think he was up to?"

Damn. Of course, Marie's sharp gaze and curious mind would have taken that scenario in. "Don't start speculating. We have no idea what he's doing, and quite frankly, I don't want to know."

Her eyes were bright while her body almost vibrated as she leaned toward him, keeping her voice low. "Oh, no, you can't pretend you aren't curious! There's been something weird about him the whole trip and this just solidifies it."

Shaking his head, he tossed money onto the table and reached down to take her hand. Leading her from the restaurant to the street, he said, "Come on."

She allowed him to lead her out but finally gave a tug on his hand, and he turned to look down at her. "Bray, we could follow him. See what he's up to. Or maybe follow the other guy. He wouldn't know us. I'd think in your career you'd always want to check things out that are going on around you."

Moving so that he was standing directly in front of her, he dropped his chin and held her gaze. "I admit, I do get curious. I also admit I'm very suspicious. But I'm not here for Gregory. I'm here for you. So, whatever he's doing, as long as it has no impact on you, it doesn't concern me."

She winced, something dark slashing through her eyes. Then her expression cleared, a veil dropping over her eyes right before she nodded. Her lips attempted to curve upward, but he noted the quiver, and the pretend smile didn't reach her eyes. "You're right. I'm sorry. I sometimes forget that I'm a job."

His gut clenched. "Shit, Marie, that's not what I meant."

She squared her shoulders as though washing away whatever negative emotions had swept over her. "So, what would you like to do until it's time to get back onto the train?" He grimaced at her change of subject, hating that he'd stolen the brightness from her eyes. He wanted to apologize, tell her that she was fascinating, fun to be with, admit to her that he enjoyed getting to know her beyond the mission. But she'd already turned and started to walk away, calling over her shoulder, "Why don't we walk down by the river?"

"Fuck," he cursed under his breath, angry that he'd hurt her. He watched as she walked down the street, her limp only slightly noticeable. Casting his gaze around, it was easy to see she captured the attention of several men in the vicinity, their appreciative stares evident to all but her. He wanted to race to her, throw his arm around her, and publicly claim her. Shaking his head, he cursed again. He needed to stay focused. He knew first-hand what could go wrong on a mission that was perfectly planned, and he'd be damned if he'd let anything happen to her. He was on an assignment, not looking for romance. Sighing heavily, his shoulders drooped slightly as he jogged to catch up with her. Silently, they walked together toward the river.

9

Marie stopped at the railing that overlooked the picturesque river, deeply inhaling the crisp air, wishing it would cool her heated cheeks. She grimaced. *When will I ever learn?* It was just like the years of rehab when she sought friendship from her hired therapists. *Well, not exactly. Some of them had become friends.* Her adolescence had been difficult, surrounded more by adults than other teens, so friendships had been searched for amongst those she spent time with. And just like when a particular therapist was finished with her and moved on to another patient, she'd missed the relationship they'd developed.

Lost in thought, she jolted in surprise when Bray's forearms braced on the railing next to her hands, and he gently shoulder bumped her from the side. She looked up, dreading to see the sympathy in his eyes, surprised when his smile appeared so sincere.

"Marie, please..."

She had no idea what he meant. *Please, don't walk*

away? Please, don't read more into this? Please, just let me do my job? Pursing her lips, she waited, but he seemed to struggle with what to say. Placing her hand on his arm, she felt the tense muscles underneath her fingertips and longed to take away his discomfort.

Strength radiated from him; she felt as though she could tell him anything and he could bear it. A trait she'd learned was so rare. "Did my brother tell you why I don't fly?"

A wince crossed his face as he nodded. "He said you were in a helicopter accident that injured you badly. I'm sorry, Marie. I should've told you that I knew."

She turned and looked back toward the water, both hands now grasping the cold railing. For a moment, she remained quiet, hating that Cory divulged what was her story to tell. She swallowed a snort. *My story?* Her accident had been in the news at the time. Easy for anyone to find and hardly a secret. *Of course, Bray would be privy to that information. I wonder what else he knows?*

She continued to stare at the river, her hands gripping the railing, the cold metal providing an anchor to her turbulent memories. "I was fourteen years old. My father was a state senator, and the whole family had been at a fundraising event. I hadn't wanted to go because I was missing a school event that all my friends were at. But the political function was one of those where it looks good for the politician to have his whole family with him, so my dad compromised. One of his business acquaintances had a private helicopter and offered to have his pilot fly me back early so that I wouldn't miss the school trip."

She leaned her head back and closed her eyes, feeling both the sunlight behind her eyelids and the chill of the breeze blowing across her face. "I wasn't even afraid. I felt so grown up. A family friend was going to meet me at the airport and drive me to my school. It's funny, but I can still remember that the trip was exhilarating even if I can't remember anything specific that I saw. I do remember the pilot was very nice and talked to me. And as we were landing, I looked down and could see everything so clearly. Funny... that, I remember."

She dropped her chin and opened her eyes, wanting to see the river rushing in front of her and not the replay of what had happened next. The story was easier to tell when she remained in the present and shut out emotions, not getting lost in the past.

"It happened so quickly, I'm not sure the pilot realized anything was wrong before I did. There was a horrible cracking sound just as we were almost to the ground. We pitched completely sideways, metal and glass hitting concrete." The color of the water in the river was deep blue, broken by the whitecaps as it rushed over large boulders. The sight was almost hypnotic as she kept her eyes straight ahead. "I remember the noise. I remember screaming. At least, I think I do."

"Fuckin' hell, Marie." The guttural words from Bray sounded dragged from the depths of his chest.

She turned and looked up at him, his breathing ragged as he stared at her, and she wanted to erase the dark clouds in his eyes. "I don't remember anything else. I've been told that I was still conscious for a while, but I have no memory of that. Sometimes, in my dreams, I can see the pilot. His body was... well, it was obvious he was dead. But when I awake, no matter how real the dream seems, I once again block that out. That's not uncommon in trauma, especially with intense pain. It's a way for the mind and body to sometimes deal with tragedy."

He nodded slowly but didn't say anything, for which she was glad. Most people gushed with platitudes, praise for handling trauma, sympathy even though they've never lived through anything like that, or more questions as they tried to dig up every macabre thought Marie could offer. She always thought it odd that so often people would ask if she remembered seeing the pilot after they crashed.

They both turned simultaneously, looking out over the rushing water. The river was so clean, reflecting the blue of the cloudless sky. With the snow-capped mountains in the background, it wasn't hard to imagine where the crystal clear water came from. The swooshing sound was both energetic and comforting.

She dragged in a deep breath, feeling her lungs shudder with the exertion. "I suppose it's easy now to understand why I never wanted to fly again." Her shoulders hefted in a slight shrug. "It's fear. I'm sure if I worked hard enough I could manage it, but so far, I've never had to push myself to do so. I travel by automobile, train, commuter rails, and buses. Obviously, I know that something horrific can occur in any of those, so I'm not immune to another accident. But somehow, I just feel better knowing that I'm close to the ground." She gave her head a little shake and offered a rueful snort. "Of course, the helicopter was close to the ground, too, so I suppose all my fears are irrational."

"I've never thought fear was irrational," Bray said. "Fear is what often keeps us safe. You're right, things can happen at any time, but as long as you don't let fear rule your life so that you don't live it, traveling however makes you feel the safest is what you should do."

She twisted her head around, nodding at his understanding. They remained silent for another moment. This time, the comfortable feeling between them settled like a warm blanket chasing the chill away.

"The reason I even brought this up," she continued, "was because, after the accident, I had years of surgeries and rehab. My leg and foot were rather destroyed. I was in and out of school, in and out of tutoring, and still managed to graduate from high school on time. But there were no ball games, dances, or the experiences of whispering with friends in the hallway about the cutest guy. So, I suppose my relationships came from the physical therapists, occupational therapists, doctors, and nurses. Many of them were friendly, and as an adult, I know there's a difference between someone being friendly and being your friend. But I'm afraid I still blur those lines."

"Marie—"

She turned fully toward him and placed her hand on his arm, giving a little squeeze. "No, Bray, please, let me say this. You are wonderful company on this trip, and I appreciate your friendliness more than I can say. I haven't had security around me a lot, but when I did, it certainly wasn't with this level of comfort. I've enjoyed spending time with you but sometimes forget that I'm a job, and in truth, that's fine. I'm still very lucky to have you with me on this amazing trip across Canada."

He opened his mouth but quickly closed it, nodding instead. She had no idea what his thoughts were. She'd love for him to declare she meant more to him than a mission, but he remained silent, a tic in his jaw the only physical evidence he was moved by her story.

A tower in the town rang the bells for the hour, and they both startled at the same time. "Oh, we need to get back to the train station."

As they turned, he reached down to take her hand. His palm felt warm against hers and his long fingers wrapped her solidly in a comforting grip as they hustled along the sidewalk. She tried not to limp but, in truth, she couldn't keep up with his long legs. He stopped suddenly, lifting his free hand, and hailed a taxi, holding the door for her as she climbed inside. He told the driver to take them to the station, and she relaxed.

"Thank you," she whispered, glad he didn't make a big deal about her limp.

He smiled, remaining quiet during their short trip. Arriving at the station, he reached into his wallet and paid the driver, then held his hand out to assist her from the taxi. His fingers remained around hers as they walked through the station, showed their tickets to the attendants, and made their way to the platform. She wondered why he continued to hold her hand, then decided it didn't matter, wanting to enjoy being with him without overthinking everything she felt.

Coming up on the back of the train, she realized it was shorter. "Oh! We've lost the extra sleeper car."

"That's why they had the Hogues and Ms. Vanders in the last sleeper car, they all got off here. I assume we're not picking up any new passengers so there would be no reason to have the extra car pulled along with us."

Enrique was waiting for them when they arrived in the lounge car, his smile beaming. "I hope you enjoyed your day in Banff! You're just in time, so no rush. If you would like to freshen up in your cabins first, tea will be served soon after we leave."

"Thank you. Hot tea sounds good."

"Are the others back yet?" Bray asked.

"The two Mr. Robbinses have returned, but Mr. Manitov has not. We have another twenty minutes before we're scheduled to depart, so I'm sure he'll be here."

Moving past Enrique, she remained quiet until they were close to their cabins. Looking up, she whispered, "Are you wondering where Gregory is?"

"Stop searching for a mystery," he admonished, but his lips twitched, giving away his mirth.

She grinned, rolling her eyes. "Fine, fine. I'll stop imagining that he was selling state secrets or drugs or that maybe his microwave parts are actually parts for some super-secret foreign missile."

His eyes flashed then shuttered as he approached her door. Now used to their ritual, she stood to the side while he stepped into her cabin first, made sure it was secure, then motioned for her to enter.

The outing had been fun but tiring, another one of the symptoms of her latest health issues. She swallowed a sigh and looked at her bed longingly, wondering if a nap was possible. Glancing at the clock on the night-stand, she dismissed that notion.

"Hey, what's wrong?" Bray asked.

"Oh, nothing."

He stepped closer, his eyes peering directly down into her face. "You're tired."

A denial was on her lips, but staring up at him, she chose honesty. "Yeah, I am."

"Why don't you rest for a while?"

"I don't want to miss it."

He tilted his head to the side, his brows lowered. "Miss what?"

It was on the tip of her tongue to say 'you,' but with a quick shake of her head, she replied, "Everything. I don't want to miss any of this adventure."

He looked as though he might protest, then changed his mind and nodded. "I don't want you to miss anything either."

His smile indicated he understood what the trip meant to her, and relief flooded her, easing the tension in her shoulders as she smiled. *Falling for the bodyguard... God, that sounds like a romance novel.* She remained quiet, afraid that if she opened her mouth she might blurt something embarrassing.

"Why don't we take a few minutes to get refreshed

and head to the observation car? I'm sure they'll serve tea to us up there."

"I think that sounds perfect. Give me about ten minutes, and I'll be ready."

With that, he left, and she hurried into the bathroom. Taking care of business, she then touched up her simple makeup, ran a brush through her hair, and was back out by the door, waiting when he knocked.

Popping out, she grinned, grabbed his hand, and said, "Let's go!"

She was prepared to let go of his hand as soon as they stepped out into the hall together, but instead, he wrapped his long fingers around hers. As they made their way into the observation car, he let Enrique know they'd have their tea in the upper deck. He led the way, still holding her hand, and even though she knew it might seem silly at the age of thirty-two, she was thrilled to feel his palm pressed against hers. She was no blushing virgin but had never felt the electric connection between her hands and deep inside her heart before. Knowing the feeling was because of the trip, the train ride, and the majestic surroundings, she wouldn't lose her heart, but she could certainly revel in the fantasy.

They settled into the settee that had become theirs, she sitting next to the window. "Ooh, we're going to start climbing, aren't we?"

"Yeah, looks like for the next leg of the journey, the mountains will be right outside our windows."

The server brought their tea, complete with delicate china, teapot, and a tray filled with little sandwiches and cookies. She ate but still felt the pull of fatigue. Leaning her head back, she relaxed with the gentle rocking of the train. Reveling in the comforting presence of Bray whose body was warm next to hers, she closed her eyes for just a moment.

Bray's arm was going to sleep but he wasn't going to move. *Not for all the money in the world. Or even the promise of a nightmare-less sleep, for that matter.* With Marie's head on his shoulder as she slept, he remained steady, offering her what support he could. Her words from earlier in the day continually replayed in his mind. The helicopter accident. Her dreams. Her recuperation. An adolescence filled with therapists and medical personnel for friends. And then her declaration that she understood his position.

He'd never had a problem keeping his thoughts squarely on the mission before. But with Marie, he did. Careful to analyze, he tried to figure out why this was different. *Maybe because there's no overt threat, and I'm able to relax more than on most assignments. Maybe because she comes with no expectations or demands. Maybe because I've been able to spend a lot of time talking with her.*

Regardless of the reasons, he couldn't escape one fact—he enjoyed getting to know her more than anyone outside his friends in a long time. She exuded strength and vulnerability tied up in a beautiful package.

He thought about her dreams. His PTSD reared its ugly head in his dreams, but when he woke, he remembered the faces that haunted him. For her, as much as he hated that she had dreams, he was glad that when she was awake her mind canceled the reality of seeing the pilot in death. It was hard enough for him as an adult to deal with the loss of military brothers. He couldn't imagine trying to deal with that as a teenager. And he knew it didn't matter her age now; trauma was trauma, no matter how much time passed.

While it appeared there was no threat to her on the trip, he was also very aware of the reason he was chosen. His medic background. He'd kept a careful eye on her, noticing that while she ate healthily, she was more lethargic. *Perhaps our outing in Banff was too difficult.*

She shifted slightly, stretched, and then yawned. Suddenly bolting upright, she swung her head around, her face close to his. A blush crept over her cheeks, and her green eyes blinked at him through her red glasses.

"How many pairs of glasses do you have?"

She sat up straighter and shoved her fingers through her hair, pushing it away from her face. "That's a strange question to ask when I've just woken and probably drooled all over you."

He laughed and enjoyed watching her blush deepen as she smiled.

"I have about six pairs. I could never choose which color I liked the best, and then I discovered the kids I've worked with really got a kick out of me showing up in different glasses. It also was an icebreaker when I needed to work with a new child who's in a lot of pain."

"I can't imagine doing what you do every day."

She settled back in the seat, casting her gaze out the window for a moment before turning back to him. "I believe we all have gifts. Different things that we're good at and different interests. Beth was right when she said that we all have careers that incorporate what we do well so that society can function."

"I agree, it's a lovely sentiment. But some careers are much more emotionally taxing than others."

She nodded slowly, her top teeth landing on her bottom lip as thoughts worked behind her eyes, and he had no idea if she was going to keep talking or if he'd pushed too hard and she might shut down. He breathed a sigh of relief as she twisted in the seat to face him more fully.

"I'm glad that I was already a teenager when I had the accident. I had a lot of pain after the surgeries, and they immediately wanted me to start doing PT and OT. My right leg and foot were shattered. Numerous surgeries literally built it back with pins and screws. It was so horrendous, I wanted to give up often. But I knew I had to keep going. And I knew that no one was trying to punish me. The pain was simply going to be part of my life. I had the most wonderful therapists, and I suppose it was a true case of me deciding what I wanted to do with my life during those hours of watching them work with me and others."

He hesitated, wanting to ask more based on her

brother's report and his research into her before the mission.

She lifted her brow and shook her head. "Why do I get the feeling that there's very little you don't know about me? Between Cory and whatever you may have learned, I'm pretty sure you know most of my background."

"I know *things* about you," he said. "But I don't know *you*."

"Is that important?"

He lifted his hand and tucked a wayward strand of hair behind her ear, allowing his fingers to glide along her soft skin. "It is. Because I *want* to know more about you."

If she wondered the reasons for his request, she didn't say. Instead, she simply nodded again. "While my teenage years were not typical, I had homeschool teachers in the hospital, rehab, at home, and managed to finish high school. I took classes during the summer and graduated from college in only three years. And then I applied and was accepted to medical school."

He'd read this in the report but remained quiet, wanting her to share her past.

"I finished medical school, but instead of starting a residency, I decided that I wanted the hands-on career I could have with a doctorate in physiotherapy. That's normally a five-year program, but my medical school qualified for the first three years. Once I graduated, I started working in Philadelphia. I just recently finished an internship in Seattle with a brilliant pediatric physical therapist. I've now been offered a position in Boston."

"And are you happy that you chose this path instead of finishing to get your medical doctorate?"

Her smile widened, her green eyes sparkling. "Absolutely! For all the therapists that helped me, inspired me, and gave me a purpose, I hope to do the same thing for other kids."

"Can you tell me about your case… the one you had to testify in?"

She rolled her eyes. "There's not much to tell. It was when I was in Philadelphia and was called in by one of the pediatric orthopedic doctors. He'd seen a young girl in the ER that had been brought in by her neighbor. Broken arm and a broken wrist. He had suspicions, but the child was frightened and in a lot of pain. I went to the hospital to see her even though it was early for a PT eval, but he thought she might talk to me. I talked about my accident. Talked about what we could do after surgery. Told her that she wouldn't be alone. And, eventually, she opened up to me. Told us that her father was the one who grabbed her by the arm, jerking it so hard she was seriously injured."

"Fuck," he breathed. It was hard to imagine someone hurting a child, any child, but especially their own. Looking at Marie, it was also hard to imagine having to deal with the aftermath. And yet, the more he listened, the more he knew she had been the perfect person for the doctor to call in. She wouldn't sugarcoat the pain that the child would have to endure, but she'd be right there every step of the way to be with her.

"Child protective services came in, and she was placed in protective care. The piece of shit dad made some wild threats. He was more of a local hoodlum than some big-time mob guy. Cory was pissed and got the local FBI to provide security for a while, but honestly, it was all hype. Just a small fish in a big pond who was trying to sound like a whale."

A bark of laughter slipped out at her description. "Damn, Marie." As his mirth slowed, his gaze lingered on her face, taking in each nuance. A tiny scar went through the edge of her right eyebrow. Pale, smooth complexion. Her fingers sweeping a strand of hair behind her ear. The perfect bow of her lips. Green eyes that peered to the side, once more taking in the setting sun vista out the windows.

She stretched her back, and he tried to ignore the way her breasts tightened the material in her shirt as she arched. Clearing his throat, he looked down at his watch. "Are you ready for dinner?"

"Oh, my goodness, I really did take a long nap." She held his gaze, and her lips curved softly. "Thank you for allowing me to rest against you. I was more tired than I realized."

"My pleasure." He was surprised at how much he meant those words. Standing, he offered his hand, glad when she placed her much smaller one into his. Palm against palm, they walked down the stairs and through the cars to their cabins. Checking her room, his gaze landed on the black bag sitting on her bathroom vanity with the pill bottles visible from the top.

He thought of the case that the man handed over to

Gregory in Banff, and he noted how so many of the cases appeared the same. Anthony and Theodore also had small black carry-on bags. Usually containing toiletries, he wondered what Gregory's bag contained.

"Is everything okay?"

He turned at her voice, seeing her still at the doorway, her head cocked to the side.

"Yes, yes. Sorry. Everything's all clear." He smiled as he stepped closer and reached down to squeeze her hand. "How long do you need to get ready?"

"Give me thirty minutes to shower and fix my makeup." His eyes widened, and she laughed. "You've been around me long enough to know I don't do a lot of primping. Certainly not like Cherelle."

"With your natural beauty, you don't need to," he vowed. He could tell he caught her off guard when her laughter slowed, and her gaze remained focused on him.

"You give the nicest compliments, Bray."

"If those are the nicest ones you hear, then something is wrong with the people you hang out with."

"You just did it again." She stared at his face, her gaze roaming before landing on his lips. Shaking her head, she grinned. "Now, get out of here so that you can be back in thirty minutes."

With her eyes on his lips, it was all he could do to keep from leaning down and seeing if she tasted as sweet as he knew she would. Jerking slightly, he nodded, hating to leave her presence, but knew she was right: the sooner he left to get ready, the sooner he could come back to pick her up.

Looking toward the end of the hall, he spied Gregory leaving the sleeper car. Making a quick decision, he slipped to Gregory's door and pulled out the universal key card Josh had developed for the Keepers. Entering the man's cabin, he glanced around for a few seconds before opening the closet. It didn't take long to find the small, black case. Opening it carefully, he peered inside. *Parts for microwaves? No fuckin' way.* He pulled out his phone and snapped pictures of the contents before closing the case and replacing it exactly as he found it. It only took a few seconds to secure the room and enter his own.

Sending a message and the photographs to LSI, he hurried to take a shower and change. He didn't know what Gregory was up to, but the man was more than just a microwave parts salesman.

Dinner was very different from the previous night. Yes, the table settings were immaculate. The food was exquisite. And Marie was even more beautiful in a pale pink silk blouse with her rose-framed glasses.

But the lively, fun conversation they'd had with Beth and Maurice was missing. Instead of the large table down the middle of the dining car, the space was set up with smaller tables for more intimate settings, which was fine with Bray. Even though he and Marie sat at a table for four, they were alone. Anthony and Theodore sat at another table, soon joined by Gregory. Bray was close enough to hear Gregory grunt occasionally while

Theodore talked. Anthony was also more subdued, but with Theodore chatting away, he may have just been used to his cousin taking over the conversation.

Bray was disquieted, but the suspicions concerning Gregory had nothing to do with Marie. She was right earlier when she wondered if he would want to know what Gregory was up to. It chafed to not investigate even when it wasn't an LSI case. Shooting another glance toward the other table, he watched Gregory scowling toward Anthony as Theodore continued to talk. *Fucker's pissed about something.* He was anxious to see what LSI pulled up on the photographs he took.

"You can't help but be suspicious, can you?"

His gaze shot back to Marie, seeing her staring at him. She reached over and placed her hand on top of his, leaning forward at the same time. "It's okay. I am, too."

Before he had a chance to reply, their dinner plates were set in front of them. She emitted a little squeal of delight as she looked down at the sizzling steak topped with shrimp. "Doesn't this look amazing?"

She was relaxed and smiling, drawing his attention to her—not that his attention was far from her anyway. The flickering from the small candle in the middle of the table made her eyes twinkle, and shadows and light danced across her face.

He was reminded that when he was very young, his father bought his mother a large emerald ring, the deep green jewel encircled with tiny diamonds. She would have preferred a family vacation, but Bray loved the way the light reflected off the many facets of the emerald. Maybe it was because of her green eyes, but Marie reminded him of the emerald. She was a constant surprise, multifaceted, and he wanted to discover all he could about her.

She related funny anecdotes from some of her patients, and as much as he would have liked to have regaled her with a few stories from some of his non-secure missions, he didn't want the others to overhear. Marie must have understood as she kept the conversation light while her eyes strayed occasionally to the table of men on the other side of the dining car.

When dessert and wine had finally been consumed, she tried to hide a yawn behind her napkin. Standing, he held out his hand, and she smiled up at him.

"I'm so predictable, aren't I?"

He shook his head as her fingers wrapped around his, and he led her out of the dining car after nodding goodbye to the others. "Not at all. I was just thinking that you are one of the most interesting women I've met."

Laughter barked out from her lips. "Interesting? Me? You're the one with the career you can't talk about." He started to protest, but she squeezed his fingers. "Hey, don't worry. I'm used to my brother's career. He could never talk about work either when others were around."

There was no doubt Marie was different from the women he usually met. Even for a fling, he discovered many women wanted to talk, try to get to know him, and when he didn't open up, they seemed to think he was a tortured soul that just needed someone to drag it out of him. He preferred the women that were there for pleasure only, just as glad to walk out the door afterward as he was. But lately, even those encounters had been few and far between.

With Marie, he wanted to talk. Wanted to share. And even in a situation when he couldn't, she understood. They walked through the lounge car and observation car to their cabins, and he completed his security check. He stood at the door, wanting to continue their conversation, but as she stifled another yawn, he knew she needed her rest.

"I'm sorry. It's not the company, I promise," she said.

"It's okay. It's been a busy day," he assured, fighting the urge to lift his hand to tuck a wisp of hair behind her ear.

"I… I was recently diagnosed with hyperthyroidism. Not Graves, but thyroiditis. It's not fatal, but I do have to deal with the symptom of fatigue as well as a few others like eating but losing weight."

"Do you have medication you have to take?" He already knew the answer but wanted her to be the one to tell him. He wasn't sure why it was important, but having her confidence was something he really wanted. A step beyond just traveling companions. A move toward… *what? Friendship?* Before he could put the halt to sliding down the slippery slope from mission to something else, she smiled up at him. Her beautiful, sweet smile soothed his rough edges and made him want to step inside her world, finding the same happy place that she managed to find each day. And then, all he wanted was to know everything he could about her.

"Oh, yes." She inclined her head toward the bathroom. "I'm still in the finding-what-works phase, but the meds I'm on now seem to help with most symptoms. Fatigue is still a problem, but," she shrugged, "I'm fine and refuse to have anything mar my enjoyment of this trip."

"That's an amazing attitude." No longer able to stop, his fingers moved forward to squeeze her hand, wanting the physical connection... needing the physical connection.

She shrugged, dropping her chin before cocking her head back up to peer at him. "So, um... what's on the agenda for tomorrow?"

It was hard for him to think about tomorrow when all he wanted to do was stay where he was that night: right by her side. Clearing his throat, he forced his thoughts to the next day's itinerary. "I think we're on the train all day tomorrow, but we're supposed to go over some amazing bridges as we move through the mountains."

Her eyes lit with excitement. "That'll make me feel like I'm on the Hogwarts Express like Harry Potter!"

He threw his head back and laughed. "Never thought of it that way, but you're right." As his mirth slowed, his gaze roamed over her face. Deep green eyes sparkled in the low lights. Lips curved into a wide smile. But a faint purple shadow colored underneath her eyes. As much as he hated to leave her presence, he knew she needed rest. No longer resisting, he squeezed her hand. "I'll say good night, Marie. I hope you rest well, and we'll spend tomorrow in the observation car, pretending we're off to wizarding school."

He loved how her smile continued to brighten her entire face as she nodded with enthusiasm.

"I'd love that. Good night, Bray, and thank you for a lovely day."

He turned, and after leaving her room, heard the click of her door lock. He started toward his own door but hesitated. The vibe from the dining car that he'd felt during dinner remained with him, and he wondered what the men were discussing. *It's not my case, not my mission.* But while he was sure it had nothing to do with Marie, he lost the battle to not check on the others.

Slipping out of the sleeper car, he was about to enter the lounge when he heard Gregory's voice. A glance around the corner gave evidence that Gregory was alone and speaking on the phone.

"He was paid, and I have the merchandise. The plan is on schedule. No, no... he doesn't suspect. And no one here suspects. It's all fine. I'll arrive on time with everything."

Bray could tell when Gregory had disconnected, and moving silently, he made it to his cabin without being noticed. Locking his door, he immediately called the intel into LSI. "I know it's not my mission, but I can't ignore something happening right in front of me."

"Looked at the pictures you sent," Walker said. "One of the photos had a serial number on one of the items. John is now our explosives expert. He analyzed them, and I'll bet it comes as no surprise to you that they're not microwave parts."

"I knew it. So, what have you got?"

"Electronics for military-grade explosive timers."

"What the fuck?" He thought of Cory's premonition and gave his head a little shake.

Mace got on the line. "That's all we've got for now, but I'm pulling in our FBI liaison and the Canadian counterpart with the Mounties. You did good, but keep your distance from him until we know what's going on."

"Don't worry. My focus is Marie." As he disconnected, those words slammed into him. *My focus is Marie.* They were absolutely true—and not just because she was his mission.

He walked over to the door that joined their cabins and placed his ear to the door. It was all quiet inside, and he hoped she had already gone to sleep. *Tomorrow will be easier on her... no walking through a town.*

Climbing into bed, he lay awake for a long time, his thoughts tangled. Images of Marie played through his mind... her smile, her excitement, her zest for new experiences. And he realized how much he was looking forward to tomorrow just to see her again.

11

Marie hadn't slept as well as she had the previous night. Even the rocking of the train was unable to keep the thoughts of Bray from her mind. She'd replayed their previous day over and over, from the fun conversation to the smiles they'd shared, to the heartbreaking remembrances of her adolescence, to her admission that she blurred the lines between friendship and professional interest... an admission that was embarrassing for someone in their thirties to confess. How her brother had managed to hire someone that held the attributes that fit her ridiculous list of the perfect bodyguard, she'd never know. But Bray not only ticked every box, he surpassed in boxes she never imagined.

And more than any other man she'd been with, he filled her thoughts. Lying in bed that morning, she couldn't help but wonder what if... *What if he was interested in me the way I am in him? What if he was attracted to me? What if he had feelings for me that went beyond the job?*

She'd climbed from the bed and hustled to get ready,

knowing the answer to those questions was simply that she was his mission. To try to make it more would only result in embarrassment for her and ruin the travel companion relationship they'd developed. And after years of practice, she was a master at pretending things were okay when they weren't.

A knock on the door had Marie throwing it open in eager anticipation of seeing him again, ready for the day in the observation car as they crossed bridges over deep gorges. They had been told that several had a spectacular view of waterfalls. "Are you excited?"

His gaze moved over her as his chin jerked back slightly. "Excited?"

"Yes! Today, we get to spend the whole day looking outside if we want." It dawned on her that he'd never said it was how he wanted to spend the day, and even though the train was not making any stops, it hit her that he might have something else he preferred doing.

Before she could backtrack, he grinned and reached down to take her hand. "Lead the way. First, we'll eat, and then we'll claim our seat and experience the majestic mountains of Canada!"

At his words, her heart leaped. Her cheeks hurt as she smiled widely in return. While they walked to the dining car, she was aware of the warmth of his palm against hers. It was such a simple gesture, one that she would be wise to assign no emotion to. And yet, it seemed so much more intimate than just what he would do professionally.

They arrived in the dining car to see it was similarly set up the way it had been for dinner. Choosing a small table for four, it was still just the two of them eating until Theodore and Anthony came in and sat nearby. Gregory chose to sit alone at a small two-seater table, barely nodding to the others.

Leaning closer, she whispered, "Looks like someone seriously needs a bit of happiness put into his caffeine."

Bray lifted a brow and nodded, his lips curving. He seemed to be watching Gregory carefully, and she wondered if he was thinking of the man's interesting interaction in the town yesterday.

"Are you going to the observation car today?"

Turning at the sound of Theodore's question, she smiled. "Absolutely. I hope the weather stays clear so we can see the waterfalls."

Theodore's head bobbed up and down. "Anthony needs to get some work done this morning, so if it's all right, I'll join you there."

Anthony looked up from his breakfast. "Oh, I'll be there, too. I'll just have my laptop with me." Smiling at the others, he added, "I'll combine work and pleasure." He turned to Gregory. "And will you join us as well? I'm sure we can have food sent up there—"

"No, thank you. I have some work that needs to get done but have no desire to combine work and pleasure. I'll see you at lunch."

Marie made big eyes toward Bray, and they stood, having finished their breakfast. With nods toward the others, they walked back to the observation car, and she led the way to what she now considered to be *their* settee.

The fog that she had seen outside her cabin window

was now starting to lift, the green forests clearly visible with only the mountaintops still blanketed in clouds. Now, as they sat next to each other, they no longer forced their bodies to separate. She loved the easy, comfortable feel of being with Bray. Their thighs touched, and he immediately placed his arm on the back of the seat, allowing him to lean closer as they pointed to sights out the window.

She inhaled deeply, once again feeling as though she should be able to catch the scent of the pine trees. Instead, she was catapulted into Bray overload as she sniffed him instead. A little spicy. A hint of coffee. And a whole lot masculine. Combined, it was everything she'd come to know about his scent.

"Did you just sniff me?"

Dropping her chin to her chest, her shoulders shook. She tried to hold back the snort she knew would erupt but was unable to keep it subdued. Finally, laughing aloud, she knew her cheeks were red with blush, and she twisted her head to look at him. "I didn't mean to, but that's what happened. When I'm up here in the top observation deck, I think I should be able to inhale the fresh outdoors, but all I managed to do was realize how great you smell."

At that, he laughed, and her vision was filled with his face so close to hers. His dark eyes held her gaze until they dropped to her mouth for just a few seconds and then jumped back to her eyes. The air felt heavy in her lungs, and she had to force her breath in and out. She wanted to lean in and kiss him, and that thought alone surprised her. While she loved being around people, she was always cautious in her love life. Getting to know someone before going out with them. Dating for a while before sleeping with them. She simply wasn't a risk-taker, and it now hit her that she'd never had such an overwhelming desire to kiss a man.

She thought about the times her brother had been home between his Special Forces missions and how women practically stalked him wherever they went. It had irritated her at the time, but now, she could see the appeal. *Is that what it's like for Bray? Women throwing themselves at him everywhere he goes?*

"I can tell your mind is working overtime, but I've got no clue what you're thinking."

She jerked at his words, pulling back so that she was sitting up straight again. "Sorry. I... um... wow... my mind was just jumping around everywhere." Twisting so that she could look out the window again, she was thrilled to see the clouds had lifted off the top of the mountains to give her something else to focus on. "Oh, look! We can see this again."

"I've asked Enrique to serve lunch up here," Theodore announced as he walked toward them.

She was glad she'd placed a little space between her and Bray, feeling the need to pull away from her over-heated thoughts. Theodore sat on the other side of the train, soon followed by Anthony, who sat at one of the small tables with his laptop but was next to the window so he could peer out every time Theodore exclaimed over something he'd seen.

The sights were as spectacular as she'd hoped, and all four spent most of the morning taking pictures, calling out for the others to look at what they'd spied. The train rattled over several bridges and through the spiral tunnels as they ascended the mountains.

"I saw the book on the Canadian railway history that you were reading," Bray said. "Learn anything interesting?"

Surprised that he'd noticed, she nodded. "A lot of these tracks follow the fur trading routes of the Hudson Bay Company and also the Great Gold Rush. The railways were started in the 1880s, and by 1890, tourists were able to see the sights that we're now viewing."

The rest of the morning was filled with sightings of bear families, elks, and eagles as well as waterfalls, rivers, and deep gorges. She sighed, settling back in the seat, the feel of Bray's arm along her shoulders comforting. "I'm so glad I came on this trip." Twisting around, she grinned. "And I'm so glad it was you who came, as well."

They held gazes for a long moment, time seeming to stand still. Bray's tongue moved along his bottom lip, capturing her attention.

"I…" he began, then hesitated, conflict moving through his eyes.

Seeing how uncomfortable he appeared, her heart plunged, and she wished she could pull the words back. "I'm sorry, I shouldn't have—"

"No, don't be sorry. Please, don't be sorry."

Confused, her brow crinkled as she tried unsuccessfully to decipher what he meant.

"I'm glad I'm here, too. It's just that I don't want to lie to you."

She said nothing but her heart continued to pound. She'd tried to force down the attraction she felt for him but had been so sure they had a friendship building. Her emotions were bouncing all over the place, and she felt trapped in a small place with nowhere to hide, keeping her and Bray close to each other. Swallowing deeply, she offered a simple chin lift, ready to accept whatever he was going to say.

"I have to be honest, Marie. When the mission came in, it was assigned to me because of a special request by your brother."

"What was his request?"

"He wanted someone with a medical background."

She opened her mouth, then snapped it shut again, understanding filling her. Sighing heavily, she nodded. "Cory... he just can't stop worrying, can he?" Tilting her head to the side, she stared. "So, you got stuck with me because of your specialty? Let me guess... medic?"

He nodded but twisted around to face her fully. "Marie, I can't imagine what it was like for your family to almost lose you when you were young. And to have to sit by and watch how much you suffered. If it was someone I cared for, I'd worry, too. And now..." His voice trailed off.

"Now, I have a condition," she filled in. Suddenly, understanding hit her and a gasp escaped. "You knew, didn't you? Before you came on the trip, you knew all about me."

He winced but moved closer. With his arm on the back of the seat behind her, his leg against hers, and his body angled, she didn't feel trapped, only cocooned and safe.

"I did. But I wanted you to trust me enough to tell me what you wanted me to know. I don't want you to feel like I lied when I said that I was glad I came on this trip. Yes, I took the assignment because I had some medical knowledge. But getting to know you has been the highlight of this trip. Spending time with you has made it more than a mission. *You're* more than a mission."

Her breath caught in her throat as her gaze moved between his eyes and his mouth. The vista outside the windows was ignored as time stood still. *You're more than a mission.* She had wanted to hear those words, and now that they'd left his mouth, her heart pounded again, this time taking flight. The space between them slimmed as they moved toward each other, drawn by pure magnetism.

"It's almost time for lunch," Anthony announced, standing from the table he'd been sitting at, stretching his back as he looked out the windows.

She jumped back at his voice, stunned that for a few minutes she'd forgotten they were not alone in the observation deck. One look at Bray's uncharacteristic surprise on his face, and she was sure he'd forgotten, as well.

Anthony continued, "I saw Gregory ensconced in the lounge car when I came up. I'll go see if he'd like to join us up here?"

After watching Anthony leave, she blew out a long breath. "Wow... I..."

A gorgeous grin slid over his face. "Yeah, wow."

Holding his gaze, she thought of all they'd talked about. Cocking her head to the side, she said, "Tell me something about yourself. Something you didn't expect to let anyone know on this trip."

He jolted slightly, his brows lifting. "Um... how major does it need to be?"

Laughing, she said, "You don't have to tell me your deepest secrets, but it only seems fair that I know something about you that you didn't plan on divulging." His lips curved, ensnaring her attention.

"Well, believe it or not, today is my birthday."

It took a few seconds for his words to reach her brain, and then she startled, her eyes widening. "You're kidding!"

Shaking his head, his smile spread over his beautiful face. "Nope. It's one of the reasons my team was glad to send me on this trip. It was true that I haven't had a vacation in a while, and it just happened to come on my birthday."

"We must tell Enrique and have them celebrate at dinner. Maybe they can make a cake with candles!"

Throwing up his hands, he shook his head. "No, no. It's cool to keep it between us. Believe me, this trip and being with you has been the perfect birthday."

A little gasp slipped out at his words, and she pressed her lips together to keep the smile from overtaking her whole face. "I'm glad. Really glad, Bray." Leaning forward, she kissed his cheek and whispered, "Happy birthday, Bray."

Theodore called out, "Anthony just texted and said we can stay up here. They'll bring lunch to us."

Nodding, she said, "That'll be perfect." She hated to leave but knew she needed a break before they ate. "I can't believe it's time for lunch. I need to pop back into my room before we eat."

Bray looked down at her, his eyes warm. "Medication?"

She pinched her lips together for a few seconds then nodded.

"You seem self-conscious," he added. "Why?"

She sighed as her shoulders lifted in a shrug. "As a medical professional, I know the importance of not being defined by a condition. I want the kids I treat to see themselves as more than just the body parts that need work or a condition that needs medication. I always felt like my family, who was so supportive, looked at me and saw the accident victim. They wanted me to get better, and it was hard because, for every improvement, there were days where I went backward. I know this is normal and learned to accept it like I hope to get my patients to accept that. But it was so hard for my family to see me struggle. And because I limp, I know it's always there, front and center, for others to see. So, I have to battle to be more than a woman with a bionic leg."

She sighed again, this time hearing the breath shudder as it left her lungs. "I didn't tell my co-workers about the hyperthyroid diagnosis. I almost didn't tell my family but finally decided to do so. But only after I made them promise to not make it a focus."

Understanding flashed across his face before he smiled. "Come on. I'll walk you back to your cabin before lunch."

Nodding to a smiling Theodore as they headed toward the stairs, she said, "We'll be back for lunch up here. I can't wait to see more of the bridges."

She preceded Bray, and when she reached the bottom of the stairs, she turned to go toward the sleeper cabins. Looking over her shoulder, she said, "I wonder if Anthony can convince Gregory to leave the lounge and to join us for lunch."

"As antisocial as he's been recently, he may just eat in the dining car all by himself."

She nodded her agreement, leaning in to whisper, "I still think he's got something sneaky going on."

Bray opened the door to her cabin and completed his sweep, waving his hand for her to join him. She walked straight to the bathroom, rummaged through her bag, and quickly swallowed her pills.

"I'm going to pop into my cabin and will be right back," Bray said.

Nodding, she was glad for the few minutes of privacy. Closing the bathroom door, she quickly took care of her business and ran a brush through her hair before stepping back into the main room.

Her bed had been made and the curtains pulled back to show the lush forests in the background. Curious, she stepped to the window and peered out just as Bray entered her room.

"What are you looking at?" he asked.

"Look at that river down there. I didn't realize we

were so close to one of the gorges. We must be getting ready to go over one of the bridges."

"We probably won't have time to get up to the observation car but I'm sure we can see some from here."

She felt his presence as he moved in closer to her, and with one of his hands on her shoulder and his face near hers, they peered out the window together as the train rounded a curve and began over the bridge. "Look! You can see our engine and the dining car up there."

She had grown used to the roaring sound and rocking motion of the train as it moved along the tracks. Just as she leaned her forehead against the glass window to look down, she felt the vibration before she heard the roaring explosion assault her ears.

Gasping, her hands shot up, her palms slamming against the glass window to steady her body against the increasing vibrations. "Oh, God! The bridge!"

"Fuck!"

Bray's curse was barely heard over the high-pitched squeal of the brakes assaulting her ears as his arms encircled her just before he threw her onto the floor. The cabin shuddered as it rocked to the side. She screamed as he rolled on top of her, pressing her flat to the floor as his body covered her from head to toe and her cheek was pressed hard against the carpet. Pain shot up her leg, and a flash of memory bolted through her of the helicopter dipping to the side. She screamed again but the sound was lost in the crash of metal and glass as her world toppled.

"Fuck! Hold on!"

The cabin tilted further, and with her eyes squeezed

shut, they rolled toward the door, unable to stop their tumble. Another strangled cry, the air forced from her lungs as the sleeper car landed on its side, careening downward, then flipped once more until the world was upside down. Sure that they would be crushed underneath the furniture, she prayed for the end to be swift. Even with her encased in his arms, her world jarred, she lost all sense of direction, and her family's faces flashed through her mind.

The car slowly stopped rocking, and she pried open her eyes. The bed along with the other furniture was bolted into the floor and managed to stay intact, although the bedspread now lay next to her head. The freestanding chair was on Bray's back, and he shifted slightly, shoving it to the side.

"Oh God oh God oh God," she chanted. The angle of the car had the blood rushing to her head, but movement was impossible as icy cold fear filled every cell in her being and vibrated along every nerve.

"Are you okay? Marie, are you okay?"

Her body shook with such force, she was unable to lift herself from her position even as Bray shifted upward. His hands were moving down her back and legs, continuing to ask if she was okay, but she couldn't seem to respond.

He leaned down, placed his face next to hers, and held her gaze. "Marie, please, talk to me."

Realizing that the train was no longer moving and another explosion had not occurred, she dragged in a ragged breath and nodded her head, jerking it up and down. "Y… yeah."

"We need to get out of here. We need to see what's going on. I don't want to leave you here—"

"No!" Panic clawed its way up her throat. Another flash of lying in the helicopter wreckage alone whooshed through her mind, causing another gasp to fly from her lips. "D... don't leave me. I'm okay. I... I can c... come with you."

Grimacing through the pain in her leg, she allowed him to assist her to her knees. The train had landed upside down on a slope, but the windows were still intact. "We're... we're trapped... we could slide into the gorge if we move." Her words were barely a whisper as she struggled to breathe. The air seemed too thick to drag into her lungs and spots appeared in her vision.

"Marie, Marie." Bray moved directly into her face again, giving her shoulders a little shake. "Stay with me, babe. Come on, breathe. Marie, breathe with me." His palm landed in the middle of her chest. "Push against my hand."

Her eyes focused on his mouth, and pushing against the pressure of his hand, she forced out the air in her lungs before sucking in more. The spots began to dissipate, and she nodded her head in jerks again. "Okay... okay... I'm okay." Pressing her lips together, she looked at the destroyed room, letting Bray take the lead.

He opened the door, climbed over the ceiling panel that was now underneath them, and entered the hall. Turning, he raised his hands to her, assisting her to crawl after him. She crouched even though there was headroom. It was as though she was in a carnival funhouse where mirrors made her feel discombobulated.

"Shit," he cursed, and she twisted her head to look behind. The end of the sleeper car that had been connected to the observation car was ripped open and facing downward, the sight of rocks in the distance with open space between all that could be seen.

"Oh, God, where are the others?" She stared at the gaping hole of twisted, mangled metal, then cried out as the car rocked slightly.

Bray squeezed her hand. "Stay still. Don't move. I'm going to go see where we are."

Afraid to move a muscle, she remained in place, her heart pounding as he crouched then crawled to the opening, horrified they would plummet further down the gorge.

"Fuckin' hell," he muttered.

She wanted to ask what he saw but fear choked any questions from her lips. Whatever it was, it couldn't be good. Disoriented, she had no idea which direction they were facing. They'd been approaching one of the bridges over a gorge and the window near her bed had faced the craggy rocks with water in the background. Uncertainty filled her, not knowing how close they were to the edge, or the rocks, or the gorge.

Bray, still in a crouch, moved back to her. Before she had a chance to ask what he'd seen, he reached out and cupped her face in his hands, getting directly in her line of vision. "We're going to go out the back. It's not good, I'm not gonna lie to you. But the back is better because that's the most stable. Less chance of injury. When we get out, I want to get you away from the wreckage so that you're safe. Then I can assess what's happened to the others."

So many questions ran through her mind, but as she stared into his eyes, dark with intensity, she simply nodded. The time for answers would come when they were not in danger of plummeting to their deaths.

When Bray had peered through the ripped-open end of the sleeper car, he'd realized they'd come to a halt against a large boulder just over the precipice of the gorge. The good news was they hadn't gone far over the edge. The bad news was that he had no idea if the car could slide further at any moment. Moving closer to peer down at the other train cars in the gorge, he grimaced as the car creaked and heard the muffled squeal from Marie.

Looking at the shredded metal, it was obvious their car hadn't simply become disconnected. *There was an explosion, but what the fuck caused it?*

Crawling to the edge, he peered straight out to see the gorge yawning before him, the empty bridge connecting to the other side. Unable to tell if any of the forward parts of the train had made it to the far side, he remembered the metal squealing he'd heard earlier. That sound indicated the engineers realized a problem and had applied the brakes. *Maybe they made it to safety on the far side.*

Maneuvering so that he could peer downward, he spied remains of the observation car crumpled on the rocks lining the gorge. There was no movement amongst the shattered glass that had been the domed ceiling.

Running down the passengers in his mind, he knew Theodore had been in that car, with Gregory and Anthony either in the lounge or dining car, both further down in the gorge near the water. He had no idea which staff might have been in those cars. He was unable to ascertain if the kitchen car and staff cars were further below in the gorge or if they perhaps made it to safety across the bridge. *No time to look now, I've got to get her out of here!*

Stealthily and moving with great care, he crawled back to where she sat, eyes wide, her chest barely breathing as though she was terrified of each tiny movement. Thankful she was not peppering him with questions, she held his gaze and waited. Stopping directly in front of her, he reached out, taking her cold hand in his.

"The gorge is wide and deep. Maybe the engine made it to the far side. Maybe the staff car and kitchen. I can't be sure until we get out and I can see further down into the gorge. Being the last car, we tumbled off the tracks, but that's what saved us. If we'd gone further, we'd be at the bottom, too. We slid down toward the embankment, so we need to get out of here. The observation, lounge, and dining cars are in the gorge. It doesn't look good, and I didn't see any movement."

"We need to go check on them." Her shaky words rushed from her.

"First, you and I need to get out of this car and onto the ground. I want to get you away from the wreckage. I need to check the other rooms to make sure no one else had come back to their cabin. Then, I'm going to make my way down to check on the other cars to see if I can find survivors."

"We're in the middle of the wilderness. How will anyone find us?"

"If the engineer is alive, I'm sure he's already called in for emergency services. If all the cars have gone down, then the railway still will know something happened. As soon as I get you safe, I'll call my people and they can pull up our location on satellite. Between my people, the train company, and the Canadian government, someone will come to rescue us. But first things first. Let's get outta here."

He shifted around to the other side of her, and with one arm around her waist, they crouched as they crawled over splintered wood and broken glass on what had been the ceiling to the door at the back of the train. He'd thrown open each door they passed, taking a look inside to make sure no one had come back before the explosion.

She whimpered slightly as they crawled along. He looked down at the strain mixed with shock evident on her face. "Your leg?"

A nod was her only answer, and he held her closer as

they continued. At the back door, he grabbed the lever and twisted, giving the door a push, grateful when it swung open. He climbed down, then turned and raised his arms. "Don't jump. Just lean forward and put your hands on my shoulders. I'll lift you down."

With the sunlight streaming down on them, he could now see her pale face, the dark circles under her eyes even more pronounced. A small trickle of blood ran down the back of her neck and over her shoulder. *Fuck!*

With his large hands spanning her waist, he lifted her from the upside-down back deck, and instead of setting her feet onto the ground, he carried her away from the wreckage. Once he was sure they were at a safe distance, he knelt with her still in his arms. "You're bleeding. Let me see what happened."

His hand shifted her hair to the side and spied a long but not deep cut at the top of her neck near her hairline. She winced as he pressed his hand against it. "Shit." His fingers bloody, he grabbed the bottom of his shirt and ripped a strip from it. With it wadded in his fingers, he placed it against the back of her neck. "Here, hold this on it. I'll go back in and see if I can find something for a bandage—"

She grabbed his arm with her free hand, her grip tight. "No, Bray! This is nothing, and we've got more important things to do. Please, let's see if there's anyone we can save."

Her pupils were still slightly dilated, probably from shock. He looked over his shoulder toward the edge of the gorge, and while he couldn't see the other train cars, he knew what they looked like. Grimacing, he clamped his jaw tight before swinging his head around to see her peering up at him, anguish etched on her face. "Okay, but there's no *we* in this. I need to know you're safe, so you stay here. Let me see what I can find, and I'll come back."

"I should come, too. I'm a doctor. I can take care of—"

"Yeah, but the gorge is too difficult for you to traverse. And as a doctor, you know when it's best to have help, so hold this on your wound, and I'll ascertain if you're needed."

Fear settled deeply in her eyes, but she nodded, her movements jerky. "Okay. Okay. Yeah... okay."

He grabbed her cheeks and leaned forward, pressing his lips against her forehead. The gesture had been pure spontaneity, something he never did. He'd wanted to offer her the physical connection of his assurances, but it was her soft skin underneath his lips that slammed into him. For a second, he reveled in their touch, her scent, and the squeeze in his chest. Dragging his lips away, he instantly felt the loss. Holding her gaze, he vowed, "I promise, I'll be back."

She stared up at him, green eyes so trusting, and his gaze dropped to her lips. Like answering a siren's call, he wanted to take them, letting both of them revel in being alive. Fighting the urge, he stood quickly and turned, walking away.

Pulling out his phone, he connected to LSI and punched in the code for an emergency.

"You're on."

Glad Josh didn't fuck around, Bray said, "Explosion.

Train derailed. Marie was with me in the sleeper car, now upside down. Assessed situation. Engine may be across the bridge. Part of the bridge is damaged. At least three cars are in a gorge, and where I'm standing, I ascertained no movement. I've gotten Marie out the back where it was more stable. She's safe and away from the wreckage. I'm going down the gorge to see if I can assist any survivors."

"Fuckin' hell!"

Similar words came from so many different voices, he had no idea which Keepers were in the compound listening.

As usual, Mace's voice cut through everything. "Pulling up location now. If the engineer is alive, he'll report to the authorities, but I want to get you and Marie out of there."

"After I check on any survivors, I'm going to come back in and grab what equipment I can carry. I'll see if I can determine what kind of explosion caused this. I'll report in with everything as I find it."

"Get to safety. Don't worry about investigating the explosion. The authorities and we can worry about that later."

Trained to keep mentally sharp during adrenaline rushes, he was surprised how his concern for Marie had delayed the idea that the explosion could have been deliberate. Now, the full force of his anger was coming to the surface. "If someone set off an explosion that nearly killed me and Marie, I'll do more than fuckin' worry about it," he growled.

Disconnecting, he slid his phone back into his

pocket and turned carefully, seeing Marie still sitting where he left her, wide eyes staring at him.

He hurried over the forest ground that quickly gave way to the rocks at the edge of the gorge and looked down, ascertaining the safest way to check the other cars. The observation car was the closest but was also upside down, the dome of glass windows that had formed the ceiling now completely shattered. Walking past, he squatted and peered in as best he could. A flash of blue caught his eye, and as he moved closer saw the partially crushed body of Theodore. He leaned in and placed his hand on his wrist... *No pulse. Goddammit!*

Theodore had been as excited as Marie to see the bridges from the observation car and had remained all morning, awaiting lunch to be served there. Passing the entire car wreckage, he did not see another body but looked around in case Anthony could be found.

Continuing over the rocks, the lounge car was next, lying on its side, partially caved in. Uncertain of the stability, he peered through the windows to see if there was anyone inside. A smaller body with a red jacket was now visible, and as he approached recognized the body of one of the dining car servers. Barely able to reach his hand in, he checked for a pulse but found none. Continuing further, he saw black pants and expensive leather shoes from underneath part of the train. *Anthony!* As he slipped down a few more rocks, the top half of Anthony's body was not visible; he checked the pulse from the ankle, finding what he expected—dead.

Steeling himself, he moved further, still looking for a possible survivor. *Where did Gregory go?* If not in the observation car or the lounge, then he must have been in the dining car. By now, the gorge embankment was steeper, and he could see the kitchen car had been pulled off the bridge as well, lying near the bottom, partially submerged. A little bit further down was the staff car, also crushed. Smoke billowed from the far side, and as he moved to a more advantageous position, he spied the engine. *Goddamnit, the whole fucking train went off the bridge.*

A shudder ran down his back, nearly taking him to his knees as the enormity of how close he and Marie came to dying hit him. If they had not gone back to the sleeper car so that she could get her medicine before lunch, their bodies would be alongside the others.

He wished he had the proper equipment to scale quickly down the boulders, but lacking anything to use, he continued to climb down slowly. He looked to the other side but saw no movement.

Finally, coming to the dining car, the last one he'd be able to inspect, he could see it had split in half. While not good for anyone who'd been inside, it did allow him to check for victims easier. Two more servers, both dead. His added weight made the train car more vulnerable as it perched on the side of the rocks, but he had to keep checking. In the front half, he discovered Enrique's body.

As far as staff, that only left the sleeper car attendants, the chef and kitchen car workers, and engineers. *Christ, how many more are dead? All of them?*

Looking down, he spied a bag of rolls. Knowing they would need something to eat, he grabbed them and tied them to his belt. Scrounging for a moment, he also took a few packages of nuts and even found a bag of dried fruit. More food was about but nothing he could carry easily.

Crawling back out of the dining car, he looked up and sighed. *No Gregory. Where the fuck was he?*

The climb back up the side of the gorge was arduous and slow. He assumed the train had an automatic relay system with the railway so they'd know it had stopped but had no idea how long it would take someone to helicopter in to rescue them.

"Bray!"

His hand almost slipped at the sound of Marie's voice. Looking up, he squinted as the sun reflected off the broken glass nearby but saw her wide-eyed face peering over the edge. "What the fuck are you doing?"

"I… there's…" She stammered, her voice dying out.

"Get back away from the edge!" He continued climbing up the large boulders, making the slope past the lounge car, checking it again but not finding any other staff or Gregory. Remembering the small refrigerator inside, he crawled to where it was located. The door was smashed, but he managed to pull two bottles of water from inside. Shoving them inside his shirt, he left the wreckage behind.

As he neared the top, the smaller rocks were more unstable, and he slipped several times. Wanting to take another look at the observation car, he passed Theodore's body and maneuvered to the end so that he could look on the lower level. Empty. *Well, at least that's fuckin' something, but I still can't find Gregory.* Now, the idea that Gregory may have been in his cabin hit him, and he scrambled the last of the way up, his hands grasping the small tree roots that grew out from between the rocks.

Hauling himself to the top of the sleeper car, he spied Marie away from the edge but not where he left her. Needing to check on her again, he climbed the rest of the way out of the gorge. He opened his mouth, but she flung herself toward him, her arms wrapping around his neck as she pressed in tight, burrowing in deeply as though she needed every ounce of his being to keep her together. He placed his hand on her wound, glad to see it had stopped bleeding.

"They're dead." Her words were muffled against his shirt.

"I know. So far, they're all dead."

"No, I found them." Her body shook, but he didn't want to wait. With his hands on her shoulders, he forced her back slightly so that he could lean down and place his face directly in front of hers. "Who, babe? Where?"

She blinked several times, then rasped, "Carlie and Frank."

He recognized the names of the two sleeper car attendants and remembered they often stepped to the back deck of the train to smoke and make out. *Christ, if they'd been out there when the car derailed, then their bodies would have been flung from the train.* He pulled the water bottles from his shirt and untied the bag of bread, dropping them all to the ground. Looking back at her, he nodded. "Show me."

He hated to make her walk any further considering her limp was more pronounced, but she didn't complain as she held his hand and led him past several large trees, close to where he'd left her. Carlie was about twenty feet from the back of the sleeper car, her neck bent at an awkward angle. He knew Marie would've already checked for a pulse, but he did so himself, nonetheless. He pulled out his phone camera and took pictures. Seeing Marie's questioning gaze, he said, "Just in case we need them for the investigators who look into the wreck."

She nodded, then pointed toward some scrub brush, and she took his hand leading him in that direction. "Frank is over there."

"You don't need to go, I can check."

"I've already checked."

He opened his mouth to protest but she jumped in, "I'm a doctor, Bray. I might not see a lot of death in my practice, but I'm not going to freak out." They silently pushed through the brush where Frank's red jacket was now clearly visible, his head also at an awkward angle.

"Christ. Fucking hell," he cursed as his chin hit his chest and his fists landed on his hips. He'd faced death. Stared it in the fuckin' face and dared it to come. Same with all the men he served with. Of course, when it did hit his team, it had shaken him to the core, but they all knew, deep down inside, it could come for any of them at any time. But Carlie and Frank were not soldiers. *Fuckin' young, fuckin' in love, fuckin' working a cool job.* He took several more photographs, then shoved his phone back into his pocket, his movements sharp with anger.

The air left his lungs in a ragged exhale. A small, soft touch landed on his back, and he jerked his gaze to the side, seeing Marie staring up at him. Understanding moved over her face, and he hated it. Hated that she, like Carlie and Frank, had to face death when they were so young and unprepared. She'd had to stare death in the face and dare it to take her, too. And like him, she'd won. But Christ, he hated that she'd had to do that.

"What did you find down there?" Her words cut through the turmoil in his mind.

Letting out a long breath, he turned to face her, placing his hands on her shoulders. Clearing his throat, he held her gaze. "All the staff that was in those cars were killed. The two dining car servers and Enrique. I also found Theodore's body still in the observation car."

Her fingers grabbed the front of his shirt, fisting. "Oh, God."

"And then I found Anthony. I was only able to partially identify him—"

"Oh, God," she repeated, her fingers now wadding the material as they curled into fists.

"I recognized his shoes."

She gasped. "The ones that Theodore teased him about paying so much for!"

He nodded, watching as she swallowed deeply. "I didn't see anyone else. All the cars were pulled off the tracks and went into the gorge. If we'd been a little bit further, we would've gone over, too. The staff car and engine were at the bottom, and I wasn't able to get to them. But the railway will know the train stopped. They'll get someone here as soon as they can."

Her gaze dropped and slid to the side, her breathing erratic. Suddenly, she jerked, her head lifting as she peered wide-eyed up at him. "Gregory? You didn't mention Gregory!"

"Christ, I forgot when we went looking for these two." He gently took her hands from his shirt and said, "You've got to let go so I can check the sleeper car again." He bent and reached inside Frank's front pocket, pulling out his keychain.

"Me, too." When he started to protest, she shook her head. "Let's go. He might need medical attention."

"Follow behind me. Only come in once I see if it's stable."

Glad she acquiesced quickly, he ran back over the dirt and rocks to the back of the sleeper car. Hauling himself up, he crawled to the last cabin door, not surprised to find it locked. He'd brought Frank's keys in case his universal card didn't work but heard the click of the lock. Pulling the door open, he peered inside. Gregory's room was in the same state of disarray that Marie's had been. Crawling over the door frame, he crouched and scanned the entire space. Not seeing Gregory, he checked the bathroom only to find it empty. Hands on his hips, he looked around. *Where the fuck is Gregory?*

A strange inkling tickled the edges of his mind, and he swept his gaze around the room once again. Moving to the closet, he opened it with difficulty. With the car upside down, the luggage on the inside of the closet was wedged against the door. Finally popping it open, he dug through the spilled contents, finding nothing but clothing. Carefully crawling to the bathroom, he peered inside the small space, finding only toiletries scattered about. *His case? His black case that had the part—fuck! Walker said John had identified explosive electronics.*

Completing a hasty but thorough search that included opening drawers where the contents immediately fell out and then shifting the bed linens to the side, the black case that Gregory had carried from Banff was not to be found.

Suspicion uncoiled, slithering through his mind, but he had no time to give headspace to Gregory's whereabouts. So far, the train car had not moved again, so he crouched at the back entrance, waiting for Marie to come to him. "I can't find Gregory. But we need to get what we can and get out of here."

As he lifted her, she asked, "Where can he be?"

"I don't know. We can figure that out later. I need to get into my room and get some of my things and then we can go into your room—"

"That wastes time, Bray. Let's get what we need as fast as we can."

The car shifted slightly, and as their legs wobbled, they reached out, grabbing each other's arms. "Fuck!"

"Okay, I'll repeat," she said, her voice barely a whisper. "As fast as we can."

He nodded. "Move slowly and carefully." He hated watching her crawl toward her cabin, but as soon as she disappeared inside, he used the universal keycard and went into Theodore and Anthony's room. The cousins had shared a room, which would have been a tight squeeze for two men. Their business was not doing nearly well enough for them to afford their own individual sleeper cabins. But right now, that made his task easier. Looking through their luggage, just like with Gregory, he only found clothing, and in the bathroom, toiletries.

Leaving their room, he crawled to his, opened the door, and stepped over the frame. Inside his luggage was an empty backpack for emergency travel. He quickly filled it with a couple of clothing items. Opening the travel safe, he pulled out his firearm and ammunition, having permission to carry in Canada. Now, he was even more glad that Mace and LSI had completed missions for the Canadian government. He jerked off his shoes and pulled on boots, lacing them in haste. Moving into the bathroom, he grabbed a few toiletries and a first-aid kit. Uncertain how long it might be before they were rescued, he made one last sweeping gaze of his room to make sure he had what was necessary before heading into Marie's to check on her progress.

With any luck, we'll be out of here soon.

13

It hadn't been long since her and Bray's world turned upside down... literally. At least now, as horrific as the sight of her room was, she was more prepared to move around the upside-down cabin.

As soon as she opened one of her drawers, the contents spilled onto the floor. Technically, they fell to the ceiling that she was now standing on, and a chortle burst forth, born from the unreal reality facing her. Besides her small purse with her identification, passport, and wallet that was still hanging crosswise over her body, she eagerly grabbed the large canvas tote that the railway had given each of them upon arrival. Digging through her spilled luggage, she grabbed several pairs of underwear, shirts, and two sweaters, shoving them inside the bag.

Not knowing how long they might be outside before being rescued, she was glad she was already wearing a pair of jeans. Searching for anything else that might be of use and easily carried, she put a few more items into her bag. Slipping out of her flat shoes, she pulled on socks and her supportive sneakers. Carefully moving, constantly aware of the car's lack of stability, she stepped into the bathroom, but her equilibrium was instantly affected with the sink and toilet upside down. Her bag containing her toiletries and medication was sitting on the floor... ceiling. Grabbing it, she turned to crawl back out.

"Marie!"

"I'm in the bathroom—" Her words were cut off as the sleeper car shifted, sliding several feet downward. She cried out, her hands grasping the doorway, terrified to move.

"We gotta get outta here," Bray said, his face now coming into view as he leaned into the room.

"That canvas bag. Can you get it? I've got my toiletries and purse." He nodded and she carefully made her way over, each step agonizing as she feared the sleeper car plunging over the edge. As soon as she was within touching distance, Bray grabbed her hand and gently led her forward. Her large canvas bag was firmly clasped in his other hand.

As they made their way toward the back, they passed his cabin's open door as well as the Robbins' open door. Glancing inside both, it appeared everyone's room was in the same condition as hers. Furniture that had been attached to the floor of the train now hung suspended while everything not attached had crashed below.

The last door they came to toward the back of the sleeper car was also open, and she could not help but peer inside of Gregory's room. Bray had made it to the back door when, suddenly, the sleeper car shifted on the rocks at the edge of the gorge. He managed to hang on to the door handle, but as the railcar tilted downward at a further angle, she cried out as all the loose items that had been thrown around in the hall slid down with her.

She dropped her bag as her hands darted out, clawing to hold on to anything, but she continued to slide toward the jagged metal of the gaping open end. "Bray!"

"Fuck! Marie!"

Certain they were going to plunge to their deaths, the car suddenly jolted to a halt. Wide-eyed, she stared up at him, her heart pounding, terrified to move.

"We must have caught on a boulder. I'm going to slide down and get you," Bray said.

Afraid to breathe for fear that the very act would rock the sleeper car even further, her heart pounded as he held on to the side of the hall by the cabin doors and lowered himself carefully. Linens and luggage and boxes and bags littered the area, having all fallen out of open cabin doorways and slid down to where she now perched.

As Bray neared, he held on to a doorway and reached out. "Grab my hand."

She wasn't sure she had the strength to obey but slowly lifted her hand until their fingertips barely touched.

"That's it, come on, Marie. You can do it. Reach up a little bit higher."

Stretching her arm further, they clasped their hands around each other's wrists, and he firmly pulled her upward until her feet could stand near one of the doorways. Looking up to the end of the car, her gaze stayed pinned on the exit to safety but wondered how they'd get there.

As though he could read her mind, Bray said, "We can do this. We're going to step on the doorways like a ladder and haul ourselves up. I've got you. We can do this."

His words washed over her, filling her, giving her strength. As hard as her heart was pounding, she felt powerful that she was conscious and able to help herself. Nodding, she watched as he placed his feet carefully and climbed up slowly before turning and pulling her up after him.

They were almost to the back door when she saw the large canvas bag that he'd had in his hand propped near the top. Her small purse was still strapped across her body, but she'd dropped the bag containing her medicine. "Oh, no!" He turned around, his gaze moving over her as though to find an injury. For fear of moving the train car, she didn't even shake her head but explained, "I dropped my bag. My toiletry bag with my medicine."

"I'm going to get you out of here, and then I'll get it—"

"No! What if—"

"No *ifs*, Marie. I know what I'm doing. Now let's go." Without giving her a chance to argue more, he hauled her to the back door, lifting her so that her ass was sitting on the doorframe. He pushed her bag to the ground, then held her as she swung her legs over and he lowered her gently. As soon as her feet touched the rocks, he nodded and disappeared back into the doorway of the train.

The quivers from deep inside threatened to take over her entire body, and she wasn't sure she released a breath until she saw his head pop up from the doorway again. He lifted a small black bag in his hand. "Got it."

"Good, now get out of there."

He tossed it over the edge of the doorway and then jumped down to the rocks next to her. She bent and snagged the bag when, suddenly, the car shifted downward even more.

"Fuck! Get going!"

Wanting to get as far away from the sleeper car as possible, she turned and hurried up the rocks, not stopping until they were well away from the edge of the gorge. Looking over her shoulder, he was right behind her, his backpack and her large canvas tote in his hands.

They waited for a moment, but it seemed as though the sleeper car had fallen as far as it was going to go. Exhausted, she fought the urge to slump to the ground. She wanted to ask what they should do now, or who would come to get them, or how long they'd be waiting, but knew the best thing she could do was remain quiet and give him a chance to plan. They'd missed lunch but she wasn't sure she'd ever feel like eating again. Her stomach churned and her heart ached. Closing her eyes, she tried to even her breathing. *I don't want to be a burden to him.*

He pulled out his phone again and quickly tapped in

a number. She leaned her back against the rough bark of a tree and waited.

"We're out. The sleeper car was in the back, and it was a miracle that we were in it. There were two staff members on the back decking of this car, and they were tossed during the explosion. Both killed. I managed to make it to the cars in the gorge except for the kitchen, staff, and engine. Found three staff, all dead. The two Robbins cousins, also dead. Theodore was identifiable and was in the location we had left him. Anthony had left to find Gregory. I can't find Gregory's body. And the case I know he had in his room, the one I took pictures of, is missing. I quickly looked at the damage as I was searching for survivors. Definitely, some type of explosive material was used. This was not a case of the cars coming unhooked. The explosion occurred at the junction between the sleeper car and the observation car. No one was in the sleeper car, so it would have been easy for him to place the device. We'd only come back so Marie could take her medication before lunch."

He paused, listening. Hearing him recite what he'd found, it struck her how he'd spent the past hour not only getting her to safety but finding five dead bodies besides the two she'd discovered. *Seven dead for sure. Probably more, if not all others.* His voice grew harsher, and her attention was dragged back to the present.

"My guess is Gregory set the explosion. He could have hidden in the sleeper car, ready to jump off just as he set the explosion. The plan would have succeeded in knocking the entire train off the bridge, but he miscalculated. The sleeper car was knocked off the tracks but didn't go all the way down."

Her chest depressed as the air rushed from her lungs. *Gregory? He thinks Gregory did this?* As crazy as the idea was, she'd suspected him of nefarious dealings. *Nefarious? God, who talks like that?* Her chin dropped to her chest as she continued to listen to his conversation.

"Yeah, maybe this wasn't where he wanted to set it off. Anthony went to look for him. Maybe he got spooked or was discovered doing something and had to set it off early. Who the fuck knows? But I've got Marie off the train. We'll get somewhere visible so that when a rescue helicopter makes it to us, they can see us."

He was quiet as he listened, grunted a few more times, and then disconnected. She waited patiently, willing to give him time to gather his thoughts, but was glad when he didn't take long.

"I was right about the rest of the train. If the engineers are dead, they aren't able to call anything in, but the railway has a way to keep track of the train as it moves. They'll know where the accident occurred. Mace, my boss, has been in contact with the Royal Canadian Mounted Police to let them know that we're here. He's also going to report that it doesn't appear to be an accident."

She nodded, but his words came faster than she could process. *Most if not all others are dead. Explosion.* Her gaze jumped up to his as her chest depressed when all the air rushed out. "I heard what you said about Gregory. Why would he want to do this?"

One of Bray's hands fisted on his hips as the other

dragged through his hair. He looked to the side, his breath heavy before he finally shook his head. "I don't know, Marie. He certainly roused our suspicions with his actions, and he was the only one today that wasn't in plain sight of the others. That doesn't make him guilty, but the fact that I didn't find a body is suspicious."

Her brow scrunched as she looked around, her mind racing. Swinging her gaze back toward him, she said, "But think about Carlie and Frank. If they were on the back of the sleeper car, he couldn't have been back there. Anyway, they were killed when the train rocked off the tracks."

Something dark passed through Bray's eyes before he erupted. "Goddammit, I didn't even check."

She stared, wide-eyed and flummoxed as he turned and jogged back up the hill where they'd found Carlie's body. Not willing to be left out, she followed him as fast as she could, ignoring the pain in her leg. "What? Bray! What are you looking for?"

He stopped next to Carlie and knelt beside her. He didn't touch anything but scanned her carefully. Marie stopped on the other side, kneeling as well. "What are we looking for, Bray?"

He glanced up, his dark eyes full of emotion she couldn't read. "Cause of death."

She stared dumbly toward him then looked back down at Carlie, seeing her head at an awkward angle. "Her neck is broken. Regardless of what internal damage may have occurred when she was thrown from the train, her neck is broken."

"I agree. But we're assuming that her neck was

broken when she was thrown from the train. What if it was broken by someone just before the train wreck?"

Gasping, she shook her head slowly. "I... I... um..."

With both of them kneeling next to the body, Bray carefully peeled back the collar of the red jacket and white shirt that made up the staff's uniform. Now that the skin of her neck was exposed, two circles of bruises were visible on the back. Bray rolled her gently to the side, exposing four more bruises in the pattern of fingertips.

"Okay, I see it," she said, her stomach churning more. "But I don't understand it. Someone stood behind her with their hands around her neck?"

"My guess is that Gregory planned on setting the explosive device and then came out to the back deck. The train would have slowed a bit as it rounded the curve before going across the bridge. He could've planned on jumping from the deck but found Carlie and Frank out here instead. His timing may have been fucked up when Anthony went looking for him. But one way or the other, he must've come up behind Carlie and killed her."

As his words sank in, they jerked at the same time, both saying, "Frank." They jumped to their feet and made their way over to where his body lay. Examining him the same way, she stared at the face and head trauma. Marie couldn't tell if anything other than the train accident caused his injuries. Bray leaned over the body closer, and she gave him room to examine what evidence he could find.

"Fuck," he breathed.

She squatted next to them and stared down at Frank, trying to see his injuries through Bray's experienced eyes. "What is it? I'm not seeing what you're seeing."

"Look at the front of his neck. Right here." He pointed to a thin red line that stretched across the front of Frank's neck. "I thought maybe Carlie and Frank were out here at the same time when the train explosion occurred and they were both thrown. But maybe Frank was out here first. When Gregory came out, he strangled him with some kind of wire. Then, as Carlie came out looking for Frank, he grabbed her from behind and broke her neck. He probably assumed that when the train wrecked after the explosion, their bodies would be down in the gorge, crushed like the others. No one would look for any other cause of death."

The air rushed out of her lungs at the idea. Shaking her head slowly, she couldn't wrap her mind around what he'd said. "But to cause an explosion, he'd have to have the... the stuff that explodes. He'd have to have a plan. He'd have to know where everyone was going to be. He'd... he'd... oh, hell, Bray, I don't know, but... Christ..."

"Shhh," he hushed, wrapping his arms around her. Pulled close to his chest, she closed her eyes and breathed in his scent, hearing his steady heartbeat against her cheek. With his lips pressed to the top of her head, he murmured, "Don't think about it now. There's nothing we can do but focus on staying safe until someone gets to us."

At those words, she jolted. Leaning her head back, she pleaded, "Can we put them into the train so their bodies aren't out here, exposed to the elements? Carlie and Frank?"

His warm eyes saddened, and he shook his head. "Marie, I'm so sorry, but we need to leave them. Technically, this is a crime scene. If we try to move them, then when the authorities get here, they might not be able to tell what happened to them to see if they were killed before the explosion."

Her breath rushed out, hating that he was right. Hating that they had been killed. Hating that Gregory had murdered so many people. Suddenly, she jumped to her feet, her legs shaking so hard she wasn't sure they would hold her up. Her mouth opened but no words came out.

Bray looked up at her, his brow lowering. "Marie? What's wrong?"

She turned her head slowly from side to side, scanning the trees all around, but saw no movement. She finally brought her gaze back to his. "If what you say is true, then Gregory's alive. He's out there, somewhere, on this side of the gorge. What's to say he's not staring at us right now? And if not, where is he?"

He stood and moved closer, pulling her toward his chest, wrapping his arms around her. Muttering into her hair again, he said, "My guess is he's already away from here. He wouldn't have wanted to take a chance on being caught near the explosion. Carlie and Frank wouldn't have been missed for a while since they were making the morning rounds cleaning the sleeping cabins. He could have killed them sometime before the explosion, left their bodies on the back deck, and jumped off."

"But where would he go?" She heard the hysteria in her voice and tried to tone it down but was sure she wasn't accomplishing that feat. "We're in the middle of nowhere!"

"In the last hour before the explosion, we'd passed a few roads. I saw a main road through the mountains in the distance. He could've had a signal, alerted a pilot where to be, and been picked up by helicopter while we were tossed over the gorge."

She leaned back, locking her gaze on his face, searching for calm. "So, you don't think he's around here looking to get rid of survivors?"

"If he went to the lengths to plan this, he'd have known these trains are in constant contact with the railway. There are cameras and signals constantly. There's no way the train could've wrecked and someone not know about it, even if everyone on board was killed."

She released a shaky breath. "So, he's gone."

"Can't swear to what I don't know, but I'd be damned stunned if he was hanging around."

"Okay. Good. So, um... what do we do now?"

"We'll move up to the track where it's clear so that when someone comes, they can see us easily."

Nodding slowly, she continued to process his words although her mind was sluggish as though her brain was in slow gear. Blinking, she jerked her head up. "Wait. How will someone come?"

His body remained still, but his eyes were active as

they roamed over her face. "Marie, honey, you said it yourself. We're in the middle of nowhere. No road can reach us here. So, we'll have to be flown out—"

It didn't matter if she understood the logic of his words. The spots danced in front of her eyes again. He grabbed her arms and pulled her back against his chest. "Stay with me, babe. Come on, stay with me. Whatever happens, I'll be right with you."

Her fingers gripped his shirt again. Cursing her fear and weakness, she sucked in a deep breath. He was right. They had to get out in any way they could. Being a wuss was only making it more difficult on him. Straightening her spine, she continued to breathe deeply until her vision cleared. Loosening her fingers slowly, she nodded. "You're right. I'm fine. Good. So, um… let's get going."

He peered into her eyes, and she prayed that the strength she wanted him to see was found, even if most of it was pretend. He must have been satisfied since he nodded in return. They walked away from the two bodies, and she grimaced, thinking of the two young lovers that had been killed. Taking each other's hands, and with their bags in their free hands, they walked up the hill to the tracks, trying to ignore the pain in her leg.

14

The rocks forming the bed of the train tracks weren't comfortable, but Bray had sat on much worse for much longer. His concern was Marie. She wasn't complaining. Instead, she kept putting her hand to her forehead to shade her eyes as she looked up into the sky. They hadn't been there for very long, and he had no idea where someone might have to travel from to get to them. He'd given her water but she'd drank sparingly.

"Hey," he said, drawing her attention to him. "It'll probably take another hour or so before someone can get to us. We'll hear the sound of a helicopter long before you can see it."

As though on cue, the whirring of blades sounded in the distance, and his gaze shot toward the western sky.

"Someone's here!" she shouted, shuffling to her feet. She waved her hands over her head, a smile on her face.

Listening carefully, he knew the bird wasn't military nor was it large. Certainly not large enough to carry survivors. *Perhaps an early scouting party.* But the railway would have been in contact with the authorities, and they'd know to send a larger rescue party.

Unease snaked through him as he watched the small helicopter dip lower in the sky, heading straight for the two of them.

Marie continued to wave her arms, calling, "We're here! We're here!"

The bird turned to the side as it neared, and Bray spied the barrel of a long-range rifle pointing out the window. *Fuck!*

"Get down!" He whirled, grabbing her around the waist, and dove for the ground. He didn't twist to keep her on top of him, wanting instead to cover her body from a possible gunshot. But that meant she took the brunt of the fall, and he hated the sound of her cry as he landed on her. Several puffs of gravel flew up around them as bullets hit the rocks.

As the bird turned to make another pass, he took to his feet with his hands under her armpits, hauling her upward in one swift movement. "Go! Run into the woods!"

Thanking God and whatever deity was listening that she obeyed instantly, she limp-ran to the nearby cover of the trees with him close behind. A flash in his mind of some of the valleys they'd traveled through with grass-covered plains all around and no place to hide in also had him sending up a thankful prayer there were trees all around.

She continued to race as fast as she was able into the thick forest's undergrowth, and he called out, "Stop,

Marie! Don't go any further until I can see what's happening."

Her chest was heaving, but she leaned her back against a wide trunk and nodded. His gaze scanned her from head to toe and back again. Her eyes were huge and her cheeks were flushed, but she was whole and unharmed.

Pulling out his phone, he connected to LSI. Not giving anyone a chance to speak, he barked, "Private bird flew in, taking shots at us."

"What the fuck?" Josh bit out.

"It was small, like a RotorWay. Couldn't identify the pilot or passenger. Firing a long-range rifle. Covered Marie, then we made it into the woods."

"Got word that rescue is on its way out of Canadian Air Force base. ETA was about fifty-eight minutes, but a storm is coming in, might delay their arrival."

"Even without the storm, that's not going to be quick enough to get us away from whoever the hell is shooting at us."

"Gregory?" Mace growled.

"That's my guess. Bird circled over the gorge after taking shots of us. But whoever was firing at us was definitely after us, and we're the only ones who would have any suspicions of him. We're the only ones on this side of the river that weren't killed. But that's not all. The two staff members whose bodies we found from the wreckage of the sleeper car were killed before the train explosion."

Sounds of *'Goddammit,' 'fuck it,'* and *'you've got to be*

shitting me,' sounded through the phone, indicating the whole group of Keepers was there and listening.

"I've got Drew, Tate, and John on their way to you. They were flying into the Air Force base, but I'll redirect them to your coordinates once they land and get a helicopter. Marie's brother, Cory, is coordinating with their RCMP."

While reporting into LSI, Bray had made his way to the edge of the woods, watching as the helicopter moved away, circled back, then moved away again. "The bird has too much time to get to us before a rescue party comes. I need to get the bags that I left by the tracks. We can't wait around. As soon as I get the bags and get back into the woods with Marie, we've got to get moving. Send me what you can, and we'll head to a safer location where we can wait it out."

Disconnecting, he shoved his phone back into his pocket. The bird flew to the other side of the gorge. Keeping low while racing forward, he snagged his backpack and Marie's bag before turning and darting back into the woods. The sound of the whirling blades grew closer, and he knew they had little time to make their escape. If whoever was firing at them decided to land near the tracks, the last thing he wanted was to be a sitting duck.

Marie was in the same place, her chest no longer heaving but her large green eyes just as wide. He stopped in front of her, his assessing gaze taking her in as well as planning. *If it was just me, I could get away. But we're in the fuckin' Canadian mountains. We can't go far, so*

I need to find a place to hide. Her hand landed on his arm, jerking him out of his trance.

"I can do this." Her fingers squeezed as she jerked her head up and down. "I'm serious, Bray. Don't worry about me because I can do whatever we need to do. I'm much stronger than you think I am."

Hating that she was the one reassuring him when it should be the other way around, he shook his head. "It's my job to take care of you, and that's what I'm going to do. We need to get away from here. We can get somewhere and hide."

"Can't we just hide here in the woods? If we go away, then the rescuers won't be able to find us."

He saw the hope in her eyes and hated to dash it. He placed his hands on her shoulders and shook his head. "If he's looking for survivors, then he's seen us. If he figures out we're the only ones, he can land and come after us."

"Oh." Her brow scrunched, and he could see her trying to formulate another plan.

"Marie, this is on me. You're under my protection, and I'll get us out of here."

For a few seconds, it appeared as though she were going to argue but then settled her features as she nodded slowly. "Okay. I trust you. What do you need me to do?"

"We need to get as far away from the tracks as we can right now. My people are sending information on our location to my phone, and I'll check it as soon as I'm sure that whoever is in the helicopter can't see us when they land."

She gasped. "They want to kill us that bad?"

"Whatever this was, it was planned. We don't have time to analyze it anymore right now. Even if he doesn't land, he can keep flying to search for us. We've got to get out of range."

He reached down to grab their bags, but she snagged hers from his hand. She slipped both arms through the shoulder straps, and even though hers was not a backpack, she was able to carry it on her back. He slung his pack on his back and pulled out his phone. Looking at what Josh had sent, he said, "We're going to head east even though that's going uphill. I hate like fuck we have to do this because I know it won't be easy, but I don't think they'll be expecting us to go this direction. I know the river curves along, and we can get to it upstream. I've got two water bottles, but we want to have fresh water."

If she doubted him or had questions, she didn't give voice to them. Instead, she dipped her chin quickly and said, "You lead, and I'll keep up." He had no idea if those words were true, but if she was determined to fight through, so was he.

Despite her best efforts, he knew she'd never be able to handle the roughest terrain that he would be able to bound over. And yet, time was of the essence. He had not a doubt in his mind that Gregory had escaped just before the explosion and had been picked up with prearranged planning and was now searching to take them out. *But why? Was he trying to kill anyone who made it out of the train wreck alive?*

Moving carefully over tree roots and pushing past

the smaller trees and brush that grew thickly on the forest floor, he kept walking but constantly looked over his shoulder to see how Marie was faring.

They'd only been hiking five minutes when she finally called out, "Stop looking at me!"

His feet jerked to a halt, and he twisted around to see her frowning up at him.

"I know I'm not a frigging super-soldier, and I know I'm not going to be as fast as you, but just focus on getting us where you want us to go and stop turning around to see what's happening with me. If I need you, I'll let you know!"

In the middle of their developing nightmare, his lips curved slightly. She looked as though a stiff wind would blow her over but she still managed to throw out an impressive glower. "Got it. And for the record, I think you'd make a great friggin' super-soldier."

A chortle slipped between her lips, knocking the frown from her face. "Yeah, that's me. FSS. Now move!"

"Yes, ma'am." With that, he turned and headed forward, battling the urge to keep looking over his shoulder while he continued to choose a path that he felt she would be able to handle.

The rise was steeper now but the thick trees kept them well hidden. Ten minutes later, his phone vibrated. Pulling it from his pocket, he nodded toward Marie. "Take a rest." Putting the phone to his ear, he ordered, "Talk to me."

"I've informed Cory and the RCMP what has happened. They're sending another team out with the intent to neutralize the threat. They've also alerted the rescue team that's ahead of them. Now, for the bad news."

Mace never wasted words, so Bray glanced toward Marie sitting nearby and steeled himself to hear what his boss needed him to know.

"A strong thunderstorm swept over the mountains to your northeast. The rescue team had to pull back. According to the radar, it's hard to tell how long it will last. The support team will lift off with them, but that leaves you and Marie without any assistance right now."

"I know the bird was circling. Probably to see if there were more survivors than us. Once Gregory sees that we're no longer around, he has to know that help is on the way and he'll need to get the fuck out of here. Whoever he's working for or whatever he's truly selling, they're going to have to cut their losses that they didn't kill everyone and get into hiding. I just want to make sure that, until that happens, Marie and I are far enough away that he can't get to us."

"Bray, we have to consider that he may not be the only one looking for you. While he may give up and get out of the area before the rescue teams come in, whoever he's working for could have others that will come after you."

Heart plunging, he heaved a sigh as his free hand fisted and landed on his hip. "Fuckin' hell! I can't believe I didn't even fuckin' think about that."

"No way you can think of all angles. That's what we're here for. Your main job is to let us worry about the angles, and you do what you can to protect Marie and yourself."

He glanced to the side where Marie was sitting on the ground, her back against a tree trunk. Other than a flushed face, she looked fine. But he knew looks could be deceiving when dealing with an illness. They'd left without food other than the rolls and nuts he'd snagged, and they had little water, both necessary. *With her condition, we've got more to worry about than just getting away from whoever was shooting at them.* "You've got me on your satellite locator. We're going to press on and get to water. Streams are coming down from the mountains that lead to the river. We'll head to the closest one."

Disconnecting, he heard a noise and turned to see Marie already standing, shifting her bag onto her back, again. "We can keep resting for a few minutes."

She shook her head. "No, let's get away from here. I heard what you were saying, and the longer we can keep him from getting to us now, the better chance we have that he's going to give up and fly away."

Nodding, he agreed. "Yeah, that's our best chance to keep him away from us." Her chin dropped just as her gaze cut away, and even though they'd only known each other a few days, he already recognized her expression of turning thoughts over in her mind. "What are you thinking?" Her gaze shot back up to his face, and she nibbled on her bottom lip. "Oh, no, babe," he said, shaking his head. "I don't want you to hide anything from me. I need to know what you're thinking when you think it."

"It's just that... How will the rescue team know where we are? If the Canadian Air Force is sending a rescue helicopter to the gorge, how will they know to look for us?"

He stepped closer, her head leaning back so that she could keep her gaze pinned on his face. He lifted his hand and cupped her cheek, his thumb sweeping over the warm skin as his fingers tangled in the silk of her ponytail. "My people, as well as your brother, are in constant contact with the Canadian military and law enforcement. They're going to let them know where we are and what's going on."

"But how will they *know* where we are?"

"Each of my coworkers has a tracer embedded just under the skin. This way, no matter where in the world one of us happens to be, our headquarters can always find us."

Her eyes widened as her mouth dropped open. "Wow... I just don't... wow." She heaved a sigh before her brow lowered again. "What did you mean when you said that you didn't even think about something?"

He hated to give her more information, but with one look at her determined expression, he figured she could handle it. "While Gregory will give up as soon as he can't find us because he'll know that someone will be coming to rescue us, depending on who he's dealing with, others may come looking for us."

"Because he thinks we know something?"

He nodded. "Yeah or knows that we know he's still alive."

"But won't the rescuers discover that when they investigate? When they can't find his body?"

"There was an explosion that took out part of the

train between the sleeper car and the back part of the observation car. They'll investigate, but without our information, they might assume he was caught in the explosion."

"But you've already talked to your people. They already know it was him. Coming after us won't do anything, will it?"

"He won't know I've talked to anyone. And with us out of the way, there's no witness to the transaction in Banff or what was in his briefcase."

She appeared to have run out of questions but simply sighed again. Slinging her bag onto her back again, she said, "Okay, let's go. FSS is ready for duty, sir."

Barking out laughter, he shook his head. She was completely out of her element but managed to be ready for anything. He just hoped they could get somewhere safe and picked up as soon as possible. "Okay, super-soldier, follow me." With that, he led the way up the path toward craggy rocks, continuing to head east. "There should be a stream nearby. Let's get some water."

15

It felt as though they had walked for hours. Looking at her watch, she grimaced. *Forty-five minutes. And Bray hasn't even broken a sweat. How does he do that?*

Marie felt every step, and even though he kept the pace slow and stayed right with her, her body couldn't keep going. Pressing her lips together, she battled the desire to cry, choosing instead to swallow the scream that threatened to erupt. *At least we're now going downhill; although, with a limp, it hardly matters.*

They'd followed the forest when they first left the train so that they could stay beneath the thick tree cover, away from prying eyes. But that led them upward in elevation. Thankfully, they soon turned and made their way down. She was sure that if Bray had been by himself, he would have taken a more direct route but was trying to find the easiest path for her to traverse. The problem was that right now, nothing was easy.

Coming to the edge of the copse of trees, they stopped. She felt his gaze on her and hoped she looked better than she felt. His next words proved her hope was fruitless.

"You look horrible. We need to stop."

Jerking her head around and up, she hit him with a glare while swiping her hair from her sweaty forehead. "You should never tell someone they look horrible!"

He appeared chagrined as he winced. "I'm sorry, that came out wrong. What I mean is that you look like you *feel* horrible."

The retort died on her lips as she sighed. Slowly nodding, she said, "You're right, I don't feel great. But I know we've got to keep going."

"Tell me what's going on. Be specific with your symptoms."

Her hands had been clutching the straps of her bag, but as she held them out in front of her, the tremors were evident. "It's pretty obvious that I'm sweating a lot, but then, I'm not used to this much physical activity. My heart rate is also fast, but again, I'm being very physical. I'm tired, but that's to be expected. I took my medicine this morning but was distracted by the view out the window and hadn't taken it again before the explosion. I'm okay for now. Honestly, Bray, we need to keep going."

"We've finished the last of the water we brought, and that's what I want to get to." With his hands on her shoulders, he turned her gently and pointed to the edge of the trees. "See that ice over there?"

She looked through the trees, across a small gorge, and could see what looked like a small glacier nestled between two mountain peaks. Nodding, she twisted her head back to him, their noses almost touching. With her gaze pinned on his warm eyes, the idea of him pulling her in close, wrapping her in his embrace, and keeping her safe filled her mind. Instead, she cleared her throat and turned to look back through the woods. "Is that where we're going?"

"Not over where the ice is, but down. There's a small river down below, and with the ice melting, there'll be fresh water for us to drink."

She nodded, glad for the water and the two rolls she had eaten as they walked, but knew their bodies needed more than just carbs if they were going to be out much longer. She looked beyond the tree line to the grassy knoll that led down to where Bray said the river lay. The sky was painted a brilliant blue, dotted by white clouds that floated along. The grass was knee-high and lush, easy to walk through. And yet, while picturesque, now that they had been fired upon, she hated to leave the safety of the thick forest covering. "Will we be safe out there?"

Bray didn't answer right away, and she swung her gaze back to him. He stood next to her, facing forward, his gaze darting around. Pressing her lips together, she waited patiently.

He finally turned and looked down toward her, but no smile curved his lips. "I can't promise what I don't know. It's quiet, calm. We haven't heard anything recently. But we've got to stay alert, not just for the threat of Gregory, but in case there are wild animals. As soon as we get far enough out to see the water, we need to take a careful look to make sure no bears or moun-tain lions are heading to the water as well."

"Oh!" The air rushed from her lungs as she jerked her head, looking around as though a bear might pop out from behind a tree. "I feel incredibly stupid. I never even thought about wild animals. All I could think about was getting away from whoever was shooting at us."

"Don't feel stupid, Marie. The two-legged threat was much more imminent than anything we were facing from the four-legged variety."

"Well, as you say, we haven't heard a helicopter." Shrugging, she hefted the bag a little higher on her shoulders and said, "I have to admit the idea of drinking some cold, fresh mountain water and washing my face sounds really good."

She held steady as his perusal moved over her, once again hoping that the strength she wanted him to see was present. With a chin lift, he turned and started from the forest, and she followed quickly behind. The sun was warm after the coolness of walking in the woods, but she was sure if they had to walk far without the cover of the trees she would've gotten overheated. As they crossed over another knoll, they could peer down and see as the grass led to the rocky edge of the river.

"I feel like Dorothy."

He was only walking a few feet in front of her to keep an eye on the terrain but turned and looked over his shoulder, his brow lowered. "Dorothy?"

"You know, in *The Wizard of Oz*. There's that scene

where she's walking through a field of poppies and she's all excited, racing toward the Emerald City."

He stopped, chuckling, and waited as she caught up. "Yeah, I know exactly what you're talking about."

"Seriously? As soon as I said that I figured a big, bad, alpha soldier wouldn't have a clue about *The Wizard of Oz*."

"I wasn't always a big, bad, alpha soldier, you know. I was a kid whose grandmother read fairy tales to me, and my sister and I would get to watch kid movies on Saturday nights while we were growing up." He lifted his hand and tucked a strand of hair behind her ear, his fingertips barely brushing her skin.

She loved thinking about Bray as a child, immersed in fairy tales and kid movies, imagining the adorable little boy who grew up to be the gorgeous man. But with the touch of his fingers along her ear, she closed her eyes and leaned her head into his palm. It was such an intimate touch, one that she might normally be able to ignore, but after the adrenaline rushes, physical exhaustion, and emotional desperation of the day, ignoring him was the last thing she wanted to do.

With her eyes closed, she could almost imagine that they weren't in the wilderness but instead, somewhere safe, perhaps having dinner together on a date. She felt his body shift and jerked her head up, embarrassed and ready to apologize for giving in to her longing. Before she had a chance to speak, he moved closer and wrapped his arms around her. He pulled her in close, and she rested her cheek against his steady heartbeat and her arms around his waist. Allowing herself the luxury of closing her eyes again, they stayed entwined for just a moment. She knew she was drawing strength from him and had no idea if there was anything she could offer in return.

She felt his lips against the top of her head. "Thank you, Marie."

She couldn't imagine what he was thanking her for. She leaned her head back and stared up, wondering how anyone could look so amazing after all they'd been through. He looked as though there was more he wanted to say, but as she waited, he remained silent. Unable to stop the curiosity, she asked, "What are you thanking me for?"

His hand had moved up over her shoulder and cupped her cheek. "For the hug."

Her lips began to curve upward even though his face remained serious. "I can't imagine that a big, bad, alpha soldier needed that hug more than I did."

"That's why it meant so much to me," he said, a smile starting to form. "Sometimes that's exactly what we need."

They continued to stand for another moment, their eyes pinned on each other, giving and taking without saying a word. Finally, both heaving a sigh, they nodded at the same time. "Let's get to the river," he said. This time, instead of walking ahead, he slid one hand down and linked fingers with her. They walked through the grass and over the gravel to where the clear, bubbling water rushed by.

He knelt on the rocks and filled the two empty bottles with water before standing and handing one to her. She knew not to guzzle, sipping instead. The crisp, cold water instantly soothed her parched throat. Looking over, she grinned. "You know the commercials that talk about their bottled water being like this? Well, they lie. This is so much better!"

Laughing, he nodded. "You've got that right." He reached into his bag and pulled out another roll. Handing it to her, he sighed. "I can't believe this is all we have to eat. Normally, I'm prepared for anything, but what happened to us was beyond anything I could have thought of."

She couldn't help but look up toward the sky, hoping to see a rescue helicopter, then realized she'd have no idea if she saw one whether it would be friend or foe. There was a large, flat boulder to the side. "Can we sit for a little while?"

Nodding, he led her over and they sat down next to each other. Pulling off their shoes and socks, they dangled their toes in the cold water. He reached inside his backpack and pulled out a small towel from the train. Leaning down, he soaked it in the cold water, squeezed it out, then handed it to her. "I don't want you to get overheated."

Thanking him, she pressed it against her neck, then winced.

"Let me take a look," he said. She bent forward and felt his fingers gently probe. "It's not bleeding, but I can't believe I forgot about it."

She shook her head. "Well, it's not like we haven't had plenty of other things to worry about." He grunted, and she hid her smile, wincing again when he placed a bandage on it.

Thanking him again, she glanced at her watch. She reached into her tote and pulled out her black toiletry bag. Unzipping it, she stared down, her tired brain taking a moment to process what she was seeing. "This isn't mine... oh, God, this isn't mine."

Bray's head jerked around, and he reached out to take the bag from her. He peered down inside, jolting. "This is Gregory's bag. This is the one that held the explosive devices."

"What? What are you talking about?" A tic appeared in his jaw as his lips pressed together. She placed her hand on his arm, drawing his attention back to her. "Bray? What's going on?" His gaze moved to her face, settling on her eyes. She could see the battle going on inside him, glad when he finally began to speak.

"I went into Gregory's room after we saw him make the deal in Banff. I found this bag and it was filled with things that I knew weren't parts for a microwave. Took pictures and sent them in. Got a co-worker who was an explosives expert, and he identified them as military-grade explosive electronic parts."

"Oh, God. So, it was him. No doubt about it, it was him."

Nodding, Bray sucked in a deep breath through his nose, letting it out slowly. "When he set off the explosion, he screwed up and didn't get away with his bag that had the rest of these in it."

"Can we turn this over to the Canadian authorities? Will that help them catch him?"

Bray jolted instead of answering. "Marie, do you have your medication?"

Eyes wide, she looked down at the bag as though just seeing it for the first time. "No! Shit... I didn't even think about it." Her gaze shot back to his face. "When we started to slide down in the sleeper car, I dropped everything to try to hang on."

"Fuck," he growled. "When did you take it last?"

"At breakfast." Her mind raced to think of what she could do to counteract not having the medication, but their situation canceled everything out.

"Goddamnit," he growled, dragging his hand through his hair. "I grabbed the wrong bag."

Her hand shot up and she wrapped her fingers around his arm. "Bray, you didn't know. Hell, you asked me if it was the right bag and I said it was. This isn't on you." She pinched her lips together. "If we need someone to blame, it's Gregory's fault!"

"Yeah, well, he isn't here for me to kick his ass!"

Blowing out her breath, she squeezed his arm. "Listen, we'll be rescued soon, and then it'll be fine. And we'll have this bag that proves what Gregory did." Doubt was evident in his eyes. "Seriously, it'll all be good. No worries."

His lips were still pinched together, his concern creeping into her. Forcing her smile to stay in place, she prayed her assurances were right.

16

Bray tried to discern the best course of action. With his Special Forces team? *Easy.* With the other Keepers? *No problem.* By himself? *Hell, yeah.*

Glancing to the side at Marie as she tied her sneakers back on, his heart stumbled. She was hindered by a leg that had been pinned the fuck together and a medical condition that resulted in overheating and fluctuating heart rate without medication. Throw in the fact that the more he was around her, the more he cared for her beyond the mission, and his thoughts were becoming muddled. *Fucking hell! I've got to stay focused.*

He didn't want to stay out in the open by the rocks near the river. *Too exposed.* He looked toward the knoll they'd crossed by the forest, but his gaze lifted to the dark clouds forming above the trees and the way the tops swayed with the increased wind. Before he had a chance to decide, his phone vibrated. "Please, tell me you've got some good news."

The hesitation on the other end had him grimace,

turning away from Marie so she would not be able to see his expression.

"The storm's turned. It's heading your way."

"Goddammit." He now scanned the area to find the best location to ride out a thunderstorm. Mountains. Large trees. Water. Open fields. "Okay, we got nowhere to get out of harm's way from lightning." He lowered his voice. "And I've got shit to report."

Mace growled but said nothing.

"Marie doesn't have her medication. We need to get picked up as soon as the storm passes or she might have some problems. Plus, Gregory will still be looking for us if he made it to the train and looked for something he's realized he's missing: the bag with the explosive devices."

"What the hell?"

Recognizing Cobb's voice, he said, "Yep. He must have screwed up royally and not taken the bag with him. It looks like Marie's toiletry bag, and I grabbed the wrong one. Our shit was all over the place and the fuckin' sleeper car was sliding down the gorge. I grabbed what I could and we got the hell out of there."

"You did the right thing. The only thing you could do," Mace assured, but it did little to make Bray feel better. "Get to safety. Drew and the others are still on their way to the AF base. If you're not rescued by then, they'll get to you."

"Got it." Disconnecting, he hesitated for a second before turning, hoping Marie's attention had been focused on something else. *The scenery. Filling her water bottle. Hell, anything.* Twisting around, he swallowed another curse. Her green-eyed gaze surrounded by blue-framed glasses peered at him, unwavering.

She didn't speak, something he'd grown used to. She talked when she was excited or had something to share. But when their situation needed his concentration, she remained quiet, waiting on him. *The kind of woman that was right for a Keeper.* As soon as that thought hit him, he blinked, jerking his head back. *Where the fuck did that come from?* The others talked about the kind of partner that was right for a Keeper, and he understood what they'd meant. *But Marie?*

With the wind picking up, his brain was still short-circuiting, and he was barely aware she had stood and walked toward him, not stopping until she was directly in front of him, her crinkled brow showing concern.

She placed her hand on his arm, and without think-ing, he wrapped his arms around her. As she stepped closer and leaned her cheek against his chest again, he breathed deeply, admitting to himself that the feel of her in his arms felt right.

"We've got to get going," he said, hating the words as they left his mouth. "A storm is coming."

She leaned back and looked up. "Thunderstorm?"

He nodded. "The forest isn't great but neither is out here in the open near the water or the meadow." He listened carefully. "I don't hear thunder, but we need to go now. By the time we hear it, we're a target."

She started to pull away but his arms tightened just long enough for him to lean down and kiss the top of her head. The act was impulsive, something he rarely was, and for the second time, he wondered what had come over him. *She's under my protection.*

But her lips curved before breaking out into a grin. Without saying anything else, they let go of each other at the same time and both grabbed their bags. They stayed together and walked as quickly as she could through the grassy knoll, not stopping until they entered the edge of the forest.

"I thought you shouldn't be underneath trees during a thunderstorm," she said, her chest heaving as they slowed their pace.

"We'll look for a grouping of shorter trees, but we'll still get in the best position." He thought about what they would need to do, and it hit him how difficult that would be for her. In a perfect world—*a world where they weren't hiking through the Canadian Rockies to get away from a madman who'd blown up the train, or a world where Marie didn't have to worry about not having her medication, or a world where they weren't looking for a way to keep from being struck by lightning*—they would be able to minimize the risk much easier.

Forcing his mind into mission-survival mode, he found a small group of trees that were less than thirty feet tall, surrounded by trees that were well over seventy-five feet tall. While the lightning could travel through the roots in the ground, this had the best chance of keeping them safe. By then, the roar of the wind had increased and the tall trees swayed above them.

"I need you to become as small as possible," he began.

Her head cocked to the side as her brow lowered. "I'm already a lot smaller than you are."

"That's not what I mean. I mean you need to compact your body mass. Don't lie on the ground or stand where you're touching a tree." He found a spot that he thought would be the best for her. He bent his knees while keeping only the soles of his feet touching the ground. "Drop your bags, and I need you to squat down like this, and put your head between your knees. You'll need to stay that way for a long time until the storm passes over."

She stared for a few seconds, then slowly shook her head. "I'm sorry, Bray, my leg and ankle won't bend that way."

He took to his feet and sighed. "I was afraid of that."

"I can kneel, which will have my knees, shins, and feet on the ground. That's the best I can do."

He admired her tenacity and willingness to adapt. Offering a smile he hoped gave comfort, he nodded. "That's all we can hope for, to do the best we can."

By now, the forest was dark, and even though he couldn't see the clouds, he knew they'd be black and rolling. The thunder was closer, indicating the lightning was near. She settled on her knees, and bent forward, her head bowed, and her hands clasped behind her neck. Admiration flowed through him. *It's more than admiration*. What he felt, he couldn't define, and at the moment wasn't going to worry about the emotions rocking him. *Keep things practical. Keep things safe.*

"I should distance myself for our safety. I'll move away about fifty feet, but I'll still be close."

She nodded while keeping her head down, and he jogged through the trees, stopping where he could still see her. Dropping his bags, he squatted and tucked his body in tightly.

It didn't take long for the storm to descend. It was a while before the rain reached them through the thick trees, but when they finally started getting wet, they were soon soaked. He kept lifting his head to keep an eye on her, but she managed to stay in position. The wind whipped around, roaring through the tops of the trees. With his head tucked, he couldn't see the lightning, but the louder the thunder boomed, the closer the storm was upon them.

Wanting it to pass quickly, he should've known with the way everything else was going that day that it wouldn't. The storm seemed to snag on their side of the mountains, staying in place overhead. He looked toward Marie again and saw that she had released her arms and bent forward so that they were also on the ground. He could have held his position for hours but knew she'd reached her exhaustion point. *Fuck it!*

He grabbed his bag and jumped up, his feet pounding the wet forest floor as he raced toward her. Her head lifted, her eyes wide as she watched him get closer. Tossing his bag next to hers, he knelt, knees to the dirt, and wrapped his arms around her, pulling her into his embrace.

"Wh... wh... what are you—?"

"Shhh," he hushed, his lips close to her ear.

Kneeling together, their torsos pressed together and their arms banded around each other. Her body shivered with cold, and he tried to rub some warmth as he moved his hands over her back and arms. As the long minutes passed, they stayed tightly enveloped. He could only imagine how much her leg ached from being held in this position. How cold she was. How tired and hungry.

His mind flashed back to Airborne course training when hardened soldiers became even more hardened. Nights where they held their position in the rain. Swimming in cold water or running over rough terrain. And how many of the Special Forces wannabes didn't make the cut. Soldiers tried and true, but they couldn't finish the training. And here Marie was, kneeling for an hour in the wet dirt on a leg that had been pinned together and still caused her pain while the storm raged around them. And she didn't complain.

He'd never met a woman like her. *Well, that's not exactly true. The Keepers with partners had found this. But I never thought I would.*

Her body fit perfectly with his, her head tucked under his chin, her cheek pressed against his heart. The desire to protect her went way beyond the mission. Somewhere along the line, it had morphed into friendship, then attraction, and now he felt the pull to keep her close. *But what does she feel?* He hated the idea that the emotions rocketing through him weren't reciprocated.

As though she heard his thoughts, she lifted her cheek from his chest and turned her head so that she was looking up at him. His eyes devoured her. Wet hair plastered against her head. She wasn't wearing her glasses, blinking the water from her lashes. Her green eyes appeared dark as the forest closed in around them. Her gaze held his and then dropped to his lips. Her breath was ragged, her breasts crushed against his chest. Her fingers dug into his muscles.

No longer heeding caution, he lowered his face slowly, giving her every opportunity to lean away. But she didn't. Instead, she tightened her grip on his waist, lifting her chin until her lips were a whisper away from his.

Taking what she offered, giving what he needed, he closed the space between them. The rain poured. The wind howled. The thunder rumbled in the distance. And he sealed her mouth with his.

Electricity jolted through his body, the vibrations moving along his spine. Was it the weather or the kiss? He didn't know and didn't care. If it was the storm and they were about to be struck by lightning, he'd go out in the arms of the woman he desired more than any other. And if it was the kiss, then he wanted that electricity every day.

Senses came alive. The feel of raindrops running down his face. The tangy scent of pine trees bending over their heads and the earthy scent of the wet dirt underneath their knees. The floral scent of her shampoo. The clashing sound of thunder echoing between clouds and mountains and the roar of the wind through the treetops. The feel of her soft body, her curves pressed against the hard planes of his. Wet strands of silky hair tangled in his fingers. Porcelain skin underneath his thumb. Soft lips moving underneath his. The taste of fresh mint as his tongue glided over hers, drinking her in. Like a man dying of thirst, he reveled in her kiss, cooler than the mountain water, more intoxicating than the strongest drink.

The kiss started slow, tentative, then quickly flamed hot. Fingers grasped and clutched. Noses bumped. Tongues danced and tangled. Swallowing each other's gasps and moans, he breathed her in.

Time ceased to matter as the thunderstorm rolled beyond the mountain range in the distance. In those moments, all other women disappeared, leaving only the beautiful one in his arms. She shivered and clarity returned, hitting him that she was probably cold. Dragging his mouth from hers, he stared at her kiss-swollen lips. Her eyes opened slowly as though waking from a dream, and he hoped it was as good a dream as he was having.

"You're cold," he whispered.

"Am I?" she whispered in return.

"You're shivering." His arms tightened about her.

She licked her lips and lifted her gaze. "It passed."

Her words were soft, barely heard as his heart pounded. A smile slipped over his face. "The storm may have passed… but not our time together."

Before he had a chance to say anything else, his phone vibrated. Keeping her close, he slid it from his pocket. "We're okay," he announced without preamble. With Mace's next words, his easy mood disappeared.

"Goddamn storm lasted till dark and has the rescue team grounded. They'll take off at first light."

Clamping his jaw tight, he glanced down at Marie,

who was struggling to stand after being on the ground for so long. A grimace marred her features, the sight tugging at his heart. "Hang on." He set the phone on the ground, then turned and placed his hands along her rib cage. Standing slowly, he lifted her at the same time, careful to not jolt her tense muscles or cause her more pain.

She gasped, her fingers clenching his arms tightly. Once he was sure she was steady on her feet, he dipped his chin and held her gaze, his brows lifted in silent question.

She nodded, her fingers slowly loosening from his biceps. She turned with difficulty and limped toward a group of bushes that provided some privacy. He snagged his phone from the ground and said, "So, we're stuck out here for the night?"

"I'm sorry as fuck," Mace said. "Cory and I have been on the phone with the Air Force Commander, but he's following protocol. Drew, Tate, and John will be there soon, and they're not going to wait. They plan on being in the air in another bird and getting to you at first light. I don't need to ask if you're going to be okay tonight, but Cory is having a shit fit about Marie."

"Assure him that I've got Marie, and I can keep us safe during the night. Drew will be able to pinpoint our location and land near us. There's a grassy meadow that will make for an easy landing. That way the Mounties can just head to the wreckage to start their investigation."

"There's something else I want to let you know. Gregory is off the grid."

Not surprised that he wasn't able to be found right now, there was something in Mace's voice that sent more unease through him. "The grid?"

"As in, he never existed in the past."

"What the fuck?"

"Josh's working full-time on it to figure out what's going on. But everything about Gregory Manitov's history has been wiped. Complete and total footprint is gone. Josh feels like he can figure out where it went, but we don't know the 'why' right now."

"Anything from the satellite about the helicopter he was in? Anything about who flew in to pick him up?"

"Rick has been working that angle, and the best we can determine was it was private, no flight plan recorded, and didn't take off from an airport. With the information you gave us about the type of bird, we're looking into that as well."

"So, a whole lotta fuckin' bad news," he breathed, his gaze now pinned on Marie limping from behind the bushes. "Okay, we're going to get settled before tonight. We'll be in contact with Drew flying in at first light."

"One more thing. Cory knows there's no way to get her out of there other than flying—"

"Tell him to stop worrying. His sister's a lot stronger than he thinks she is. If there's one thing I've learned about her, she's going to be able to handle whatever comes at her." Disconnecting, he watched as she continued to limp toward him and prayed his words were true.

17

That kiss. Holy hell. With her lips still tingling—along with every other part of her body—Marie limped toward the bushes so that Bray could take his call in privacy. Plus, she needed to separate herself from him, or she'd whirl around and throw herself into his arms again, begging for more.

While she'd never met anyone in her past that she wanted to plan forever with, she'd had some relationships with men she thought were great kissers. Not only did Bray dominate them in every aspect, but if there was an Olympics of kissing, he'd take gold, silver, and bronze all by himself.

Making it behind a clump of small trees and scrub brush, she turned to assure that she couldn't see him anymore. Her foot, ankle, and leg screamed at her for the immobility of the past hour and now for daring to move at all. Unable to squat properly, she managed to take care of her business without peeing on her already-soaking wet jeans, praying that she was hidden from

Bray's sight. Holding on to a tree trunk for a moment to regain her stability, she tried to breathe through the pain.

I hate peeing in the bushes. Considering she and Bray had survived a train explosion that appeared to have killed the others—a thought that made her squeeze her eyes tightly shut as nausea rolled through her at the loss of life—and they had survived a madman shooting at them from a helicopter, *and* survived a violent thunderstorm in the middle of the forest, peeing outside in the bushes was little to be concerned with. But still, as much pain as she was in, she could barely make her way back out to where he stood.

His tight jaw that greeted her indicated he wasn't happy. *Christ, how much more can we take?* As soon as his gaze landed on her, he immediately moved to her so that she didn't have to take more steps than necessary. Without thinking, she lifted her hand and placed her palm flat on his chest as he stopped in front of her. Searching his face, she waited.

"You okay?"

Nodding, she licked her lips. "Yeah. I discovered I prefer indoor plumbing, but I'm okay."

A small grin slipped over his face, and he cupped her cheek with one hand and reached down to link fingers with his other. "Middle of a fucked-up vacation, and you manage to make me smile."

Her lips curved as well, and it felt good to smile. Used to Bray's way of operating, he didn't make her wait before giving her the news.

"We've got to spend the night out here. The storm

fucked up the rescue, and they had to turn back. They'll come at first light."

She sucked in a deep breath through her nose, keeping her lips pinched tightly together.

"My guys will have made it to the base, and they'll take off early. They'll get to us, and that'll allow the Canadians to start investigating."

Swallowing deeply, she nodded, knowing more was coming.

"We'll need to get settled here for the night. I need to get us cover and make sure we're safe." He ducked his chin. "Can you hang on a bit longer?"

She rolled her lips in, her gaze searching his in the dim light.

"Come on, Marie. I need to know what you're thinking."

"I trust you, Bray."

"Okay, that's good. But that doesn't mean I don't want you to give voice to your concerns. One of the things I learned in the Army is that it's important to work as a team. Everybody had their own specialty, but we all needed to work together to get things accomplished. Same thing with the Keepers."

"I'm curious about why you call yourselves Keepers. I know it's not the right time, but I hope that sometime, you'll tell me about your job."

He nodded, and his thumb swept over the apple of her cheek. "It'd be an honor. But first, we need to make sure we're safe for the night, and I can't do that if my teammate isn't letting me know what she's thinking or how she's feeling."

Sucking in another deep breath, she let it out and nodded. "Teammate?" A little snort escaped. "Okay, yes, I can make it. Am I in pain? Absolutely. Will it cause me permanent damage? No. And if I can help, then I need you to tell me what to do." He smiled, and she couldn't help but smile in return. Continuing, she added, "I said that I trust you, but it's a little scary to think of staying out here for the night. Mostly, I'm scared of bears. Then wolves. And then probably creepy things like snakes and bugs. And let's not forget the cold." She sighed heavily. "Part of me wishes I was back on the train in my luxurious cabin. And another part feels ashamed. I'm alive and the others aren't."

Something dark moved through his eyes; she caught it even with the lengthening shadows of dusk. She inhaled quickly, wanting to ask what he was thinking, but knew there were more important tasks that needed to take place first. "So... um... what do you need me to do?" He opened his mouth, and she quickly added, "And don't say there's nothing for me to do. After all, you said it yourself—we're teammates."

He laughed, his mirth reaching his eyes, and she was mesmerized.

"Okay, the biggest problem we have right now is that we're wet. The temperature is going to drop. Thankfully, not below freezing but enough that it could be dangerous. I'm going to gather wood to make a lean-to against one of these large trees. If you can start collecting smaller pieces of wood so that we could build a fire, that would be great."

Scrunching her nose, she looked to the side, peering

at the wet world they were standing in. "But all the wood is wet."

"The storm was fast as it moved over us, so the outside of a lot of the sticks might be wet, but they're not soaked through. They'll be dry underneath."

Nodding, she straightened her shoulders. "Okay. I'm on it."

As though breaking from a huddle, they moved in separate directions. The light was fading fast, so she began searching in earnest. Besides the lack of clear sight, bending and stooping were hard on her leg. Refusing to buckle under the pain, she collected an armload of small sticks that didn't appear to be water-logged. Looking over her shoulder, she called out, "Where should I put these?"

"You can bring them here."

Walking to where he was standing, she spied a pile of branches, many of them taller than she was. "Good God! Where did you find all these so quickly?"

He walked by, tapped his finger on the end of her nose, and said, "Years of practice foraging in the wilderness. We never knew when we might need that skill."

Seeing what he had accomplished gave her energy. Searching faster, she brought two more armloads of small sticks and branches, dropping them in a pile on the ground near where he was. As she collected another armload, she cursed the weakness that crept through her body. Shivering, she hoped they would be able to have a fire soon.

"You're shivering."

She jumped as Bray came up behind her, his hands landing on her shoulders. "Geez, you scared me."

"I want you to rest while I get the shelter up. Lean your back against the tree, and I'll have a dry place for you in just a few minutes."

She wanted to argue but knew it was pointless. He was able to work much faster than her, and making herself more ill was not going to do him any good. She hobbled over to a large, wide tree trunk and leaned back. Her gaze naturally fell to him, and soon, fascination took over, taking her mind off her pain.

Bray stood in the middle of several massive tree trunks, and it became obvious he did so with great purpose. Using his boot, he scraped the wet topsoil to the side, creating a circle in between the tree trunks where the earth was now dry. The long limbs and branches he'd gathered were soon balanced in a teepee shape supported by the trunks on the outside. He deftly wove the branches with foliage among the larger stakes, soon filling in the space. He walked away again and within ten minutes came back with his arms full of smaller pine branches that he'd stripped from larger trees. Weaving those in as well, the thick branches filled with pine needles created walls.

He grabbed their bags and moved forward, dropping them at the small entrance he'd left open. She stood and walked toward him, her eyes darting between the structure he'd created and his face.

"I'm absolutely stunned." She looked around, shaking her head slowly before bringing her gaze back to him. "I watched you make all this, and it's still hard to believe you created it."

"Let's get inside, and I'll get the fire going."

Eager to sit down on the dry dirt floor, she ducked and followed him through the small opening. The structure was almost five feet tall in the center, so they continued to crouch once inside. She moved to the far edge and managed to keep her groan to a minimum as she settled onto the dirt. Within a few more minutes, he'd used his boot to dig a smaller circle in the middle and lined it with a few rocks. Once again, in fascination, she watched as he piled many of the smaller sticks inside. Reaching inside his bag, he pulled out a first-aid kit.

Grinning, he said, "I hope you'll still be impressed even if I cheat."

He pulled out a lighter, and it didn't take long for him to have a small fire blazing. Laughing, she shook her head. "I'm not even going to tease you and say that you failed at doing everything by hand. Honest to God, Bray, you're so amazing!"

As the smoke curled upward, she tilted her head back and realized he'd left an opening in the very center of the survival shelter so the smoke could escape. The area was so small that the fire's warmth was soon felt. She was still cold and shivering but held her fingers out toward the fire, hoping to chase the icy tingles away.

"I'll step outside, and you change into something dry."

Nodding, she jerked off her thick sweater and began peeling her jeans off, but as wet as they were, it was proving to be difficult. "Shit," she muttered, leaning toward the fire then pulling back quickly.

"You okay?"

She sighed, dropping her chin to her chest. Giving a mental shake, she shoved her dignity down and called out, "Bray, I'm going to need help."

He popped his head in, his gaze sweeping over her bra-covered chest to where her soaked jeans were just past her hips before settling his dark eyes on her face. Coming in all the way, he immediately dropped to her side. So that she could maintain her balance and neither of them fall into the fire, she placed her hands on his shoulders, and he worked her tight jeans the rest of the way off

Digging in her bag, he found her dark slacks and slid them over her feet and up her legs. Completely aware that his face was at her crotch, she blew out another sigh. "I'm really sorry about this, Bray—"

He stood, still stooped, and held her gaze, a smile playing about his lips. "I promise I didn't see anything. I wasn't even looking. Just doing my duty, ma'am."

She burst into laughter, playfully slapping his arm. "You're so full of shit."

"Fine, fine... I'm a red-blooded male with a drop-dead gorgeous woman half-naked in front of me. I peeked a little."

Their laughter erupted, easing the day's tension. "Well, I appreciate your dedication to your duty."

Now that her wet clothes were off, she immediately felt the warmth of the fire chase away the chill. He stripped quickly and pulled on dry clothes as well, looking over his shoulder to see her staring up at him. She had been ogling his fantastic ass but managed to jerk her gaze up just as he turned. He wiggled his eyebrows, and she had a feeling he knew exactly what she'd been staring at.

It took several more minutes for them to move their items around to maximize their space. The few minutes of distraction and mirth had dissipated, and she longed for more room, more heat, more food. *But we're alive.* Guilt once again speared through her as did the memory of the look Bray had on his face earlier.

"You lost someone, didn't you?"

He jerked around, his brow furrowed. "What do you mean?"

Hesitation caused her to stumble, but she'd started and wanted to finish. "Earlier, when I said I felt guilty that I was alive and the others weren't. Your expression. Your eyes. I knew you understood and wondered who you lost."

For a long moment, he held her gaze, a tic appearing in his jaw. She thought he wasn't going to answer, then, finally, he released a long-held breath. He shifted in the small space, settling down on the other side of the fire. He was only two feet away, and yet, she felt as though he purposefully placed as much space between them as he could. His legs stretched out, his calves and feet right next to her. She longed to reach over and touch him. Hold him. Pull him close. Tell him he didn't have to say anything. But she remained silent and still, hoping he would speak... and fearful of what he'd say. She had her own nightmares. Knew what death looked like. Saw it in her dreams. *Had he done the same?*

"One of my last missions." His voice was low, gravelly. The firelight cast his face in a dance of light and shadows. Even with the flickering movement, she could see the anguish in his eyes.

"Fuckin' fabulous team. We'd all been together for almost three years. Everyone was perfect in their specialty. In SF, we're all trained to do what needs to be done and fill in, but each team is made up of different specialties."

"You were the medic but could do what the others did as well?"

He nodded. "Yeah. I had the medical training and mostly used it on rescues that we completed. Sure, my guys would have some injuries that needed treating, but I was the one who had to patch up someone we rescued."

He leaned his back against one of the tree trunks that made up part of the walls. "Our missions were expertly planned but there are always contingencies we couldn't count on, and that's why we were one of the best. Our captain was brilliant at fast planning, and we could change direction on a dime."

"Kind of like this trip?"

He dropped his chin and sighed before lifting his head and holding her gaze through the firelight. "Yeah. Easy mission, taking a train ride. And now look at us."

"Hey, don't knock the Canadian Rockies experience. From the train ride, to soaking feet in a river, to camping out under the trees."

A smile crossed his lips and it reached her heart. She knew there was more to his story and it wouldn't be good. *Perhaps making him smile eased his pain for just a few seconds.* She knew that sometimes in life, the few seconds of lightheartedness could chase away the darkest nightmares. She remained quiet, giving him time to sift through his memories, to decide which ones to share and what needed to stay buried. A wince passed over his face, and she longed to smooth the lines that appeared.

"The mission is, of course, confidential, but essentially, it ended up FUBAR." He must have noticed her look of confusion because he added, "Fucked up beyond all recognition."

"Oh," she nodded in understanding. "You're right. A lot like this trip."

"Yeah. And there's nothing I can say to keep this from fucking with your mind, Marie. You're right... we're alive and a lot of great people on the train aren't."

She blew out a shaky breath, nodding slowly. "I know." She might wish his words weren't true but they struck deep into her heart. Clearing her throat, she asked, "And that happened to your team?"

"Not to this percentage of dead to alive, but yeah. Intel in the field can change very quickly, and while we're trained to expect the unexpected, we were ambushed. We lost two of our team, and two more were injured. I did what I could for the injured, and we managed to get our fallen brothers out of there. But with twelve people on a team, we were down by a third. And it completely fucked with the rest of us. One of the guys didn't re-up and got out a few months later. Within a month, he killed himself—"

A gasp erupted before she could hold it back, and her hand darted around the side of the fire to land on his outstretched leg. "Oh, my God, Bray! I'm so sorry. I'm just so, so sorry."

Anguish filled his face, his jaw tightened as his chin lowered, and his gaze seemed to focus on his hands now clasped in his lap. "It rocked the rest of us. We hadn't completely dealt with the grief of the loss of our other team members before we had to deal with another loss. And we should have done something... should have known. Our command was concerned about us. There was a lot of discussion about breaking up the remaining team members and dispersing us to other teams. They'd already added more to keep us at twelve, but nothing felt the same. It was as though I was wearing a skin that just didn't fit right." He lifted his hand and scrubbed it over his head, his elbow cocked, squeezing the back of his neck. "Remember when you said you didn't quite fit?" She nodded, and he continued. "That was me. I was coming up on the decision as to whether or not to reenlist when I got a call that changed my trajectory."

Fascinated, she shifted slightly on the dirt so that her legs were stretched out on the same side of the fire, glad for the warmth that was finally penetrating. With her back against a tree trunk also, she held his gaze as well as her breath, waiting for him to continue his story.

"On one of my missions a few years before that time, I'd had the opportunity to work with a soldier considered legendary in our circles. The special mission we worked on didn't last very long, but we clicked. His life took several twists and turns after that, all covert, and then he finally got out. Once a civilian, he decided to pull together a team of former military and start his own security and investigation firm. He doesn't take just anybody. He handpicks the ones he thinks will fit into what he's trying to do."

Leaning forward, hanging on his every word, she squeezed his leg. "And you got a call from him, didn't you?"

For the first time since beginning his tale, she watched his shoulders relax as he nodded and the lines in his forehead softened. His dark eyes shimmering in the firelight captured and held her attention. *God, to be looked at like that every day...* She jerked slightly, pulling herself to the moment, knowing that would never happen.

"I did. He'd heard, of course, what happened to our team, and we got together. He explained what he was creating and paid for me to take a trip up to Maine while on leave. What he showed me fuckin' blew me away. As soon as I saw what he'd built and heard his mission for the company, I knew exactly what I needed to do. Turned in my paperwork to get discharged as soon as my time was up. Three months later, I was employed by Lighthouse Security Investigations."

"You referred to Keepers earlier. What is a Keeper?"

He leaned forward, his unwavering gaze causing her breath to halt as she waited for his answer.

"A Keeper? It's fuckin' everything."

18

Fuckin' everything. It wasn't until the words bolted from his lips that Bray realized how true they were. Another spear of guilt moved through him. _But how can that be?_ In the Army, he considered his teammates to be his brothers, closer than blood. _And that was true... then._ There had still been the brashness of youth. The idea that they could conquer all and never be conquered. Invincible. He winced and dropped his chin, his focus on his hands fisting against his thighs.

"Steel comes from fire."

His head jerked up at Marie's words, his eyes snapping open as he looked at the beautiful green-eyed woman sitting on the other side of the fire as the light danced over her face, her legs pressed next to his.

She continued, "You couldn't have become steel if you hadn't gone through the fire."

His chest depressed, and he struggled to keep his breathing even. Thoughts flew at him, fast and furious, making it difficult to untangle emotions.

"You love your job. And you're good at your job. And you get to enjoy your job but can never get away from the knowledge that some of your former teammates can't have what you have. And that's the guilt that we survivors live with. Our lives continued. Their lives didn't."

Understanding moved in to replace the confusion, and he nodded slowly. "I loved my team. I loved my brothers. But it wasn't until this very moment that I realized that it's my job *now*, being a Keeper, that's everything to me. And you're right. This opportunity came at a price."

"While I've never walked in your shoes, Bray, I understand. The pilot had a wife and two kids. Why I was spared and he wasn't, I'll never know. But life is a series of events that can give us the highest highs and the lowest lows. Sometimes, we can't understand why we get to enjoy the highs when others can't." Shrugging, she added, "And, sometimes, we can't understand why we have to go through the lows. And I've got no answers to that other than to say that's just life, and we try to make the best of the hand that's dealt to us." She leaned forward, her fingers landing on his leg again. "And it sounds like becoming a Keeper is exactly what you needed to do."

She leaned back, her hand leaving his leg, and he missed the touch, but her words gave him a modicum of peace and understanding. "My boss grew up near a lighthouse and said his grandfather used to tell him tales of famous lighthouse keepers. Men, women, and families who often lived in isolation for years just to keep the lights burning. Guiding ships to safety and, when necessary, going out and risking their own lives to save others. When he created his security business, he called it Lighthouse Security Investigations, and the men and women who work for him are known as Keepers. I think that's what appealed to me. It wasn't just a job. Hell, there are lots of security jobs available. But it was his mission. His goal. His life's purpose. All that appealed to me and what I wanted to do with the rest of my life. So, yeah, I hadn't really thought about it until just now, but it's everything."

She smiled, her face so beautiful, her green eyes so brilliant. His heart squeezed again, only this time, it was with something warm. Comforting. Easy. He couldn't remember the last time he'd ever talked about his special forces team or his job with LSI. *And sure as fuck not with a woman.*

She lifted her hand toward the warmth of the fire again, and this time, he noticed the tremor. *Damn!* He leaned forward and took her hand in his, noting the clammy feel to her hand. "Marie, you're shaking. We need to get more water and food down you."

Shifting to his knees in the small space, he opened one of the bottles and helped steady her hands as she held it to her lips. She drank several long gulps before nodding and pushing the bottle away, mumbling her thanks.

"We've got several more packs of nuts." He ripped open one and handed it to her. "Eat as much as you can. We'll be out of here in the morning."

"You're sure?"

He heard the fear in her voice. Nodding, he assured, "Yeah. My team will be here. The weather won't matter. They'll make it in."

She sucked in a deep breath and let it out slowly, her lips finally curving upward. "Good. I look forward to meeting them." Her pale face made the dark circles underneath her eyes appear starker.

"We need to get some rest."

Her brows lifted. "I'm not sure that's going to happen. I don't want you to think I'm ungrateful for the accommodations because I am extremely relieved to have a shelter and a fire. And I am also extremely grateful for the company I'm keeping. But sleep?"

"What's the most comfortable position for you to sleep so that your legs don't hurt as much?"

"I guess I usually sleep on my back or roll to my right side so there's no pressure on my left."

He shifted their bags to the far side and then settled on the opposite, reclining before opening his arms. "Come here." He hadn't meant for his request to come out as an order, and just when he was about to amend his statement, she acquiesced, moving stiffly.

Her movements were ungainly, but she managed to lay on her back with her head on his arm. She was closest to the small fire, ensuring that she would stay warm, and he was on the other side, wrapping his arms around her.

"None of this seems real."

He looked down to see her staring up at him, her features still beautiful even though fatigue fought to mar them.

She lifted one of her hands and laid it on his chest, right above his heartbeat. "If I had to have a companion on my train ride, I'm so glad it was you. If I had to survive a train wreck, I'm so glad you survived with me. If I had to run for my life, I'm glad you're the one protecting me. And if I have to spend the night in a tiny shelter in the middle of a Canadian Rocky forest, I'm glad it's your arms I'm lying in. I have no idea what that says about me, but there it is."

He brought his face closer and smiled. "You believe in fate?"

She sucked in her lips and pressed them tightly together for a few seconds before answering. "When I was lying in a hospital bed after my third or fourth surgery, my grandmother gave me a book on literature written by Nobel laureates. I couldn't imagine why. To a teenager in pain and frustrated with life, literature above my head seemed like a pointless gift. But, in between therapies, I was desperate for something to take my mind off the pain. And in that book, there were many poems that I didn't understand, but sometimes, I came across something that struck me. One of them was by Hermann Hesse, a German poet. 'Whatever good or bad fortune may come our way, we can always give it meaning and transform it into something of value.' So, I'm not sure if that answers your question about my belief in fate, but those words burrowed deep inside of me and stayed."

He smiled, moving his face even closer. "My Italian grandmother use to despair that once I left Catholic elementary school, my reading education was going to consist of auto magazines and Playboy—"

Marie's fingers squeezed his arm as a giggle slipped out.

"So, she'd give me books to read, mostly by priests. Usually, I ignored them, but when I was on my first overseas tour, she mailed a small paperback by a Trappist monk, Thomas Merton. I remembered it and thought about it when I'd found my brotherhood in SF. 'We do not find the meaning of life by ourselves alone – we find it with another.'"

The tiny gasp from her lips captured his attention, and he lowered his mouth until he was a whisper away, giving her control. And just like before, she responded by shifting her hand to his jaw and pulling him down to her face.

The first kiss they'd shared in the middle of the storm had rocked him. He'd never had such a reaction to a kiss before, making him think it must have been the pent-up adrenaline, the electricity from the storm, or the churning emotions from the day. But this... this was a slow burn kiss and just as powerful.

She'd called him *steel*, and right now, his steel met silk. Soft and pliable, her mouth moved under his. He drank her in like a man dying of thirst, but no matter how much he took, it would never be enough. He shifted his arm underneath her head, curling to bring their bodies closer. His free hand gripped her waist, then slid upward, careful not to touch her breasts. Not that he didn't want to. But Marie was not a woman he was going to cop a feel with no matter how much he desired her body. When they had sex, it was going to be all in, not fumbling like teenagers in the backseat of daddy's car.

Continuing its upward path, his palm cupped her cheek. His fingers dove into her tangled tresses as he held her close, hoping the warmth of his hand soothed her face. He lifted her glasses from her face and carefully laid them to the side. Turning his head slightly, he sealed his mouth over hers, his tongue darting out to lick her lips. Like answering a magician's command, her lips parted, and the tip of her tongue met his. She moaned, and as he swallowed the tiny sound, it vibrated through him.

Shifting slightly, she pressed her body tightly against his. It was a perfect fit. She was petite, but with his mouth dipped to hers, her breasts crushed against his chest and his cock was cradled against her stomach.

As their lips continued to meld, he was struck with how different the experience was than what he was used to. Kissing was rare the times he'd had sex just for the physical release, implying an intimacy that wasn't part of the experience. And the few relationships he'd had, none lasting beyond a couple of months, kissing had held more meaning but tended to be the precursor to sex. Something to be expected, but when the blood ran south to his cock, the only thing on his mind was taking care of his partner so he could get in and get off.

But now, knowing there'd be no sex tonight, all of his energy and focus pinpointed on the sensual dance of their lips.

His tongue lazily explored her mouth, dragging over

her tongue, memorizing her taste and feel. As she grew bolder, her tongue tangled with his. *Jesus, her taste was a slice of heaven, and kissing her was the closest he'd come to finding perfection in anything.*

Her hand was clutching his arm, each fingertip like a brand. But he wanted to be branded by her. That thought alone should have had him looking for an escape, but instead, he eased her gently onto her back to keep the pressure off her leg, rolling over her just enough to help her stay warm.

Slowly, he lifted his lips away from hers and dragged his gaze over her face. Her lips were slightly puffy and moist from their kissing. Her pale cheeks were now tinged with a hint of blush, and as her eyelids slowly fluttered open, her gaze remained unfocused for a few seconds before she smiled.

And more than the feel of her lips and body pressed to his, more than his desire to strip their clothes off so he could explore and worship her body, and more than his desire to vow promises he had no business making, he wanted her to rest.

Shifting so that she was mostly on her back, he curved his body into hers. She reached up and touched his face. "May next year's birthday bring you all you'd love to have, Bray."

Kissing her forehead, he kept his lips pressed to her soft skin. "Try to get some sleep, babe. Tomorrow is going to be busy, but I'll do my damnedest to make it a hell of a lot better than today was."

Her continued smile warmed his heart, and she

nodded, closing her eyes. Grateful when her breathing slowly evened and he knew she'd found sleep, he rested fitfully, knowing somewhere out there, Gregory was looking for them. And wanted them dead.

19

Marie blinked and tried to stretch. Her body ached and her leg barely moved. Nausea swept over her, and a groan slipped out.

Something shifted behind her. "Marie?"

Licking her lips, she tried to smile as she twisted her head around to see Bray's face so close, concern filling his eyes.

"What do you need, sweetheart? What can I help with?"

Swallowing, her gaze landed on his mouth. Last night, he'd called her *babe,* and just now, *sweetheart. Endearments? Or throwaway words that guys often used when talking to any woman?* She was always honest with herself, and the truth was... *I really want it to be an endearment.* His kisses had catapulted her into the stratosphere of kissing heaven, and she never wanted to return to earth unless she could claim more of his kisses. She winced at that thought. *God, that sounds needy.*

"You're in pain. Let me help you up."

Her wince had come from the exaggerated thought of wanting to stay with him, but he wasn't far from the truth about her pain, either. He shifted upward, and she immediately felt the rush of cold. Glancing to the side, the fire had gone out. The warmth she'd felt during the few hours of sleep had come from his body. Now, the chill of the early morning slammed into her.

It was embarrassing to need assistance again, but she'd so often needed help after her injury that she'd learned to accept it with grace. "If you can help me stand and hang onto me while I walk around to get the stiffness out, that would be good."

They had little room in the shelter, but with great gentleness, Bray lifted her to her feet while keeping a hand on top of her head so that she wouldn't bump it on the wooden branches as they crouched to move outside. A breeze blew past them now that they were no longer within the confines of the shelter, and she shivered.

Bray helped her prop against the large trunk of a tree before he turned and began to dig through her bag. He returned with a shirt and sweatshirt of hers. Sliding the shirt over her arms, his fingers definitely made quick work of the buttons. Within a minute, she had the sweatshirt on as well.

He bent to pick up her coat, but she threw out her hand and halted his movements. "Not to be indelicate, but I've got to use our luxurious outdoor facilities first."

He chuckled, and as she pushed off the trunk felt his gaze pinned on her. She couldn't help the severe limping in the cold morning but hated for him to see her so vulnerable. Lifting her hand, she waved him back, glad she didn't have to verbalize that she wanted privacy and would do whatever it took to handle the situation herself, and just as glad he gave that to her.

Hobbling to the far side of a clump of trees with thick undergrowth, she fumbled with her clothes, then managed to take care of business with only a modicum of difficulty. *Okay, I admit it. I am desperate for a shower, a toilet, and a meal.* Gathering her strength for the short trek back to where Bray awaited, she dragged in a shaky breath, knowing her heart rate was fast. *And my meds. I need those more than any of my other wishes.*

Walking back, she stretched out the kinks in her body, hoping she returned to him in better shape than she'd left. His gaze stayed pinned on her, the intensity almost burning. But, instead of the cold feeling she'd get when a doctor or therapist was evaluating her, it was warmth pouring from him that she enjoyed.

"Let's get you into your coat," he said, holding it out for her. She'd shunned it yesterday as they walked, and the sun kept them comfortable. But now, in the pre-dawn chill, she was glad for its fleecy down.

"My people are on their way. I need you to be prepared."

She closed her eyes, steeling herself for what was going to happen. Letting out a ragged breath that misted between them as she opened her eyes, she nodded. "I'm not sure I can ever be prepared for what's going to happen, but then, I have little choice."

"I'll be right with you. You know that. I promise I won't leave your side."

The intensity of his gaze shot through her, but she couldn't imagine he felt the heat the way she did. "Gotta see the mission to the very end," she said, trying to smile to keep him from seeing that her joke wasn't real.

Thinking he might be relieved that she wasn't taking things too seriously between them, she was surprised when Bray ducked slightly so that his face was directly in front of hers, his dark eyes pulling her in. She couldn't look away if she'd wanted. But then, looking away from him was the last thing she wanted to do.

His hand had remained on the lapel of her jacket but now slid up to cup her face. "If you still think you're just a mission, then I've done a piss-poor job of letting you know that you're not. For the record, I've never kissed anyone on a mission. For the record, I've never wanted to. You've been more than a mission for a while, but I wasn't willing to admit that even to myself until last night."

Before she had a chance to say anything, his head cocked to the side, listening. A few seconds later, she could hear the whir of helicopter blades in the distance. The mere sound made her fear her knees would buckle, and she locked them steady as he bolted to the shelter, kicking the dirt over the cold coals. Turning, he jerked his backpack on and hefted her bag.

Feeling the need to do something as the helicopter approached, she reached out and pulled her bag from his hand. "I've got this." She was referring to her bag but realized her words needed to apply to everything they were getting ready to do. Swallowing deeply, she turned to find that Bray had stepped directly into her space again.

"You do have this," he said, wrapping his arms around her and pulling her close, kissing the top of her head. "You're fuckin' strong and fuckin' brave. And if you weren't scared, you'd be a fool. And baby, you're no fool. But you're not alone. We're going to do this together."

Her arms had wrapped around his waist as she allowed his words to seep inside. Leaning her head back, she nodded. They turned, and with their hands linked, walked quickly beyond the edge of the woods to where they could see the helicopter lowering to the ground. *It's huge!* The helicopter was much larger than the one she'd been in as a child. The tall grass whipped around as the force of the blades sent the air whirling. She stared at the helicopter, her heart pounding with fear, waiting. It didn't hit her for a few seconds that she was waiting to see if it would flip over and crash. But it didn't. It simply lowered to the ground.

Once again, Bray turned to face her, his hands cupping her face this time, tilting her chin upward. "Remember, we've got this. Together, we've got this." He lowered his mouth to hers, and she clung to his waist as his kiss sealed her lips and sealed his vow.

A sound met her ears that she couldn't identify, and they turned together to see the side door of the helicopter slide open, a smiling face greeting them.

"It's go time!" Bray called out and linked fingers with her again.

He started forward, and she had no choice but to

follow. The closer they came, the more her heart pounded. Bray wrapped one arm around her waist and held her hand, bending her forward so they crouched as they approached.

The noise was deafening. *Oh God oh God oh God.* She had no idea if she'd given voice to her thoughts, but Bray gave her no time to hesitate. Before she knew it, she'd been hustled to the edge. Arms reached down as Bray grabbed her waist and hefted her up.

She was lifted and carefully set on her feet but she twisted her head to see Bray hauling himself easily into the open doorway. Her hand grasped at the man standing in front of her. He was tall and his wide smile greeted her, his eyes carefully assessing. "Dr. Brighton, welcome aboard," he called out. "I'm Tate. We'll get you strapped in safely and get you out of here."

Managing what she thought might be a nod, she discovered her fingers wouldn't loosen from his arms.

"I've got her." Bray's voice was a soothing balm to her racing heart. His hands gently pried her independent-minded fingers loose from Tate's shirt, then wrapped his arms around her. Bending, his breath warm against her ear, he said, "Stay with me, babe. I've got you."

This time, she was sure her nod was actually a nod but no words came forth. With one arm still banded around her, his other hand reached out.

"Tate, good to see you, man." They shook hands, then Bray did the same with another man standing near Tate. "John, looks like Mace got you in the field quickly." He leaned over slightly, calling out to the pilot, who twisted around with a wide grin on his face as well. "Drew, thanks for getting the bird to us. Looks like you brought luxury with you."

"Only the best," Drew called out, laughing.

Before she had a chance to process more of what was happening, Tate pulled the door closed. Bray linked fingers with her and led her to a seat. "Let's get you as comfortable as we can, and then we'll get going."

Just those words brought her heart crashing against her ribs, so nodding was the only reply, still not trusting her voice. He divested her of her bag from her shoulders, slid her coat down her arms, and after she sat down, helped her buckle. Without sitting himself, he called over his shoulder, "You bring what I need?"

"Got it," John said, handing a black bag with a red cross on the side to him.

At the sight of the familiar bag, she winced as embarrassment flooded her. "This is ridiculous," she muttered under her breath. Bray's gaze jumped up to hers, his brow lowered. Sighing, she shook her head. "Not you. Me. I'm ridiculous." Before she had a chance to explain, the blades of the helicopter increased in rotation, and there was a slight shudder as it lifted off the ground. Her hands clutched the arms of her seat, and she cursed her weakness as fear flooded her being and she slammed her eyes closed.

"Open your eyes." Bray repeated his request as his hands cupped her face. She acquiesced, and he'd moved so that as he knelt directly in front of her, his face only a few inches from hers. "Stay with me. Keep your eyes on me."

As she stared into his face, she memorized every nuance. His square face and hard jaw. His thick black hair that she imagined he gained from the Italian side of his family. The dark eyes that could flash with anger, twinkle with mirth, and warm her like an embrace.

"You can do this, Marie. I believe you can do anything you want."

He shifted back ever so slightly, and she darted her gaze to the side, looking out the window. They were in the air, but the ride was smooth. She knew nothing about aircraft but shooting her gaze to the other side realized what they were in was a large helicopter with eight comfortably spaced seats and a middle aisle. It was nothing like the small, two-seater helicopter she'd been on years before.

Seeing John and Tate sitting to the side, she offered a weak smile. "I'm afraid I haven't given a very good first impression, but please, know I'm so grateful that you came for us."

"Hell, you put up with this guy on your vacation! Kudos to you, Doctor!" Tate joked.

"Seriously!" Drew called out from the front.

John didn't say anything, but his wide smile indicated he appreciated their humor. Bray flipped his friends off, eliciting a bark of laughter from her. He grinned and said, "I'll keep flipping my friends off if that keeps making you laugh."

Glancing down at the blood pressure cuff in his hand, she sighed. "I can already tell you that my blood pressure is elevated, and I'm sure my heart rate is fast. It's okay, Bray."

"Hey, you might be the doctor, but it's a well-known fact that you all make the worst patients." Leaning closer, he whispered, "Anyway, I've been dying to play *Doctor* with you."

Another chortle slipped out and she shook her head. "How the hell can I be in the air, terrified, and you make me laugh?"

"Because I'm just amazing like that." The look he gave her was one where his eyes sparkled, and she loved that his gaze was locked on her.

"Yeah, you are." With that, she watched as his eyes now flared. She had no idea where they were going or what would happen when they landed. After this, she feared they'd go their separate ways and she might never see him again. That thought made her heart squeeze as much as being in flight.

After checking her temperature, blood pressure, and heart rate, Bray pulled out a bottle that Tate handed to him. Calling out the name of the medication, she nodded, eyes wide. "You brought it?"

"I know it's not all you take, but it's what we could get our hands on quickly," Tate explained.

Taking the extended water bottle, she drank deeply, swallowing her pills.

John opened another bag before offering it to Bray. "There's food in here if you feel like eating."

She shook her head, gripping the seat arms again as the helicopter dipped slightly. "I'm so sorry. I'd love to eat but I don't think I can keep it down."

"Take a bite, babe," Bray encouraged. "So the meds won't make your stomach worse."

She pressed her lips together, uncertain whether either choice would work with her stomach, but decided to nibble a cracker.

"We'll be on the ground in about forty minutes," Drew said.

"We can eat more then," Bray offered, and she nodded her agreement.

"Damn!" Drew cursed, then quickly added, "Sorry. Bray, you might want to take a look."

Marie didn't budge, but Bray, Tate, and John looked out the side windows, mumbling curses under their breath. Hating to be left out, she stretched her neck up and tried to peer down. "What? What is it?"

Bray's gaze jumped back to hers. "We're flying over the gorge, babe."

As terrified as she was, curiosity won over, and she leaned to the side just enough to peer downward. The scene before her could have come from a disaster movie, something from the mind of a screenwriter and filmed by an expert crew. Unable to take in the entire scene without moving closer to the window, she could see the twisted tangle of railcars below. Several military helicopters were on the ground, and people in uniforms moved around.

"They'll investigate what they find and will want to interview us back at the base."

She gave no response but nodded slowly. Bray turned and opened her bag, pulling out the smaller black vanity bag. Handing it to John, he said, "See what you make of this before we have to turn it over."

Her gaze cut away from the window to John. He

opened the bag carefully, then took out one of the objects, turning it over in his hands. "Wireless electronics. The kind used in the mining industry as well as military. You can make wireless detonators, but these are high quality." He looked over at Bray. "Do you think Gregory was buying and selling these? Black market?"

Bray's jaw tightened and Marie wondered if his teeth wouldn't break from all the tension rolling off him. "Don't know. Just know that whatever he used them for, the explosive on the train was enough to kill a helluva lot of people." His gaze shot over to hers before he added, "And two died by his own hands."

The memory of finding Carlie and Frank's bodies yesterday slammed into her, and she closed her eyes, a grimace tightening her jaw.

Bray moved to sit next to her, taking her hand in his. Rolling her head to the side, she looked at him, squeezed his hand, then closed her eyes, praying for the trip to end soon... and safely.

20

Bray kept a close eye on Marie, his fingers resting lightly on her wrist, not liking her rapid heart rate. Her hands were clammy again but her eyes were closed, and he didn't want to interrupt whatever peace she might have found.

"Bray."

Drew's quiet voice shot his attention up to the front. Offering a quick nod, he turned toward Marie, not surprised to find her eyes open wide as she gripped his hand.

"What? What's happening?"

He unbuckled and moved to kneel in front of her again, placing his face close. "Marie, keep your eyes on me. We're getting ready to land—"

A whimper escaped but she cut it off almost as quickly as it erupted.

"Stop trying to fight your feelings. You're scared, so be scared. No one here judges you for that. Hell, we've all got shit we're scared of. But what I do want you to do is keep your eyes on me." He moved closer until he made sure his face was all she could see. But what hit him was that she was also all he could focus on. Ever since she'd woken in his arms this morning, he wanted to experience the beauty of seeing her wake when they hadn't been on the cold ground in a branch shelter. He wanted his body alone to keep her warm, not needing the fire embers. He wanted to see her smile first thing upon waking in a bed, not having the horrid stiffness from not being able to move. And mostly, he just wanted to keep waking with her morning after morning.

Not moving so that she had no choice but to maintain eye contact with him, he knew Drew was landing expertly and probably more gently than he'd ever landed just to make it easier on Marie.

With a thud, they settled and he smiled. "We're on the ground, babe. We made it."

Eyes wide, she gasped and looked around. "Oh, God, we did."

He'd barely unbuckled her when she grabbed his hand for assistance to stand and then threw her arms around him. He wrapped her in his embrace, holding tight. She finally let go and swiped at the few stray tears that had escaped. Turning, he led her to the door and allowed Tate to help her down. John followed, the bag of black-market explosive electronics securely in his hands.

She hugged the others, holding tightly to Drew. "Thank you so much. I'm so sorry I was such a wimpy passenger—"

Drew waved away her concerns. "Don't give it a thought. As Bray said, we've all got shit that scares us. I just consider it an honor that I was able to have you as a passenger."

Bray slipped up behind her and said, "We need to get inside."

"Where are we?"

"We're at the closest Canadian Air Force base. They've got a hospital here and you need to get checked out. We're going to have to be interviewed by the RCMP, and John will turn over the explosive electronics."

"I don't know what they think I can tell them. I was never alone with Gregory."

"They're going to want to know what we saw in Banff. We'll just tell them exactly what we saw. No embellishment. No suspicions. No speculations. They probably want to know what we noticed him doing and who he spoke to when we were on the train. Don't worry. Once we do that, they'll turn us loose and we can get out of here."

She opened her mouth but her attention was drawn to the group approaching, men and women in suits and uniforms. He wanted to know what she had almost said but now was not the time. Turning, he introduced them. "Allan Bray, Lighthouse Security. This is Dr. Marie Brighton. She needs medical attention."

One of the women in uniform stepped forward. "Dr. Brighton, if you'll follow me, I'll escort you to our medical facilities—"

"We'll both go," Bray announced.

The suited man in the front glanced sharply at him. "I'm Frederick Barclay, RCMP. You'll need to give your statement while Dr. Brighton is examined by the doctors—"

"No. She doesn't leave my sight. You can obtain our statements when she's cleared by the medical personnel."

Frederick's hard stare lasted a moment before moving to Marie, then finally, he nodded. Turning, Bray inclined his head toward John. "What my teammate has is what will interest you until Dr. Brighton is checked out." With a nod toward John, Tate, and Drew, he wrapped his arm around Marie and they followed the uniformed woman to a nearby SUV.

Once inside the hospital, Marie turned to him and whispered, "I'm okay, you know. You don't have to stay with me."

"But I want to."

She blinked at his simple declaration, and he held his breath for a second, wondering what her response would be. Just as he was about to capitulate, she smiled. It started slow, the simplest curve of her lips. Then her smile widened, and he reached over to grasp her hand, holding it close.

Once inside the base's medical center, she was taken into a room to meet with a doctor. She relayed her condition and reviewed her current status. Bray stayed to the side, watching as she interacted with the personnel, her voice calm and sure. Her gaze strayed to him, her smile still in place, and his heart squeezed. He had no idea if the future held anything for them, but he wasn't willing to give up until taking them as far as they would go.

As soon as she had been cleared, they were taken to a conference room in the facility where Frederick waited for them and protein bars were offered.

Bray looked down at her, his hand cupping her face. "They'll want to interview us separately. But I won't leave here without you. Make sure you eat and drink plenty of water."

Nodding, she whispered, "What happens after this?"

He didn't know if she meant where they would go for the night or what would happen between them when they returned to the States. Deciding to keep his response simple for now, he said, "We'll get a good night's sleep. Somewhere with a warm bath and good food."

Her smile widened. "God, that sounds good—"

"Dr. Brighton?"

He glared at Frederick over her shoulder then gave his attention back to her. "Don't leave without me. Wherever my people have us booked for tonight, we'll be together." Her obvious relief didn't pass his attention, and his chest swelled with pride. Giving her a nudge, he watched her go inside the room and the door closed.

"Mr. Bray?"

Turning, he headed into the conference room across the hall. Sitting down, he looked at the two investigators in front of him and began. Giving the information as asked, he thought of Marie in the other room and hoped she wasn't getting too tired. Anxious to be with her, he answered the questions presented and relayed his knowledge quickly, glad when he was released. Stepping into the hall, he found her standing with Drew, laughing at one of his tales, probably of when Bray screwed up on something.

Walking over, he threw his arm around her shoulders and pulled her in close, ignoring Drew's grin.

While she had a smile on her face, he could read exhaustion written all over her. Turning toward Drew, he lifted his chin. "What's the plan?"

"Got rooms booked at one of the hotels in town. Nice. You know Babs, only the best. If y'all are ready, we'll go there now and then fly home tomorrow."

He felt Marie's body stiffen but knew they could approach the trip home after eating and resting. "Sounds good. Lead the way."

Thirty minutes later, they walked down the hall of the hotel, their footsteps making little noise on the carpeted floor. Drew, John, and Tate had gotten off the elevator on the second floor while he and Marie had continued to the third. Stopping at her door, he opened it and ushered her just inside. "Stay here until I check it out." She was either used to their routine or exhausted because her only response was to nod. He swept the room before moving back to where she stood with her back to the door. Lifting his hand, he gently brushed her hair back from her shoulder. "It's all good."

Her gaze had stayed pinned on him but she now glanced to the side as though taking in the room for the first time. King bed. Small table with two chairs. Settee on one side. Dresser with TV perched on top. Wide windows with a view of the town below.

"Hey," he called, drawing her attention back to him. "You need to eat. Do you want to go to the restaurant downstairs?"

Fatigue appeared to weigh heavily on her shoulders. "Honestly, I really want a shower… or a long, hot bath. I don't think I have the energy to make it downstairs."

"Okay, then, you take a bath, and I'll order room service to be delivered. What would you like to eat?"

She tilted her head to the side, peering up at him. "Will you eat with me?"

A smile slipped over his lips. "If you want me to, then absolutely."

Nodding quickly, she smiled in return. "Yes. Please. And order whatever you want to eat. I'll eat anything."

With his hand still on her shoulder, he longed to cup her cheek, but now that they were back in civilization, he was uncertain. *The kisses they'd shared… were they just because of the extreme circumstances? Did she feel the same spark that he did? The same interest? The same desire?* Not willing to push her in a direction she might not desire, he stepped back, his hand sliding down her arm to squeeze her fingers for a few seconds before letting go. "I'll order food to be delivered here for you and then I'll head next door to my room to get cleaned up."

Her brow furrowed, and she reached out to grasp his fingers that had just released hers. "You're coming back, aren't you?" Before he had a chance to respond, she startled, standing up straighter, two spots of red dotting her cheeks. "I'm sorry, I don't know what got into me. Of course, you want some time to yourself. You don't have to worry about ordering, I can certainly do that for myself—"

"No, I'd like to eat with you, but I didn't want to overstep my boundaries."

Her shoulders relaxed again, and she smiled. "Oh, good. I'd like that, but I don't want to be needy. If you'd like to eat with your friends, I can certainly take care of myself."

Snorting, he laughed. "I can eat a meal with them anytime. What I'd much rather do is spend more time with you. I'll order the food to come to your room in an hour. Until then, take a long bath or shower, get comfortable, and rest. I'll be over when the food comes."

He handed her the key card that he'd used to open her door, but she wrapped her fingers around his hand and pushed it gently back toward him. "Keep it. Come back as soon as you've showered, and we can hang here together until the food comes if you'd like."

If he wasn't mistaken, there was hope in her eyes, the same hope that was mirrored in his. "Okay. I'll be back in a little bit." He leaned forward and kissed her forehead, knowing he'd much rather kiss her lips. But if he didn't leave immediately, he wasn't sure he'd ever get out of her room. Turning, he slipped out and walked next door. Entering his own hotel room, an exact duplicate of hers, he was surprised at how much colder it felt without her smile to warm the space and his heart.

Thirty minutes later, he lounged in one of the chairs in her hotel room, the sound of the shower still running. It had been hell thinking of Marie naked just on the other side of the door.

A knock on the door gave him the perfect excuse to try to drag his mind away from her. Checking first to ascertain it was room service, he opened the door quickly when he saw it was Tate. Stepping back, Tate followed him into the room. If he was surprised that Bray was in Marie's room, he gave no evidence.

Keeping his voice low, he asked, "What's up, man?"

"We've been in contact with Mace. He wanted me to pass along that Josh still can't find anything new on Gregory. Josh is going fuckin' nuts, but it's as though the man has disappeared. He's even been looking at Interpol, CIA, Canadian feds, military... you name it, and this guy's gone off the grid. So stay sharp."

A quick chin lift was his only response, knowing Tate expected no other. "It makes no sense that he'd still be after us. He's got to know that everything has been turned over to the authorities."

"I agree, but until we know for sure—"

The sound of the running water in the bathroom shut off, and Bray glanced over his shoulder before looking back at Tate. "In light of what you just said, I'll be here tonight."

"Drew said we can fly back whenever you're ready tomorrow morning. Just give us a heads up and we'll head to the airport."

With another chin lift, he threw open the door to let Tate out. Tate turned and held his gaze for a moment, but before he had a chance to speak, Bray got there first. "You don't even have to say it. I know what you're thinking. But we haven't gone there, and I don't know that we will. Not that I wouldn't be interested. First time I've been interested in fuckin' forever, but I don't know what she's thinking."

"Fair enough," Tate acknowledged. "But take it from the rest of us. When you find it, it's worth fighting for." With that, he turned and walked down the hall.

Seeing the room service staff rolling the cart down the hall, Bray waited. "I'll take it from here." He tipped the young man generously, then rolled the cart in and locked the door. The scents emanating from the covered plates were tantalizing, but his mind was still back on the notion that Gregory Manitov was out there somewhere.

The sound of the bathroom door opening jolted him from his thoughts, and he turned to see Marie walking into the room. Her long dark hair was wet, combed back away from her face and down her back. Dressed in flannel pajamas and thick, fuzzy socks, she was almost covered from head to toe, and yet, she was so desirable. She'd traded glasses, and he was glad she'd grabbed them from the train when packing. Now, her purple frames matched the pajamas. Her gaze held his, uncertainty written across her face.

"Damn, you look amazing."

Her smile widened until she burst out in laughter. "I think you've been in the wilderness too long if you consider this to be amazing!"

He crossed the room in five steps, standing directly in front of her, looking down. Not hesitating, he lifted both hands and cupped her face, tilting it upward. He waited for her to give him the sign that she wanted this as much as he. When her hands snaked around his neck, he lowered his mouth to hers. She molded her body against his, but he forced the kiss to remain short. Lifting his head, he chuckled at her little mew of discontent. Nuzzling her nose, he whispered, "I don't want to stop, but I want you fed." Not giving her a chance to argue, his hand glided down her arms and linked fingers with her. Walking backward, he led her over to the table.

Once she was seated, he began lifting the covers off the plates. "First, we eat." He caught the questioning gaze she sent his way but remained silent. Whatever was going to happen between them afterward was yet to be discovered.

21

Marie had stood inside the bathroom, staring at herself in the mirror. She'd started with a hot shower to rinse away the effects of yesterday as well as wash and condition her hair. Then, she'd wrapped her hair in a towel and filled the tub with more hot water and bath oil, closing her eyes as she'd allowed her muscles to relax. Once out, she'd moisturized, glad for the products the hotel provided considering she had none of her toiletries. Dressed in warm pajamas with her favorite fuzzy socks, she'd wondered what Bray would think about her now that the mission was over.

The kisses they'd shared had tilted her world off its axis. She'd never believed it was possible to fall for someone with just a kiss. As soon as that thought hit her mind, she shook her head. *No, that's not right. It was a helluva lot more than just a kiss.*

It was the way he'd taken charge without taking over. It was the way he'd shown care without smothering. It was the way he was always present without crowding. It was the way he asked questions as though coveting the answers and was then willing to share himself. It was the way he stayed with her that went beyond security. It was the way he looked at her with interest as much as desire. *And yes, I'm falling.*

Squaring her shoulders, she'd thrown open the door and stepped into the room, halting as soon as her gaze landed on him. The scent of delicious food was tantalizing, but she'd been more interested in the man stalking toward her, telling her she looked amazing.

His black T-shirt stretched taut across his muscles, the bottom of his tattoo barely seen below the sleeve of one arm. Faded jeans that fit like they'd been made just for him and worn often had her longing to see what was hidden beneath. His dark hair was still damp, the ends curling around his ears, and his heavy five-o'clock shadow had drawn her eye. Her ridiculous pirate-romance fantasy came true just in the way he moved across the room. And when he took her hands, leading her forward, she had no doubt she would've done the same if he'd simply crooked his finger toward her. She didn't know a man alive where that maneuver would have worked, but if Bray ever tried it? *Hell, yeah.*

Now, seated at the small table, she watched as he lifted cover after cover, exposing the perfect meal... hamburgers, french fries, onion rings, roasted carrots and broccoli, and for dessert, chocolate pie. Eyes wide, she clapped her hands. "Oh, my God! This is absolutely the best food!"

Laughing, he nodded. "I thought about ordering all

breakfast food because that's also perfect, but I figure we'll have a good breakfast in the morning."

Her smile faltered at the thought of tomorrow and all it would bring... another flight, this one much longer. And worse than that, which was crazy considering she didn't think there would be anything worse than flying, was the idea of saying goodbye to Bray.

He knelt in front of her, his hand cupping around the side of her neck, and brought his face close to hers. "Don't worry about that now. I'll get you through the flight, I promise."

Pretending the flight was her only concern about tomorrow, she nodded. If there was one thing she'd learned about Bray, it was that he would keep his promise. The only thing she didn't know was how her heart was going to take the goodbye.

He walked around to the other side of the table, and she pushed those thoughts to the back of her mind and focused on the food in front of her. Taking a huge bite of the perfectly cooked hamburger topped with melted cheese, pickles, lettuce, and tomato, she groaned, closing her eyes. She chewed slowly, enjoying each flavor as they glided over her tongue, then swallowed before licking her lips. When she finally opened her eyes, she caught Bray's almost black eyes staring at her, his jaw tight. Afraid she might have something on her mouth, she licked her lips again and grabbed the napkin.

His gaze was focused on her lips, and it hit her... *He's turned on.* That tiny bit of knowledge gave her power, making her want to jump him. But, unwilling to keep him from finishing his meal, she looked back at her plate, dipped a French fry in ketchup, and shoved it into her mouth. They talked little while eating, but the sexual tension grew with each moment until she thought they would snap under the pressure.

By now, the evening had darkened the sky outside their windows, and the soft lights from the nightstand and over the table cast the room with a tantalizing combination of soft glows and shadows. She was reminded of the way his face had appeared last night in the flickering firelight, and while she'd never wish for them to be back in that time and place, she could not forget the way he'd looked. Or the way he'd looked at her.

She swallowed the sip she was taking and set the glass back onto the table. Glancing down, she saw that their plates were mostly empty; only the pie was left. "Are you interested in dessert?" she asked, her voice soft, almost hesitant, knowing when the meal was over, he would probably leave, and it would signal the beginning of their end.

His head nodded slowly, the movement mesmerizing. "Yeah, I am."

She reached toward one of the dessert plates but his fingers wrapped around her wrist, stilling her movements. Not saying anything, she waited as his thumb raised over her racing pulse.

"I want dessert but not the pie," he finally said. His voice was low as though each word had been dragged over gravel before being released.

"What do you want?" She wished her voice was

confident and sultry but knew her shaky, whispered question could barely be heard.

He shifted his hand so that their palms were together, fingers linked. "I want you."

He opened his mouth as though to say more, but she offered a quick shake of her head. "You don't have to say anything else. Those three words are the only words I've wanted to hear. So, if you're going to take them back, you need to do so now. If you're going to mar them with more explanation, I don't want to hear it."

Her breath halted in her lungs as she waited to see his reaction to her pronouncement. In typical Bray fashion, he didn't make her wait long. His slow, heart-stopping, blood-pounding, pheromone-inducing smile gave her his answer. And it was exactly what she'd wanted to hear.

She leaped from her chair at the same time he did, not caring that the furniture almost tipped or the cart with empty dishes was bumped as he shoved it out of the way. Their bodies crashed together in a rush. His arms banded around her waist, pulling her flush against his body, her curves fitting perfectly against the hard planes. With no shoes on, the height difference was more pronounced. Unable to lift on her toes, she reached her arms upward so she could clasp her hands behind his neck, adding pressure to pull him forward.

He acquiesced, bending easily, but instead of taking her lips, he lifted her straight off the floor until their faces were equal. She squealed, then clutched him tighter, even though she knew he would never drop her.

She closed her eyes and angled her head, wanting to

feel his lips on hers. He leaned back slightly, keeping their lips from meeting, and she jerked her eyes open in surprise.

The intensity of his gaze held her captive, halting any words of protest at the delay to what she knew was going to be the best kiss of her life. But it was obvious he needed a moment, and she'd give him anything.

"I don't want to take advantage of you."

Once again, his words sounded as though they were pulled from the very pit of his gut and the gravel voice slammed into her, not rough but soothing. She wanted to beg him to speak to her every day for the rest of his life just so she could feel the way she felt at that moment. Instead, she tried to drag her mind back to the moment but wasn't sure she could accomplish that feat until he spoke again.

"Marie, you know you've been way more than a mission to me, and I want to take this forward. But you've been through a lot, and I don't want to have any regrets between us—"

"Shut up and kiss me," she ordered, her hand moving to grasp his jaws. He continued to hesitate, so she dove her fingers toward the back of his head, gliding through his silky hair that was way past needing a haircut. She hoped there was a way to keep it exactly like it was at this moment. "The past day has been a helluva trip for both of us, but believe me when I say that it was far easier than what I've gone through before in my life. I'm a grown woman and no blushing virgin. And I'm along for this ride with you. If we've got a night, I'll take it, even though I'll hate it's so short. But what I'm telling you is that there's no advantage to be taken with me. I'm freely coming to you, wanting whatever you're going to give me." She shifted in his arms to where her face was only an inch away from his and smiled. "And you need to decide what you're going to give me because I want it to start right fuckin' now."

With a whoop, he twirled her around as their lips met. Her giggle was quickly swept away when his tongue entered her mouth, delving deep and stealing her breath. The electric tension that had filled the room while they ate now sparked out of control between their joined lips and her core. So lost in the sensations, she was barely aware of moving when suddenly, she felt her body falling, then realized he was laying her down on the bed with his arms still securely around her.

His movements were so careful, so gentle, she was quickly nestled on top of the soft, plush comforter with his hard body above. She couldn't imagine a more perfect place to be. His hips settled between her thighs, his pelvis against hers, but his upper body weight was held just off her chest with his forearms planted next to her and his hands cradling her face.

Their lips molded together, nibbles and licks, tongues diving and sweeping until her chest heaved with the exertion of trying to breathe. His mouth left hers but didn't go far. He kissed his way over her cheek, nibbled her earlobe, and continued down her neck, sucking gently at the tender spot where her neck and shoulder met. Her pulse raced beneath his lips, and her fingers grasped at his hair, her short fingernails digging in slightly.

Her chest suddenly felt lighter, and he'd shifted his weight to his legs as he knelt between hers, his fingers unbuttoning her pajama top. Blush hit her cheeks and she covered her face with her hands. "God, my choice of nightwear is hardly sexy. I just wanted to stay warm."

His palms smoothed the material back, exposing her breasts. She knew her curves were more modest, not lush by any stretch of the imagination, but the way his eyes flared as they devoured her made her feel both feminine and powerful. He glided his hands over her breasts, his fingers circling her nipples that had budded into points.

The electricity jolted along the nerves that moved between her breasts and core, and she undulated her hips, seeking any relief to the need for friction that plagued her. He chuckled, the sound erupting from deep in his chest, and she added that sound to one that she wanted to hear every day, just like that—deep and low, caressing her body with the tone that met her ears.

He leaned down, his lips hovering above a nipple, and grinned. "Patience. Good things come to those who wait."

She groaned and shifted her hips again. "I want to respond to that by telling you to fuck off, but what I really want is for you to fuck *me*."

This time, his chuckle erupted into laughter, but before she had a chance to say anything else, he licked her nipple then blew air over the taut bud, eliciting another groan from her lips. He repeated the action with her other breast before latching on and pulling the nipple deeply into his mouth, gently dragging his teeth over the hard point.

Tortured and loving it, she grabbed the bottom of his T-shirt and began tugging it upward. He leaned back for a few seconds, just long enough to reach behind him, and snagged the material before pulling it over his head. Where it fell, she didn't know and didn't care as long as her eyes could feast on his muscular chest. His pecs bulged, and his abs had ridges she couldn't wait to lick and count.

With her pajama top partially over her shoulders and down her arms, she felt trapped, unable to get her hands on him the way she wanted. With his help, she wiggled her arms the rest of the way out and dropped the material to the side to join his T-shirt. Now, both topless, their gazes and hands were free to roam and appreciate.

"Christ, you're beautiful," he said.

Dragging her gaze up to his face, she smiled. "I was going to say the same thing about you."

He kissed her long and hard and wet, then once again trailed his mouth down her neck, giving attention to both breasts, and then down over her flat stomach. He shifted back on the bed and dragged her pajama bottoms and panties down her legs. She watched as his eyes flared again. She'd had attentive lovers in the past but she'd never felt the heady power of being the complete center of someone's attention before.

His gaze moved over her legs, and she watched him carefully as they moved to her scars. He neither avoided them nor focused on them, choosing instead to simply maintain his devotion to her as a whole body, not just the sum of her parts.

He shifted down, his shoulders pushing her thighs apart, his face resting just above her mound, his gaze pinned on her. "I told you I wanted dessert."

Before she could come up with an appropriate response, he licked her with the flat of his tongue and she flopped back on the bed, a gasp leaving her lips. Again, she'd had talented lovers, but oral sex had always been hit or miss with her. But this... there were no words to describe what Bray was doing to her other than 'holy-fucking-moly.' She wasn't sure if the devil was dancing or angels were singing, but whatever he was doing between her legs, it was magic.

He circled her clit with his tongue before sucking deeply, two fingers inserted inside her core, tweaking to find the spot that had her slapping her hand over her mouth to keep from screaming his name. The coil tightened inside, but he backed off just before she shattered, teasing her until she was coiled once again. Finally unable to take the tension, she leaned her head up, grabbed handfuls of his hair with her fingers, and threatened, "Enough! I'm so desperate, you'd better give it to me!"

He chuckled again, but this time, the deep rumbling came when his mouth was covering her sex, and she felt that sound reverberate in a place she'd never felt before. With her head pressed against the pillow and her hand pressed against her mouth, she cried out as her body shook with the intensity of her orgasm. The vibrations continued as he slowly kissed his way from her clit over her navel to each breast and to her mouth where she tasted her essence on his lips.

Uncertain if she would ever move again, all sexy and seductive words left her as she lay exposed in front of him, a silly grin on her face.

22

Fuckin' hell... what was that? Bray hadn't even sunk into Marie's body. His cock hadn't gotten to play. He'd had no orgasm. And yet, just watching her fall apart with nothing more than his mouth and fingers on her, he'd been rocked with the force of her orgasm.

Now, lying underneath him, her mouth wide with a grin that was far from sexy, and yet, the sexiest thing he'd ever seen, he stared as his chest heaved. "Christ, woman. I'm so hard for you and we've barely begun."

He didn't think she could be more beautiful, but as her smile widened and her hands grasped his shoulders with her fingers dug in slightly, she was gorgeous. "Well, then, handsome," she said, "looks like we need to get a move on."

"Hell, yeah," he agreed, keeping his weight on his hands pressed into the mattress next to her shoulders. He bent his elbows and dipped down to take her lips in a searing kiss before lifting up again. Continuing his sexual push-ups, he bent and dipped down to suckle each breast, kiss her neck, nibble her ear, and take her lips again. And when he didn't think he could take it anymore, her fingers moved to his jeans button and she fumbled trying to get them undone. Considering his cock was ready to burst through the zipper, he decided she was right. *They definitely needed to get a move on.*

He slid back from the mattress and lowered his zipper. She lifted on her elbows, her gaze pinned to his crotch. Considering the idea of taking it slow and teasing her, her tongue darted out and licked her lips, and he was a goner. With his thumbs hooked into the waistband, he shucked his jeans and boxers down his legs, springing his cock free.

He paused just long enough for her gaze to roam freely over his body. He'd had women do that before and he'd been cocky enough to like their blatant appreciation. But there was something about Marie's wide-eyed gaze and gently curved lips that made him want to crow with pride.

She lifted her eyes to him and shook her head slightly. "Damn, Bray. You're like a Michelangelo sculpture come to life. You could pose in front of a group of medical students just so they could study and memorize your musculature." She scrunched her nose and shook her head again. "But then, I'd have to kill all the other students just for drooling over you."

He threw his head back and barked out laughter. "I never know what's going to come out of your mouth, babe. But I gotta tell you, that's the most original compliment I've ever had, and it is by far my favorite." Her nose scrunched again, and he realized he'd just mentioned the fact that others had complemented his body, something most women didn't want to think about. *Hell, he'd never been jealous in his life, but thinking of men who'd come before him made him see green.*

Placing a knee on the bed, he crawled back over her, dipped to kiss the tip of her nose, and said, "Not only is it my favorite because of the originality, but honest to God, it's because it came from you."

Smiling, she slid her hand down his shoulders, over his pecs, tickling his abs, before her fingers encircled his cock. If there was any blood left in his head, it rushed south, erasing all ability for rational thought. As she glided her hand up and down his shaft, he dove for her mouth, his tongue moving in rhythm with her hand.

He shifted his hips until they were nestled between her thighs, his cock at her entrance. Her fingers dug in slightly, and he felt her tense. Lifting so he could see in her eyes, she didn't make him wait and wonder.

"Um... I'm clean and on birth control but—"

Jolting, he cursed, "Shit! Christ Almighty! I can't believe I forgot!" Embarrassed at his lack of finesse as well as his forgetfulness, he jumped from the bed, his head swinging around as he looked for his pants. Grabbing his jeans off the floor, he jabbed his hand into the back pocket and pulled out his wallet. Reaching inside, he pulled out several condoms and tossed them next to her. "I'm so sorry, Marie. Jesus, babe, I've never gone ungloved before. I'm clean, too, tested at work. But I can't believe just being with you has my brain so muddled I didn't even think about it."

A giggle slipped out as he climbed back over her, and

her hands moved to hold his jaws. "I like thinking about muddling your brain."

He kissed her again, loving the feel of her smile against his lips. As their lips melded together, he could only assume that some blood must've stayed in his head as thoughts slammed into him. Lifting his head, he stared down, his hands smoothing the hair away from her forehead. "Before we get ready to do what we're doing, I've got to say something first. Which is crazy because this is not normal for me. Hell, none of this is normal for me."

Her brow lowered, and it was plain to see his words were confusing. *Shit, I'm fuckin' this up.* Sucking in a deep breath, he let it out slowly, gathering his thoughts. In typical Marie fashion, she said nothing but simply rubbed her hands over his shoulders, giving him time to sort out what he wanted to say.

"I don't sleep with missions." As soon as those words left his lips, he watched her eyes widen and he winced. "I know I told you that some of my fellow Keepers have met their women while on missions. But you need to know that I've never crossed the boundary of professional and personal before. Never. And while I've never gone ungloved before, it's also important for me to say that while I was less discriminating with partners in my younger years, those days are behind me. What I'm feeling for you goes way beyond physical. I can't define what it is, I just know it's different."

Her smile was soft, her green eyes twinkling in the pale light of the lamp. She lifted a hand and smoothed the hair from his forehead, holding him close. "I'm not looking for you to define what this is, Bray. We're two adults with their own professions and lives that have crossed due to extreme circumstances. But, like you, what I feel for you is more than I've ever felt for anyone, and it's real. Where we go or what we do after this, just know that for me, it's different, too."

With her smile piercing his heart, he rolled on the condom and eased his cock forward as she clung to him, her velvet sex sheathing him. He wanted to go slow, careful, but she lifted her hips to meet his and he plunged to the hilt. Hearing a gasp, he was stunned to realize it came from him. So tight. So warm. It was as though her body had been made just for him.

Thrusting in and out, he wanted to cast all thoughts from his mind but was completely aware that instead of the total focus being on his cock, he wanted to make sure to give as much as he took. He'd always tried to be a considerate lover, but ultimately, his cock ruled his thoughts. But with Marie? He prayed that every thrust felt as good to her as it did to him, and if not, he wanted to make it better.

"What the hell are you thinking?"

His gaze jerked to her face, seeing concern. "I was just trying to figure out how to make this as good for you as it is for me because babe, this is fuckin' amazing."

The tension in her face left as she smiled. Pressing her hips up, she said, "The best way to make it good for me is to keep doing exactly what you're doing. Hard, fast, and deep."

Grinning, he had no response to that other than to do exactly what she asked. He thrust hard, fast, and deep. Her breasts bounced in rhythm, the nipples peaked and taut. He bent to take one in his mouth, tugging gently before soothing with his tongue. The fire that built low in his back had his balls tighten but he wanted her to come again. Rocking slightly to the side, he kept his weight on one hand while reaching down with the other, finding and tweaking her clit.

Her legs lifted to tighten around his waist, and she flung her head back but kept her eyes open, pinned on him as she cried out her orgasm. Her skin pinkened, the blush covering her breasts and rising on her neck to paint her cheeks. Her green eyes held him captive. Her short fingernails dug small crescents into his shoulders. *God, she's so beautiful.* He was sure he'd never seen a more beautiful sight in his life.

He felt the pulsing around his cock and gave himself over to the physical need of his body emptying into hers. With a few more thrusts, his release had his body tightening, his neck muscles cording as he groaned, and her name left his lips. As every drop was wrung from his body, he was acutely aware of her, something else that was new for him. Aware of the feel of her toned legs around his hips. Aware of her breasts lightly pressed against his chest. Aware of the scent of their coupling filling the air. Aware of the slightly damp hair framing her face. Aware of her hands soothing over his shoulders.

And maybe more than anything, aware of her smile that was open and honest.

He wanted to crash on top of her and let their sweat-slicked bodies cool together. But first, he needed to take care of the condom. "I'll be right back. Don't move a muscle."

As he headed into the bathroom, he heard her mumble, "I may never move again." Grinning to himself, he quickly dealt with the condom and stalked back into the bedroom, pleased to see that she indeed hadn't moved. He scooped her up into his arms, bent to grab the covers in one hand, jerked them down, then laid her gently on the soft sheets.

"I'm not going to fuck around, babe. I don't want to leave you tonight. I'd love to lay in bed with you and hold you all night long, but if that's not what you want, I'll sleep on the sofa—"

She grabbed his wrist and held on tight. "If you try to walk away from this bed, I'll tackle you to the floor."

He glanced down at the massive size difference between the two of them and lifted his brow as he looked back at her. "I'm not sure you'd be able to tackle me, babe."

"Well, it might not be successful, but I can sure as hell try!"

Chuckling, he turned out the light and crawled under the covers, pulling her tight against him. "The last thing I want is for you to get hurt trying to tackle me, so it looks like I'm sleeping with you tonight."

He had no idea what her reaction would be, but she remained quiet, speaking volumes with her actions instead. She snuggled in tightly, wrapped her arms around him, and pressed her body close, allowing him to envelop her in his embrace. Finally, she whispered, "Happy Birthday, Bray."

Then, he felt her lips press a kiss right over his heart. It didn't take long for her breathing to even out, and he knew she'd fallen into an exhausted sleep. He rested, but sleep didn't come easy for him. When slumber finally settled, it was with the memory of that precious kiss that stayed with him all night.

"It's whatever she wants. If she wants to go by car, I'll rent something and drive her."

Bray had woken early to the sound of his phone vibrating on the nightstand. Slipping into the bathroom, he talked with Drew. "I want to make sure she's feeling okay and get some food in her, then I'll ask her. I'll let you know what I find out. I don't want to hold you guys up but I don't want her to make a decision that she's not happy with." Gaining the easy agreement he knew he'd obtain from his fellow Keeper, he ended the call. Quickly using the bathroom, he stepped back into the bedroom, surprised to see Marie sitting up in bed. Trying to ignore the sex-and-sleep tousled hair, her rosy lips, the sleep crease along her cheek, and the way the sheet barely covered her breasts, he lifted his gaze to her eyes. That didn't help much considering he could still remember the way she looked at him when his mouth was on her sex. His cock jumped, and he grimaced, forcing the blood back to his brain.

"Who was that on the phone?"

"Drew."

"He wants to know when we'll be ready to fly out, doesn't he?"

Nodding, he said, "Yeah, but there's no rush to make a decision."

Tilting her head to the side, her gaze remained steady. "What decision is there to make? He needs to file flight plans and get the plane ready. It's not fair to make him wait."

"I told him that if you'd prefer to take the car, then we'd rent one and I'll drive you back."

At that, she visibly startled and the air left her lungs in an audible rush. "You'd drive me all the way to Boston?"

He stalked toward her and sat on the edge of the mattress, leaning to plant one hand on the far side of her hip and lifting the other to cup her jaw. "Babe, I'm not about to make you do anything you don't want to do. If you prefer going by car, then that's exactly what we'll do, and I'll count it as an honor to be the one to drive you."

She swallowed deeply, her gaze still not wavering. "I know that fear is real even if it's not rational. But I also know that I've given in to some of my fears for a very long time. I've fought so hard and accomplished so much, but it seems ridiculous to allow this one last fear to rule my life. I realize that in a few hours, when we're up in the clouds, I might curse my decision, but you can tell Drew that we'll fly with him."

"Are you certain? You can wait and make that decision after you've eaten breakfast and had a chance to really wake up."

Laughing, she leaned forward and placed her lips against his, kissing him lightly. "The only decision I want to make this morning is if we're going to save time and water by taking a shower together."

Blinking, it took a few seconds for his brain to catch up to her invitation. Suddenly jerking, he stood and whipped the covers off of her and lifted a squealing Marie in his arms. Kissing her fast and hard, he stalked into the bathroom and set her gently onto the floor. Leaning in, he flipped on the water of the shower. "Easiest decision we'll have to make all day, babe."

23

I'm insane! That was the only rational explanation Marie could offer to herself as she unsuccessfully tried to still the quivers running rampant throughout her body. She didn't want to know their altitude. She didn't want to know how much longer they had to go. And she was more thankful than she could express that Bray and the others had closed all the window shades in the plane.

By the time she and Bray had taken their long shower that included washing each other's bodies as well as sex against the wall where he was so careful with her leg even though she'd promise to let him know if anything hurt, she was warm and sated, ready for anything. That feeling continued through their room service breakfast of French toast, scrambled eggs, bacon, juice, and coffee.

As they greeted Drew, Tate, and John in the lobby of the hotel, she was all smiles, ready to face the day and conquer her fears.

And then they left the comfort of the airport and walked out to the small plane. Her feet had stumbled to a halt, and she'd stared, wide-eyed, heart pounding, palms sweating. "Oh, my God," she'd whispered.

Bray had whirled around and stood directly in her sight, lifting her chin with his knuckle. "You don't have to do this, sweetheart. We can turn around and walk away and get a car and drive. Honest to God, we can do that, and I'll be fine with it."

She'd wanted to cry at his generosity. Sucking in a deep breath, she'd closed her eyes and let it out slowly, repeating the calming gesture several times. Finally, she'd opened her eyes, held his gaze, and said, "Let's fuckin' do this."

His lips had slowly curved into a wide smile that turned his handsome face into a devastatingly gorgeous picture. She'd had no idea if she'd be able to make it onto the plane, but if her words had the power to make him smile like that, she was damn sure going to try.

Now, she sat with Bray's hand held tightly in hers. Aware that she was gripping, she tried to loosen her fingers occasionally, then the plane would wobble and her grip would tighten once again.

"Have I told you that I think you're amazing?"

At Bray's words, she rolled her head to the side, seeing his face close to hers. "I'm a mess."

"No, you're not," he replied, smiling gently. "You're smart, brave, caring, generous, fun."

All of those words were lovely, but it wasn't until he continued that she felt him down to her soul.

"You tune into me, something I don't think I've ever

had before," he said. "You seem to know when I need time to gather my thoughts and you don't try to force answers from me before I'm ready. You catch me by surprise with some of your questions or comments, making me think of things I haven't pondered before. You're in a field that's demanding, and yet, you find time to relax, something I never saw my father do. You're generous, walking away from a higher-paying career to use your medical knowledge in a way that would make you happy as well as help others. You have scars but don't let them define you. You make me feel as though I could do anything while not making me feel that I have to."

By now, her breath barely left her lungs as she stared at the intensity in his gaze, hearing that same intensity in his voice. His words swirled inside, making her long for... *what? Promises?*

She wanted to ask him what was going to happen now between them. A *'thank you, it was lovely, goodbye?'* A *'maybe I can see you again sometime?'*

She knew what she wanted. A *'let's make plans to continue what we've started'* conversation. It was on the tip of her tongue to say the words that ran through her mind, but sitting on a plane with some of his coworkers close by, even though they had headphones on, didn't seem like the right time or place for that conversation.

The plane dipped again, and she tightened her grip on his hand. Casting an apologetic grimace his way, she said, "I'm so sorry. You won't have a hand left by the time we land."

Leaning closer, he kissed her lightly. "It's all good,

babe. You just hold onto me. We'll get through this together."

True to his word, they finally landed in Boston even though she was certain her heart would stop from fear. As Drew touched down smoothly and they coasted to the hangar, she finally managed to pry her fingers from Bray's hand and take a breath that wasn't strangled deep in her chest.

With shaking legs and his help, she exited the plane, then hugged Drew, Tate, and John for all their support. Turning, she smiled at Bray's extended hand and reached out, glad to link fingers with him that didn't involve holding on for dear life.

They walked as a group toward the hangar's wide-open door. She'd talked to Cory, and he said he'd meet her here before driving her to her new apartment, staying a couple of days to make sure she was fine. She'd tried to tell him that she didn't need his hovering any more than she'd needed a security person's hovering. Glancing at Bray walking next to her, a small sigh escaped. *I would no longer mind him hovering.*

"Marie!"

The shout came from the side, and she looked over to see Cory running toward her. Bray immediately let her hand loose, and she limp-jogged straight into her brother's arms. He picked her up and twirled her, kissing the top of her head. Laughing, she hugged him tightly, knowing how much he'd worried.

By the time he finally set her feet back onto the concrete, the Keepers had approached. She turned, beaming toward them, her gaze settling on Bray. "Cory, I want to introduce you to the pilot that helped me deal with my fears, Drew. This is John and Tate, rescuers extraordinaire." Reaching out to take Bray's hand, she added, "And this is Bray, my security *traveling companion* that you sneakily hired."

Cory shook their hands, offering his thanks. When he moved to Bray, he glanced down at their clasped hands, and she stiffened, ready to smack her brother down if he said anything. Thankfully, he simply thanked Bray, his voice sincere.

"Sis, I wonder if you'd mind letting me talk to these men for a moment."

She blinked, uncertain she'd heard Cory correctly. "I'm sorry?"

"I need to talk to Mace's men and thought you might like to take a trip to the ladies' room."

She released Bray's hand and plopped both of her fists onto her hips. "Shall I go powder my nose while I'm at it? I certainly wouldn't want my delicate ears to hear what the men talk about in my absence."

"Marie, that's not what I mean. It's just that some things have come to light, and I don't want you—"

"Stop right there," she bit out, her hand lifting, palm facing him. "If you say another word, I'll tell Mom it was you who broke her heirloom antique vase from great-grandma instead of letting you blame it on the cat."

"Sis, come on, you wouldn't!"

A snort erupted from behind, and she had no idea

which Keeper it was but didn't care. "May I remind you that it was Bray and *me* on the train that exploded? *I* was involved in getting to safety. *I* discovered two dead bodies." At that, Cory winced, but she was on a roll. "*I* was shot at. *I* had to spend the night in the wilderness, although," she turned and smiled at Bray, "it was Bray who made a shelter, built a fire, and made sure I was safe. But," she turned back to level her glare onto Cory, "*I* flew in a helicopter and a plane to get here. So, if you think my delicate sensibilities can't handle what you have to say, then just try me!" Her tone grew softer, but each word was more punctuated by the time her speech was finished.

Cory's hand shot up as he rolled his eyes. "Okay, okay, I get it!" Sighing heavily, he opened his arms, and she accepted his invitation, knowing he acknowledged that he didn't need to keep her in the dark as well as wanting her close.

"Okay, I've been in contact with Mace, and what he's found out about Gregory Manitov is the same thing I'm being told from my counterpart in the RCMP. There's no trace of him. It's like he didn't exist."

"What?" she barked out, her gaze shooting from Cory over to Bray. "How is that possible?"

Cory shared a look with Bray, incensing her. "Don't keep me in the dark!"

He turned her toward him and said "Sis, I don't know. None of it falls under my jurisdiction, of course, but I called in as many markers as I could and kept running into a brick wall. There's not much else I can do. We can hope he got to whatever island he's probably retiring to with the money he's earned or stolen. For you, sis, I'm taking you to your new apartment and already talked to the security there. We'll call Mom and Dad. I know they're anxious to talk to you."

She stared into Cory's face, her heart aching for the concern she saw. Offering a small smile, she squeezed his hand then turned and walked over to Drew, Tate, and John, her smile warm and heartfelt as they said goodbye and walked back toward the plane, giving her and Bray privacy.

Bray held still, not reaching for her. Not willing to part so publicly, she held his gaze, his dark eyes intense. Unable to read the emotion swimming in their depths, she said, "Can we talk?"

Nodding, he led the way to the side but held himself stiffly. Standing in front of him, she hesitated, aware that Cory's gaze was on them. "This isn't how I planned on saying goodbye," she admitted, glad when her words seemed to penetrate the shield that Bray had erected. She reached out and took both of his hands in hers, twisting her wrists so their palms met and fingers linked.

He sighed and nodded. "I guess I preferred not thinking about it."

Her body was strung tight, exhaustion warring with a multitude of emotions she knew would take months to untangle in sessions with a counselor. "I know this isn't private, but I need to know if what you said to me is true. I just need honesty, Bray. If what we had was a... well, for lack of a better description, a *dramatic vacation fling*, please, let me know. My feelings haven't changed, but I really need your honesty." She wanted to throw her arms around him and beg to see him again. She wanted to make promises she hadn't thought through, vows she wasn't sure were reciprocated. She wanted to feel his arms around her pulling her close, his lips on hers in another kiss that tilted her world, and more chances to feel his body rocking into hers.

But mostly, she needed him to be honest. If what he wanted was not the same, she needed to know. Swallowing deeply, she stared up into his black eyes, unable to read what he was thinking.

His gaze never wavered but neither did his hardened expression. The muscle tick in his jaw that she'd grown familiar with was present. She sighed, then forced her lips to quirk upward. "It's okay, Bray. I'm just glad we met—"

"I don't know how this is supposed to go."

At those words from him, she snapped her mouth shut, chin lifting slightly as she steeled herself, waiting to hear what else he needed to say.

"I guess I thought I'd have a chance to say goodbye in private."

Her heart sank as his meaning moved over her, but she couldn't disagree with what he said. *Goodbyes are always better in private... especially permanent ones.* Determined to not fall apart until she reached the solitude of her apartment, she nodded.

"It's just that there's so much more I thought I'd have a chance to say," he continued.

She grimaced at the thought of what he would have said if they'd had the chance. *You're a lovely girl but I'm just not ready for a relationship.'* Or *'I don't do long distance.'* Or *'I can't compete with your career.'* Or *'I didn't mean for things to go so far.'* Shaking her head, she shoved those thoughts down. *We never made promises. We never defined what we felt.* This time, she squeezed his fingers and her smile was more sincere. "Bray, it's fine. Really. Being with you was amazing, but I'd rather part as friends than make you feel like you have to run away from me."

The expression of relief she expected to cross his face didn't occur. Instead, his chin jerked inward as his brows jerked down into a severe V, and his eyes narrowed.

"Run away from you? Why the hell would you think I wanted to run away from you?"

She blinked, head moving back slightly as she held his gaze. "Uh… because…" She tilted her head to the side, still uncertain of his thoughts. "Because you seemed to be having trouble with… this."

"This?"

A ball of anger was replacing the dread that had lodged in her throat. "Yes, *this*, Bray. You're stiff, didn't initiate a PDA, which wasn't a problem in front of your friends. You can't figure out how to say goodbye, and I get the feeling that you're trying to let me down easy with whatever bullshit line you finally have the balls to say."

At that, his eyes narrowed even more, and he bent slightly at the waist, bringing his face directly in front of hers. "Did we mean any of the shit we said to each other about wanting to see where this would go?"

Blinking again, she nodded. "I did. I want you in my

life, Bray. If that's only as a friend, I'll take it, but it'll be hard not having all of you when that's what I really want."

He dipped his chin sharply. "Damn right."

Still not having a clue what his exact thoughts were, she was shocked when he kept hold of her left hand but dropped her right, leading her back to where Cory was waiting. It didn't escape her notice that he walked slow enough for her to not limp, even though energy was vibrating from his body. Stopping directly in front of Cory, he continued to hold her hand. Twisting her head and looking up at him, she had no idea what to expect, but from the equally brow-lowered expression her brother had on his face, she was fearful of an alpha smackdown between her two favorite men.

"Cory, because you hired LSI to do a job, and I was the employee tasked with the mission, plus because you're Marie's brother, I have no intention of hiding our relationship."

Cory's brows snapped upward, and she gasped, surprised at the turn of events. "Do you think you could've told me that first? This isn't the dark ages, Bray. I don't need my brother's permission to date someone!"

He squeezed her hand and dropped his now-warm gaze to her, speaking softly. "This isn't about asking permission, Marie. This is about showing respect. To you and your brother." Shifting his attention back toward Cory, he said, "Your sister and I haven't defined what we are or what we feel other than we want to continue exploring a relationship. From now on, what happens between us is between us. I don't report to you. I don't report on it to LSI. The courtesy I'm giving to you and I'll give to Mace is to admit that feelings developed during the mission. Now that the assignment is over, we're just a couple who are ready to move their relationship forward."

No one spoke for a moment, Cory's gaze moving between Bray's intensity and her face, which she had no doubt expressed surprise, elation, and an internal fight against the desire to twirl in happiness.

She was aware the other Keepers had walked back over, forming a semicircle behind them, and loved that they had his back even if it wasn't necessary.

"Marie?" Cory's voice was gentle, and she heard the multitude of questions expressed in just his calling out her name.

Nodding slowly, she smiled first at Bray and then toward Cory. "He put it perfectly. What we experienced was intense, but feelings were already developing before the train wreck. The bottom line is that we're not ready for a permanent goodbye."

Cory continued to hold her gaze, then his lips curved as well. Stepping forward, he pulled her into a hug and kissed her forehead before turning toward Bray with his hand outstretched. "I appreciate this. Your protection and your honesty." Looking to the other Keepers, he said, "I get the feeling they'd like a private goodbye. How about I buy the three of you a cup of coffee before you have to head back to Maine?"

Drew, Tate, and John laughed, accepting his offer. As

the four men walked away, she turned her attention back to Bray.

"Nothing will ever be boring with you, Allan Bray."

Laughing, he nodded. "Funny, I had the same feeling about you."

24

Bray stood at the wall of windows at the front of his house, pacing as he'd done for the past hour. It was Marie's first visit since they'd parted at the airport two weeks ago. She was driving the three hours to get from Boston to his home, claiming that she loved to drive. It had seemed like a good idea at the time, but considering he was wearing a path on his rug, he now wished he'd gone down to get her.

He'd missed her as soon as she'd driven off with her brother. Climbing back into the airplane with his fellow Keepers, he'd kept the conversation on the events that had taken place in Canada. But he should've known Drew wouldn't be hushed.

"Nice touch," Drew had said, his grin wide. At Bray's scowl, the others had laughed, and Drew continued. "Talked to the brother. Got the family's okay. Squared it with the man who'd hired you. Hell, Bray, you took care of all bases and still got the girl."

"You gonna fuckin' shut up anytime soon?"

Drew had laughed harder and shook his head. "Nah, got nothing to do for an hour other than just fly us home. Hell, I could do that in my sleep!"

"Yeah, well, I'd rather you focus on your shit and not on me. But, until then, I'll drown you out." With that, he'd gone under headphones and listened to music, hiding his grin. His teammates could tease all they wanted—he *did* get the girl.

Now, his feet stumbled as he heard the sound of a vehicle coming down his driveway. Throwing open the door, he jogged down the stairs, his gaze landing on Marie's smiling face through her windshield. Burgundy glasses framed her green eyes, and he was struck with how much he'd missed her face.

She'd barely put her car in park when he opened her door and leaned in, his hands cupping her face, his lips landing on hers. And just like the first time, he poured everything he had into the kiss, and his senses fired with a jolt. Her delicate scent commingled with the salty crisp air blowing off the water. Her lips were soft, perfect for plundering, which he did as soon as she opened to him and he swept his tongue inside. Still clutching her face, his shoulders were branded by her fingertips as she grasped to pull him closer.

He wanted more of her, but as common sense slid into his consciousness, he realized she was still buckled into her seat. Lifting away from the kiss, he pressed his forehead to hers. "Sorry, babe. Let's get you out of the car and into the house."

She popped open her trunk, and he grabbed her

small suitcase. Linking fingers, they turned toward his house.

"Holy moly, Bray. This is amazing!" She squeezed his hand, casting her gaze up at him, her smile wide. "And your property backs to the water?"

Nodding, he gave a tug on her hand. "Let's go in, and I'll give you the tour."

"I never pictured you with something so modern, but now that I think about it, this fits."

When he'd relocated to Maine, he'd looked for a place that would keep him close to the LSI compound but eschewed the idea of an apartment, townhouse, or God forbid, even a close-knit neighborhood with cookie-cutter houses. He'd told the realtor he wanted a water view, a fairly new house so that upkeep would be minimal, woods around so that he had less yard to mow, and he couldn't see himself in an old-fashioned house. When this property came onto the market, he took one look and jumped at it, even though the price was more than he'd originally wanted. But it was in perfect condition and checked every box he had, plus some he hadn't even thought of.

Relating that to Marie as they walked inside, she nodded again. "Oh, my God! This place is fabulous!"

The front door was set in a full wall of glass, the pale wooden floor leading straight back to a hall that opened into a two-story living room with full back windows facing the water. His furniture was minimal, keeping with the modern space. Low-slung, comfortable sofas and chairs. A large flatscreen TV was over the fireplace and bookshelves lined the wall. To the right was the large eat-in kitchen with another wall of windows over-looking the water and back deck. The cabinets were white, the countertops marble, and the decorations neat.

She stood in the middle of the space and turned slowly as though trying to memorize every inch. His family, friends, and teammates had visited, all expressing appreciation for his house, but until that moment, he'd never cared about someone else's opinion. But standing next to Marie as she carefully perused his home, he waited nervously to see what she would say now that she was getting a close-up view.

A smile spread over her face as she shook her head. "I'm still in awe. This place is absolutely magnificent, Bray. It's like a dream house come true."

"I never thought to ask you what you think of your new place in Boston."

She rolled her eyes and shrugged. "It's an apartment. There's just not much to say about it. It's not even mine."

Jerking slightly, he looked down. "Not yours?"

"I'm just subletting right now. I couldn't see signing a year-long lease in Boston until I'd lived there long enough to make sure it was where I wanted to stay. I've visited Boston lots of times, but it's my first time living there. I had originally wanted to rent an old Victorian house, but Cory convinced me that I'd be safer in an apartment building with security." She shrugged again. "It has a pretty view even if it's not very large. It's nice enough to sublease for now, but it's definitely temporary."

Squeezing her fingers, he asked, "Do you want to see more?"

"Oh, yeah!" They walked into the master bedroom where her gasps sounded out once again. Small fireplace with a large flat-screen TV. The same pale floors. A master bathroom with a huge shower and sunken tub and lots of space. "I cannot wait to try out your tub!"

His feet stuttered to a halt at the thought of her in his bathtub. Grinning, he said, "I may not get that thought out of my mind until I see you in that tub. But I gotta tell you, you won't be alone. Thank God, it's big enough for both of us." Now that that thought was firmly planted in his mind, it was hard to think of anything else. He quickly showed her the rest of the house. Guest bedrooms, the upstairs loft, the room he used as an office, and then they ended up on the back deck filled with comfortable furniture. A boardwalk extended from the deck through the woods down to the water where he had a small dock, two kayaks, and a canoe.

Once they were back inside and he'd set her suitcase in the master bedroom, she turned and wrapped her arms around his waist, pulling him close. With their bodies flush together, he looked down and grinned.

"So, now that you've got me in your lair, what's on the agenda?"

"Tomorrow, I've invited the other Keepers and the whole LSI family over. It'll be simple... beer, brats on the grill, and most will bring side dishes and desserts. Everybody wants to meet you."

She jerked, her fingers grasping his shirt. "Everyone wants to meet me?"

"Hell, yeah. Babe, you're famous. You survived the train wreck, a night in the middle of the Canadian Rockies, and a helicopter rescue. You'll find out pretty quickly that means you fit in just perfectly around here."

"Okay," she said, dragging the word out. Tilting her head to the side, she crinkled her nose. "So, that's tomorrow, what about the agenda for the rest of today?"

"It's totally up to you. This is your weekend, and I want to spend it doing whatever you want. If you want to sightsee, we can go out. If you're hungry and want dinner, we can go to a restaurant or order in. If you want to get on the water, I've got kayaks."

A slow smile curved her lips and his heart beat faster at the sight.

"Anything I want?" she asked.

"Anything."

Her fingers clenched the bottom of his shirt, then her hands slid upward, smoothing over his skin. He felt the warmth from her touch on his back zip straight to his cock. *Please, let her want what I want. Please, let her need what I need.*

"Well, Bray, what if I said I'd like you to show me the master bedroom again? Particularly the big king-size bed."

With a whoop from him and a squeal from her, he scooped her up and stalked straight into the bedroom. "Thank fuck!" The kiss they'd shared the moment she'd arrived had stayed on his lips and his mind and had his cock pressed against his zipper. He wasn't lying when he'd said he'd do anything she wanted, but wanting to hit his bed first... *Hell, yeah!*

Reaching his bedroom, he slowly lowered her while keeping her feet just above the floor, allowing the front of her body to drag along his. With one hand banded around her upper back, her breasts were pressed against his chest. His other hand cupped her ass, sure that she could feel his need for her against her stomach.

Her hands clutched his face, bringing him closer as she angled her head. Her lips landed on his. As with all their other kisses, the crackle of electricity seemed to fire about the room as their mouths fused together. Her tongue darted out and traced over his lips, sending tingles straight to his cock. A long, low groan was pulled from his chest, allowing her to take advantage, gliding her tongue into his mouth, dragging it over his. Her taking charge of the kiss was hot as fuck, but after a moment, he decided to take control back.

Lowering her feet the rest of the way to the floor, her fingers were already grasping at his shirt, trying to lift it up. Separating just long enough for him to assist in flinging the material between them and down his arms before tossing it to the side, he was glad she was wearing something easy to remove. "Lift your arms, sweetheart."

Grinning, she lifted her arms into the air, giving him a chance to gently pull the material up and over her head, allowing it to join his shirt on the floor. He pushed her dark hair off her shoulders so that nothing was impeding the feel of her skin against his lips as he kissed down her neck, his fingers gently tugging the straps of her pink satin bra down her arms. Within an easy flick of the front closure clasp, the bra fell open, her perfect breasts beckoning. Answering the call, he dipped his head and sucked a nipple deeply into his mouth.

She dropped her head back as her fingers clutched his shoulders, digging in as though that was the only thing holding her upright. Moving back and forth, his mouth paid equal homage to both breasts as his hands glided over the curves of her waist to unfasten her jeans. Dropping to his knees as he dragged them down her legs, the scent of her arousal hit him. With her hands still on his shoulders, she lifted each leg as he pulled her jeans and panties completely off.

Still on his knees as he looked up at her naked body presented to him, his cock throbbed, but it was the pounding of his heart that caught and held his attention. The truth was, almost any naked, beautiful woman in his bedroom could make his cock swell with need. But it was only Marie that made his heart beat faster, needing everything that she could give him while wanting to offer her the world.

"Christ, babe, you are so beautiful." He bent and kissed the scars that ran along her leg before nuzzling her sex.

She dropped her chin, holding his gaze, her fingernails digging into his shoulders, and smiled. Without hesitation, she slid her legs apart, and the gift she presented would have dropped him to his knees if he wasn't already there. Licking her folds, he dove in like a man starved. Sucking, licking, tonguing... He played her sex like a fine instrument, tuning it perfectly to make the most beautiful music. And when she shattered, he held her in place, letting her juices coat his tongue as her body shook with desire.

Looking up again, he grinned. "Like I said... beautiful."

"Does it make me sound too needy to say that I missed you more than I ever thought possible?" she whispered.

He stood, towering over her, wanting to envelop her in his embrace as he shook his head. "No. No more than me counting down the days, hours, and minutes until I could have you in my arms again."

He bent, jerked the covers down, and then turned, lifting her again and placing her gently onto the soft sheets. He shucked his jeans and boxers faster than he'd ever stripped and fisted his cock as she leaned up on her forearms, her lust-filled gaze watching him until she finally cried, "Please, Bray... now!"

He reached for a condom, but her fingers landed on his wrist, stilling his movements. She held his gaze as he waited to see what she wanted to say.

She licked her lips, her gaze darting to the side. "What is it, babe? Seriously, Marie, we'll never do anything you're not comfortable with."

"No, no, that's not it," she said, shaking her head. "I just wanted you to know that I'm clean... I've got my test results on my phone. And I'm on birth control. I know we're new, but—"

"I trust you. I've got my test records, too. So...?" He held his breath, wanting to hand over all control to her.

"If you want, I'm fine with no condom," she said, her lips curving.

His gaze roved over her body, once again humbled at the gift she was offering. He'd never gone bareback... ever. And the idea of being completely natural with her had his imagination firing. "Yeah, baby, I'd love to have nothing between us."

Settling on her back again, she lifted her arms to him, her smile wide. "Okay. Nothing but you and me."

Her words speared through him... *nothing but you and me.* He placed a knee onto the mattress and covered her body, lining up at her entrance. Thrusting deeply, the air rushed from his lungs at her tight sex sheathing him. *Jesus!* Nothing had prepared him for the feel of skin on skin. Her inner core was slick with her arousal but the muscles still added the friction to send electricity vibrating throughout his entire body.

As much as he wanted to lose himself in the sensations, he cradled her face with his hands, and just like the last time they'd made love, he kept his gaze locked on her, not wanting to miss a second.

He slowed the motions of his hips, taking his time as he lowered his lips to hers, nibbling the corners of her mouth before gliding his tongue over hers. His pelvis dragged over her clit as she lifted her legs to wrap around his back. Swallowing her moan, he angled his head to take the kiss deeper.

Her fingers lightly danced over his back, soothing over the muscles before gripping his arms as her body shuddered, the pink of a blush rising from her breasts to her cheeks. His cock swelled even more as his release was imminent. Lifting from the kiss, his gaze stayed pinned on hers as they fell off the precipice together. Spots danced in front of his eyes. Her inner core squeezed, wringing every drop as he emptied himself.

He managed to fall to the side, hoping he didn't crush her, but was uncertain he could move again. The sound of his ragged breathing filled his ears, and it was a moment before he realized she was breathing just as hard. Not having to deal with the condom, time ceased to matter as his cock slowly slid from her body. They lay, arms and legs tangled, heartbeats together, breaths mingled.

Brushing her hair back from her face, he kissed her gently. "Welcome home, babe."

25

Marie sat on Bray's deck, surrounded by a group of women that she had immediately felt comfortable with, and yet, was in awe of. All sweet. All smart. And all beautiful.

Yes, the other Keepers were much like Bray: tall, muscular, handsome. So much so, she wondered if Mace specifically chose them for their prowess or if all Special Forces members were like them. But now, she wondered if the women were specifically chosen by their respective mates from an I'm-a-badass-woman website that she didn't know about.

Mace's wife, Sylvie, told her tale of meeting him when her son witnessed a murder and Mace protected them. Helena offered a hilarious story of how she met Rank when she dropped into the middle of one of his investigations. Julie met Walker when he came to Mexico to escort her and three teenagers when an earthquake trapped them. Babs, the most bad-ass of them all, was a Keeper, having served with Mace, and got with Drew when her vacation from hell landed her with real-life pirates on a Caribbean island. Then there was Sara, who Blake rescued when they were together in French Guiana, and she'd been kidnapped. Nora had been Tate's high school girlfriend, but after years estranged, he came to save her when her job in a Wyoming hospital landed her in the middle of a jailbreak escape. Claire was running for her life when Levi rescued her from the side of the road. Christina, a violinist, needed Clay when her life collided with drug dealers. Josie had met Cobb in New Mexico, needing protection when her clinic was faced with an embezzler. Lucy was a local teacher who'd met John before he became a Keeper but, like Christina, her life collided with drug dealers from Canada and he came to her rescue.

By the time their stories had been shared, Marie's mouth hung open, and she had no idea what to say other than, "Good grief! No wonder the Keepers think you all are amazing."

"Honey," Marge said, peering at her over her glasses. "You and Bray survived a train wreck and an assassination attempt. I'd say that qualifies you for joining the sisterhood."

She wasn't sure about that sentiment, but coming from Marge, she took it as high praise. Marge and Horace filled the role of 'keepers of the Keepers' as Bray explained.

"Well, I don't know... I mean, Bray and I haven't known each other long... well, we just started..." The others laughed, and she shrugged, having no idea what label to put on her and Bray.

He'd taken most of the Keepers down to the water to check out the improvements he wanted to make to the dock. Some of the women walked down to join them and others headed to the kitchen to set out dessert. Marie looked into the living room and spied David, Mace and Sylvie's son, piled on the sofa, a scowl on his face, crutches on the sofa next to him. When they'd arrived, Sylvie explained he'd injured himself playing soccer.

While polite, he'd given off typical preteen vibes of *don't mess with me*. She walked inside and into the living room and sat down near him. "David, I know you don't know me, but I wondered how you're doing with your injury. I'm a doctor who works with young people who have injuries to help them get better." She could see the warring on his face, the desire to blow her off mixed with the good upbringing he'd had that told him he needed to be polite. "I also know it sucks to miss the rest of your soccer season."

His face darkened, then he sighed heavily. "I'll still go to practice and games to show my support, but even that makes me angry. I mean, not to brag or anything, but I'm one of the best on the team. The coach and the others say so. But because of this stupid ankle, I'm stuck on the sidelines. And not to be rude, but there's no way you can understand even if you do work on kids."

"I know that the exercises the doctor gave you to do are important. You don't want to overdo it, but you need to keep to the physical routine they gave you for complete recovery." His lips pinched together, and she was reminded of a younger version of herself. *Angry. Frustrated.* "You know, David, I really do understand." Just as he was about to retort, she lifted the bottom of her pants leg, showing the horrific scars that ran from her knee to her ankle and foot.

His eyes widened as he gasped, followed by, "Wow!" He immediately winced, mumbling, "Sorry, Doctor Brighton."

"Please, call me Marie. And *wow* is probably the exact right response," she laughed, glancing down at her leg, the familiar scars no longer shocking.

David's eyes cut over to her. He opened his mouth then shut it without saying anything.

"You want to know what happened, don't you?"

Nodding, he said, "Yeah... uh, yes. If you don't mind."

"Not at all. I was in an accident when I was fourteen. My leg was crushed and had to be pinned back together."

"Pinned?" He sat up straighter, his interest piqued.

"When the bones can't be set easily or there is too much damage, then the doctors can add metal plates and screw them into the bones. In my case, I have some plates, but then, I also have some places where the bones just fused, but I lost mobility."

His eyes moved between her face and her leg. "And you were only fourteen?"

"Yes. I lost most of my teenage years to the injury. I had to be homeschooled for a lot of high school, and because the surgeries covered about two years, I had physical therapy for almost four years. I did what I could, of course, and my family didn't want me to miss out on things, but the reality is my life was very different."

"You… um… you still limp a little."

"That's right. Because my ankle fused with limited mobility, it's hard to bend it all the way. But what you have to understand is that if I hadn't done the therapy that the doctors wanted, I wouldn't be able to walk at all now without a cane or crutches."

Now sitting up completely, he twisted to look at her more fully. "Did you miss out on sports?"

Crinkling her nose, she nodded. "Oh, yeah… soccer."

At that, he blinked, his mouth dropping open. "No way!"

"Yes, way!"

"Man, that sucks! Like you didn't get to play at all as a teenager?" His voice held the surety that she'd just announced the worst thing he could imagine.

"That's right. I never played soccer again."

Shaking his head slowly, David's face held sorrow. "I'm really sorry." His brow lowered as though deep in thought, then he looked back at his ankle wrapped in an elastic bandage. "How did you handle that? Weren't you pissed… uh… mad?"

She nodded slowly, pressing her lips together, casting her mind back to a place she tried not to think of often. "Yeah, I was. But for me, my accident was pretty severe, and I had lots of bad dreams for a long time. At first, I just wanted the pain of the surgeries to be over, and then when I had to do exercises and they hurt, I got mad again. Why did everything have to hurt so much? But I was tired of hospitals and staying in bed and not being able to do anything. I finally realized that while the accident was not anything I had control over, I did have control over what I did with my body afterward. I could do the stretches. I could do the exercises. I could eventually hobble and then walk. So, being pissed just made me want to take charge of my recovery more."

His brow lowered, churning emotions crossing over his face. Finally, he asked, "You work with kids who have sports injuries?"

She nodded. "Sports injuries and all kinds of injuries."

"The doctor gave my mom some papers with a few exercises on them for me to do but I haven't looked at them. We have to drive almost an hour to get to the therapist and that suck— um... stinks."

She remained quiet but nodded slowly, giving him a chance to think.

"Would you take a look at them to see if they're what you'd recommend for me to do? And if I do them, will they get me back on the field sooner?"

"Sure, I'll look at them. I'm only here through tomorrow but—"

"Mom's got 'em in her purse. I'll get 'em!" He pushed off the sofa with the help of his crutches and hobbled toward the kitchen, calling, "Mom! I need those exercises the doc gave you. Doctor Marie is going to see if it's what she recommends for me to get back out on the field!"

She followed him, her feet stuttering to a halt when

she realized the sliding doors to the deck were fully open, and the large gathering had become quiet, all appearing to watch the exchange she'd had with David. Her gaze immediately landed on Bray, and the warmth pouring from his eyes filled her heart. She smiled, and he walked to her, not stopping until his feet were directly in front of hers and her head was tilted back to hold his gaze. In one fluid movement, his arms encircled around her and he dropped his mouth to hers. The kiss started to flame, and just as she was ready to give in to the heat, he lifted his head. Realizing they had an audience, she was glad he'd managed to maintain control. If it had been left to her, they would have morphed into kiss-overdrive, the kind that would have forgotten their guests and taken them straight to bed, if they'd even made it that far.

She was exhausted by the end of the evening but couldn't remember the last time she'd had so much fun. As she and Bray stood at the front door saying goodbye to everyone, the words he'd said the night before after they'd made love shot straight into her mind. *"Welcome home, babe."*

She'd thought at the time that he was just welcoming her to *his* home, but with his arm casually draped around her shoulders as goodbyes were given along with handshakes from him and hugs from her, a new interpretation wormed its way into her heart. *Not just his home, but our home.*

Before she traveled down that rabbit hole of thought, a hole that would undoubtedly be filled with twists and turns that made no sense, Mace, Sylvie, and

David moved to them. While Mace and Bray shook hands, David stopped in front of her and grinned.

"I'm really glad I met you, Doctor Marie. I wish you didn't have to leave because I told Mom that I'd give anything for you to do my PT."

"Thank you, that's sweet, David. But with the exercise list that was given to you along with those examples and a few tips that I've shared, you should do really well. And if it's okay with your mom and dad, I'm only a phone call or email away if you ever want to chat."

He smiled and offered a chin lift, emulating a gesture she felt sure he'd seen from the other men. Sylvie wrapped her arms around Marie and hugged her tightly. "I'm so glad I got to meet you, not just because you're with Bray, but I can't thank you enough for what you did tonight for my son. He's been so down in the dumps and didn't want to do any of his exercises. You helped him regain the spark that was always part of David and I've missed during the last week." Smiling, she cocked her head to the side. "And if I can throw my two cents then, I'd love for you to relocate here as well!"

Sylvie walked out with David, and she was ready to wave goodbye to Mace when he turned to face her directly. Dipping his chin so his eyes met hers, he said, "I appreciate you taking the time to talk to David. What you said to him made an impression, and that's not easy with kids his age."

"Injuries are tough at any age," she replied, mesmerized by the deep voice of the take-charge man. "But he's too old to be babied and too young to be able to imagine the long-range goal being met with short-term successes." Shrugging, she added, "Although I find kids of all ages often respond to therapy better than adults."

"It was really nice to meet you, Marie." Mace took her much smaller hand in his and offered a gentle shake. "I hope we get to see a lot more of you." With that, the last of the guests walked out and Bray closed the door.

He turned and wrapped his arms around her, his smile wide as he kissed her forehead. "Did you have a good time?"

She rested her cheek against his chest and nodded. "I like your friends. What you all have built is nothing short of amazing. I've always enjoyed my fellow doctors and coworkers, but I've never seen such camaraderie." Leaning back, she held his warm gaze. "Do you think it's because each of you started in the military?"

"I have no doubt that had a lot to do with it. But a key component has been Mace handpicking the people he wanted in his company. We all joke about our egos, but honestly? When we walk through the door, egos are checked, and we all work for the common mission."

Hating to change the subject, she said, "Speaking of mission... I overheard you and Josh talking about Gregory. Anything new?"

He sighed, lifting his hand to brush her hair behind her ear, then his fingers stayed, cradling the back of her neck. She leaned into his warmth, loving the simple gesture.

"Our Canadian contacts are strangely quiet so we don't know if they are on to something that they're keeping close to themselves or if they have no idea where he is either. But, by now, he's got to know that whatever we had was turned over to the authorities. If he lost a ton of money on his electronics, then it's gone, and he won't recoup it from us."

"So, no more looking over my shoulder. Good!"

He bent and kissed her shoulder, nuzzling her neck at the same time. "Such a delicious shoulder."

Laughing, she inclined her head toward the kitchen. "Since our guests made sure the place was spotless before they left, we have nothing to clean up. So, you could snack on my delicious shoulder if you want."

His hands spanned her waist and he lifted her in his arms, kissing his way down her neck to the soft skin exposed by her pink tank top. "There's more deliciousness here than just your shoulder. I might have to sample the entire meal."

As his mouth continued its path downward, she wrapped her legs around his waist and ground her core against the crotch of his jeans, electricity driving her need. With her fingers clutching his hair, she groaned, "You can lay me out like a charcuterie board and sample everything on the platter."

Laughing, he twirled her around, glanced over her shoulder to make sure the front door was locked, then stalked through the house, carrying her to his bedroom. The bedroom that she couldn't help but imagine she'd one day consider to be hers as well.

26

A week later, Bray returned from an assignment in Texas with Cobb where they'd worked to develop the security needs for an oilman whose teenage daughter had been threatened by someone she met online. Besides the system for the entire ranch, he'd also reviewed the basics for staying safe in the world of teenagers and social media. The girl listened carefully, and while he was sorry she'd been terrorized, she and her parents intended to ensure her continued safety.

Now back in Maine, he stopped by LSI before going home, wanting to see if there was anything he needed to work on before the next day. Walking into the compound's main room, his phone vibrated. Smiling, he connected. "Hey, babe."

"Hi, Bray. I'm almost to my apartment but wanted to let you know that I got a call from the security desk at my building. The Canadian railway must have been going through the wreckage and they found my toiletry bag and had it delivered to the address I'd given them. Of course, I'll just toss the medication since it's been out of my hands for three weeks, but I don't mind getting some of my personal belongings back. Not that I had anything expensive in there, but it had two pairs of earrings that my grandmother had given me."

"That's great, sweetheart. Did they return anything else?"

"That was the only thing that the security guard said had been delivered. I told him just to lock it up in the manager's office, and I'd get it when I get there."

"Speaking of work, how's it going?" Marie had only been at the new clinic in Boston for a couple of weeks, and while she'd tried to keep her comments positive, he could hear the strain in her voice when they spoke on the phone. And when she'd visited last weekend, she'd mentioned her disappointment in the job while admitting it was too early to truly see if it was a good fit.

Her sigh spoke volumes. "It's fine."

"Babe."

He heard a slight huff. "How do you make one word mean so many different things?" she asked. "Depending on how you say it, it can mean *you need to tell me more*, or *I don't believe you*, or *are you serious*, or *let's hop in bed and rock each other's worlds.*"

Belting out a laugh, he caught the eye of the other Keepers in the room and dropped his chin to focus on just her words. "So, which one did I mean?"

"You don't believe me when I say my job is fine."

"That's because *fine* is a chicken-shit description. No woman is fine when they say they're fine."

"You did not just classify me with such a sexist comment!"

"Babe—"

"Oh, no, now you're going to growl *babe* when you mean *seriously?*"

He took a deep breath and let it out slowly, ignoring the chuckles from several of the others around him as well as Babs walking by, patting his arm and whispering, "Chill, man."

Starting over, he said, "Sweetheart, honest to God, I'm not trying to piss you off, but it seems like you're pissed already and not about me."

A few seconds of silence descended, and he wondered if he needed to apologize, make an impromptu trip to Boston, or just stay quiet and see what she needed to get off her chest.

She finally sighed. "You're right. Work isn't fine. But I've only been on the job for a couple of weeks so I haven't given it a chance."

"Can you identify what's wrong?"

"The clinic has a stellar reputation but it's so corporate. It's like the director is more concerned with everyone's reports and expenses being filed on time than actually spending time with patients. He's also pushing volume. Quantity over quality. If we can hand a parent a list of exercises and show them once what to do, then he's satisfied. I'm used to being able to take time with the kids I work with, making sure they're doing things right and looking at the whole person."

"I can't imagine you're the only one that feels that way."

"The other doctors and therapists seem to fall into two camps. Either they feel the same way I do, or they love paper-pushing more than hands-on therapy. But before you suggest I talk to him, I can let you know that's been tried by others. He's definitely a my-way-or-the-highway kind of director."

"What do you think you should do?"

She sighed heavily, and he wished they were together having this conversation so that he could pull her into his arms. He longed to offer her comfort but wanted to connect with her fully when they talked.

"I don't know, but I'm really looking forward to your visit next weekend. Until then, I'll just suck it up and see if I can figure out how to make sure the patients get what they need from me."

"I'll head home in about an hour. Once you get home, have a glass of wine, and we'll talk again. And maybe I can say *babe* in the way that says let's rock our world."

"Oh, you're on!" she replied, her voice immediately brighter.

"Don't forget to get your toiletry bag from the manager's office," he reminded.

"I'm just walking in now. Let me grab it, and I'll call you later."

Laughing, he said goodbye and disconnected. Turning around, the smile left his face as soon as he saw Mace's expression as he stalked into the room. The others noticed as well and everyone's attention was riveted on their boss' tight jaw and flashing eyes.

"Just got off the phone with my contact in the

RCMP." Mace waved his hand toward the main conference table, and everyone quickly sat. He pinned Bray with a look that Bray could not begin to interpret. "Many of the bodies they recovered from the train wreck were identifiable. There were a few that they took DNA samples from to make sure they were identified correctly. I know you said Anthony Robbins was mostly trapped under the train. There were also a few of the staff that need to be identified by DNA as well. They fast-tracked those results, but no positive ID yet. They hope to have the initial results very soon." Mace grimaced and held Bray's gaze. "But there's more, and you're not going to like it."

Bray felt the room crackle with frustration and anticipation as they waited for Mace to continue.

"There is no Gregory Manitov. At least, not anymore." No one spoke, and Mace held Bray's gaze. "The man you knew as Gregory Manitov was undercover with the Mounties. As soon as the accident occurred and he went silent, all information about him was deleted."

Josh leaned back in his chair heavily. "I can't believe they were able to keep me from digging that information out!"

Mace looked over at Josh and said, "Don't worry about it. We can hack into most things, but there are always some things that'll be out of our reach, at least for a little while. And this was one of them. His real name was Roberto Evanitch. He was on the trail of stolen electronic munition equipment."

Shaking his head, Bray was still trying to wrap his

mind around everything. "So the *deal* that Marie and I watched happen in Banff was him at work in his undercover capacity? Making a payment and receiving stolen munition equipment?"

"That would be my guess," Mace said.

"So, where is he? Why don't the Mounties know where the fuck their undercover man is?"

Mace growled, "No clue or they're not saying."

"Fucking hell, can this get any more complicated?" Bray barked just as his phone rang again. Looking down at the caller ID, he said, "It's Marie."

Mace nodded. "Take it."

"Hey, ba—"

"Bray!"

Her screech set his teeth on edge, sending his heart rate rocketing. "Marie? What's wrong?" Barely aware of the other Keepers around him, he grasped the phone tightly.

"My bag! It's not just my things!"

"Wait, putting you on speaker for the others." He hit the button and then said, "What else is in your bag?"

"It's got my medicine and other items, but there are some of those wireless explosive electronics we found in that other bag! What are they doing here? Who put them here?"

"Shit, I don't know, but don't touch anything! Where are you?"

"I'm in my apartment. I came here first and then opened the bag," she said, her voice shaky.

"Take a picture and send it," John said. Looking at Bray, he said, "Let's find out what we're dealing with."

"Marie, John says to take a picture and send it to me."

"Okay… um… hang on."

The phone was silent for a moment other than a few mumbled curses coming from Marie before a photograph came through to Bray's phone. He sent it to Josh to put on the large screen for John to look at while he got back with Marie.

"Babe, leave the bag where it is right now." Turning to John, he watched as John nodded.

"It's the same as what was in the bag we turned over to the Canadian authorities," John confirmed. "Whoever had these must have slipped a few into her bag, either by mistake or to make sure they got to their destination."

"Bray, what do I do?" she asked, her pitch rising with each word.

"Stay in your apartment, locked in. No one comes in or out. Let the security guard downstairs know I'm on my way." She started to protest but he cut her off. "Babe, not up for discussion." He shot a look toward Mace, who nodded.

"I'll fly you," Drew said, already standing.

"I'm in, too," John added.

"Babe, I'm flying in and should be there in a little over an hour."

―――――――

Drew and John waited in the lobby, telling Bray to go to Marie first. He eschewed the elevator and took the stairs to the third floor. Once there, he walked down the quiet, carpeted hall until he came to her door. Surprised when the door opened an inch with just the force of his light knock, unease snaked through him at her lack of security, considering the sound of her voice when she'd called after discovering what was in her case.

Reaching his hand in his pocket, he pressed a code into his phone, then pulled out his weapon, pushing the door open a little more.

"Come in, Mr. Bray."

At the sound of a man's voice and Marie's whimper, he stepped inside the doorway with his weapon drawn. His gaze landed on Marie standing in the middle of the living room, eyes wide in her pale face, her hands lifted slightly to her side.

Behind her, with a gun fitted with a silencer held to her head, was a man. Heart pounding, his chest squeezed as he stared at a ghost. Locking down his emotions, he shifted his gaze to Marie, offering a small chin lift. "Babe, you okay?"

Her body shook as terror filled her eyes. "I'm sorry," she whispered.

"You're not the one holding a gun, sweetheart. You've got nothing to be sorry for. As far as I can tell, it's that piece of shit behind you that's the problem."

"Considering my gun is currently pressed against your sweetheart's head, I'd advise you to lower your weapon, Mr. Bray," Anthony Robbins said.

Bray ran his tongue over his bottom lip before inclining his head slightly and dropping his hand while keeping his gun ready.

"I'm not a fool, so don't treat me like one. Lay your weapon down on the table."

He walked to the table nearby, continuing to face Marie and Anthony, then set his gun down. Ignoring Anthony, he walked forward, stopping several feet away from Marie, forcing his facial muscles to ease as he kept his breathing slow. Her gaze latched onto his, seeming to take in his stance and mimic his breathing. Looking past her shoulder to Anthony, he said, "Let her sit down. If you want to keep the gun on me, then go ahead, but let her sit down."

"I quite agree, Mr. Bray." He nudged Marie with his gun.

As though her legs wouldn't move, she remained frozen in place. Bray reached out and took her hand, finding her fingers icy cold. Without saying a word, he encouraged her to sit down in the closest chair. Anthony moved along, his gun still trained on her.

As much as Bray wanted to wrap his arm around her and offer her comfort and warmth, he needed his arms and legs free to move quickly. She shifted slightly, staying close but dropping his hand. He had no idea if she understood what he was trying to do, but she gave him what he needed.

Anthony remained next to Marie, waving his gun. "Step back, Mr. Bray."

Bray stepped back, shifting slightly so he could keep Marie, Anthony, and the front door in sight. He observed the toiletry bag on the coffee table. Holding Anthony's gaze, he said, "I have to admit, I'm impressed. You had a fuck of a lot to plan and a fuck of a lot that had to go just right for your plan to work."

Anthony laughed and nodded. "The planning wasn't as hard as I thought it was going to be. The timing?" He shrugged and continued to nod. "That caused me the most angst, but even that worked out impeccably. The only thing I hadn't counted on was survivors. If you two had stayed in the observation car with Theodore, you would've been killed as well, and things would've been easier."

A slight gasp sounded from Marie and she twisted her head around to stare open-mouthed at him. "You killed your cousin? You planned on killing your cousin all along?"

Anthony's hand that wasn't holding the gun lifted and waved it dismissively. "My cousin was naïve. He had expensive tastes, big dreams, and thought that if we worked hard, we would reap the benefits. But I handled the money. We would never make the kind of money we both wanted with our little company." He sighed. "I had hoped at one time that the venture might work for both of us but had to abandon that notion. If I thought he would have gone along with all my plans, I would've gladly considered involving him. But I knew he never would, and to be honest, I would never have completely trusted him to not have a fit of guilt and bring the entire plan to a halt."

"You killed Carlie and Frank!" she added, her voice still shaky but gaining strength.

"Ah, young love... it was the death of them," he said, chuckling. "I hadn't counted on them having a rendezvous on the deck at the back of the train. Carlie caught me by surprise, but she had no suspicions other than I was just getting a breath of fresh air. I couldn't let her go back inside and alert anyone, so snapping her neck solved that problem. Of course, I realized that Frank would be coming, and I was ready for him." He pinned them both with a calculating stare. "I'd hoped their bodies would be found and thought to have just been slung from the back deck. I didn't count on you two investigating."

"And you obviously killed Gregory," Bray said, his words harsh.

At that, Marie startled. "I never thought about that," she mumbled under her breath, her voice shaky.

"Ah, yes, the intrepid undercover agent. He was grossly underprepared. He was supposedly going to be buying stolen electronic parts for munitions, and then he and I would make a deal. I had him pegged from the beginning."

"You planned on killing him ahead of time," Bray prompted.

"It was so easy to set him up. I simply reminded him that it would look bad for us to be chummy. So, we had arranged for him to avoid all of us the day we were going over the gorges. I sent him a text to meet me in the lounge, supposedly for us to talk." A little smile slipped over Anthony's face. "It was truly effortless."

"You had to make sure he was dead but wanted everyone to think it was you," Bray continued.

Anthony laughed as he nodded. "It was so hard to put my expensive shoes on that lowlife agent. But when

I killed him, I made sure to obliterate his body enough that the investigators would think it was me and assume he'd gone rogue."

"That might've worked except they've done DNA testing." For the first time since entering the apartment, Bray noted Anthony's eyes widen in surprise. "Oh, yes, the Canadian Feds know that Gregory was killed in the wreckage, and you're the one at large." Nodding toward the bag on the coffee table, he said, "Seems like the agent was better than you expected. After all, he stashed some of the stolen explosive parts in Marie's bag after making the sale with you. You got the money, and you got the bag from him, but you realized you didn't have all the items."

"After I set the explosives on the train, I saw him coming out of Dr. Brighton's room, and I knew—just *knew*—he had something he was hiding. But he didn't see me, so it was easy to draw him toward the empty lounge car before killing him. But first, I managed to get him to tell me what he was doing in her room. By the time I killed him in a way that would make him unrecognizable and switched shoes, I had just enough time to get to the back of the sleeper car and search her cabin before the explosion. Unfortunately, I ran out of time before checking your bathroom. I had planned on going back to see if I could find them, but…"

"Instead, you saw us on the tracks and knew you hadn't managed to kill everyone."

"Oh, Mr. Bray, you have the whole of it. I should be glad that you weren't on the case instead of Gregory."

Marie glanced to the side where Anthony was standing. She gave her attention back to Bray, but her normally expressive face was blank. The muscle in his jaw ticked, and he hated she had to go through more trauma because of this prick.

Anthony looked at his watch, a bored expression on his face. "All good things must come to an end, and I need to meet with my buyer, who is waiting for these last items."

As Anthony leaned forward to grab the case off the coffee table, Marie held Bray's gaze, and to his amazement, her lips curved slightly… and he offered a barely perceptible nod.

27

Marie's body had been strung tight, not knowing what Anthony was doing behind her. She'd sat, barely breathing as she'd listened to his impassioned explanation of planning the deaths of so many for financial gain, like a Hollywood screenplay that most would consider to be so fantastical it would never be real.

Bray hadn't moved, and yet, she'd been aware of minuscule changes... his breathing slowing, his muscles tensing, energy flowing from him. Afraid to even twitch, she'd stayed perfectly still while trying to match her breathing to his. Slow and even, barely noticeable.

Finally, she'd glanced to the side and realized how close Anthony was standing just behind her. His crotch was practically at her shoulder. Shifting her gaze back to Bray, a crazy thought popped into her mind. She had no way to communicate anything to him, but he lifted his chin in a tiny nod.

"Well, boys, what took you so long?" Bray asked, looking toward the door.

Anthony threw his head back and laughed. "Oh, my God, Mr. Bray. I thought you were smarter, but you're really just as cartoonish as Gregory was."

"Hell, there's only one!" came a voice from the door.

Marie later wished she'd had a camera to record what happened because it occurred so quickly. When Anthony jumped at the voice coming from the door, she whirled around with her elbow raised, hitting him in the crotch just as Bray leaped forward, his body crashing into Anthony's. She fell to the side to get out of the way, landing on the floor behind the coffee table. By the time she peeked over the top of the table, Drew and John, both with weapons drawn, were standing inside the apartment as Bray pressed a writhing, groaning Anthony to the floor. Tossing Anthony's weapon toward the other Keepers, Bray held his hand out for the zip ties Drew gave him and quickly had Anthony's wrists secured behind him.

Bray looked over at her, his gaze scanning her face. "Babe? You okay?"

She nodded, her head moving in fast jerks. "Yeah. You?"

He smiled, and her heart stuttered. Blowing out a breath as he lifted Anthony to his feet before shoving him toward Drew, he turned and immediately pulled her into his arms. With one hand holding the back of her head and his other arm banded around her middle, he held her close. She breathed him in, loving the feel of him in her arms and his steady heartbeat against her cheek. He pressed his lips to the top of her head before he lifted, and she missed his touch.

"You get all that?" he asked.

She leaned back to ask what he meant but he was staring at the others.

"Yeah. FBI is on their way. Should be here in just a moment," Drew said. "Mace called just before you pressed the emergency signal. The DNA came in and proved that the body with Anthony's shoes was Gregory, and that meant that this piece of shit here was the only one unaccounted for."

"These are part of the same lot of explosive electronics," John confirmed, handling the bag carefully. He turned at the noise and stepped back as the room soon filled with more men and women in suits and others in jackets with ATF, FBI, BFD, and BPD on the back. With the FBI in charge, it didn't take long to determine which woman was leading the investigation as she directed the others. She was soon on the phone, then walked over to Marie with her hand extended.

"Dr. Brighton? Your brother wants to talk to you."

Her chin jerked back as she accepted the proffered phone. "Cory?"

"Sis! Are you all right?"

"Yes, yes, I'm fine. Bray got here, and the other Keepers, and they took care of Anthony. It's over, Cory. I'm good." Bray's arm banded tighter around her waist. Gathering strength from him, she repeated, "I'm good."

Later, being interviewed by the lead FBI agent, she grimaced when admitting she'd opened the door to Anthony without checking first. "I'd put Bray on the visitor's list. It never dawned on me that someone else would come up."

"We will be talking to security," the agent said, her words clipped.

Marie pressed her lips together, not envying the security guard having the agent questioning him. Soon, the apartment emptied, leaving her with the Keepers.

Drew walked over first, bending to kiss her forehead. "You gotta come back to Maine soon, darlin'. Knew you'd fit right in and today just proves it. Can't wait to tell Babs about your elbow to the crotch maneuver." Chuckling as the heat hit her cheeks and she rolled her eyes, he moved over to clasp hands with Bray.

John hung back until Drew moved toward the door before he approached. "Gotta tell you, Marie, the way these guys operate is still a little new to me, but from what I can see, Drew's right. You need to come back soon. I know Lucy would love to have more time with you." With a hug, he joined Drew at the door where they pow-wowed with Bray before leaving.

Bray finally closed the door and turned, his gaze finding hers. The apartment was now empty, strangely quiet, and she stayed rooted to the floor, her chest heaving as he filled her sight.

"Babe," he rumbled, taking a step forward.

A bubble of laughter slipped out as she flew as fast as she could across the room. He locked his body tight in anticipation, and she didn't stop until landing in his arms. His body caught hers easily, not even rocking back a little. Holding her tight, she looked up and grinned. "You said *babe*, but I knew you really meant *come here.*"

Now it was his turn to laugh. She pressed her face

into his neck, breathed him in, and slowly, their mirth ended. Sighing, she whispered, "I can't believe he killed all those people just to get away with his crime."

"If the crime had been traced back to him, he hoped the explosion on the train and his faked death would keep anyone from trying to find him, giving him time to get his money and end up on an island somewhere. He was always going to make it look like his contact was him, and since Gregory showed his hand, he was the perfect one for Anthony to kill. Two birds with one stone."

Suddenly exhausted, she gave her weight to Bray, who easily took it. He nuzzled her hair, and she closed her eyes, wanting to memorize everything about this moment. His strong arms around her, offering the feeling that he'd move mountains for her. His broad chest with his heartbeat pounding against her ear, knowing that their hearts beat together. The light kisses he pressed against the top of her head, something no man had ever done other than her father. Emotions swirled, and she sucked in a deep breath as her heart squeezed.

"Babe."

The word rumbled from deep in his chest and she grinned, loving the feel of it against her cheek. Leaning back, she peered up and cocked her head to the side in question. "And what does that *babe* mean? I'm not sure I've perfected my man-speak understanding."

He chuckled, and again, she felt it roll from his chest to hers.

"What are you thinking?" he clarified.

She pressed her lips together for a moment, wondering how honest he wanted her to be. But as his intense gaze penetrated, she knew she could not give him any less than her total honesty. No matter what came afterward, she had to lay it on the line.

Swallowing deeply, she began, "I'm standing in an apartment that isn't mine, in a city that doesn't feel like home, having come from a job that isn't professionally satisfying, living through another traumatic event, this time with a gun held to my head…"

His gaze softened, and he lifted one hand to cup her face.

"But all I can think of is how much I love you, Bray."

His arm squeezed and the blazing intensity returned to his eyes. "Babe," he breathed just before his mouth descended, and he crushed her body to his.

Kissing him, giving her whole body and soul to him, she decided she liked this '*Babe*' the best.

Three Months Later

Bray looked over to the edge of the field and spied Marie talking to David. The Keepers were playing an impromptu soccer game on the grassy lawn near the lighthouse after work. Sylvie had shown up with David, who'd been out there with the rest of them but had run over to greet Marie when she showed up after work.

After Anthony's arrest, Bray had stayed the weekend in Boston, and on Sunday morning, Marie had pronounced as soon as she woke that she was turning in her resignation. "I know it's early, but I'm unhappy at that clinic and want to find a position that suits me better."

He'd suggested she look near where he lived, and she'd smiled before whipping off the T-shirt of his she'd worn to bed. Before he'd known what hit him, she'd pounced. It had been one of the best wake-ups he'd ever had. Now that she'd moved in with him, every morning he woke to her beautiful face was the best.

She'd found a job at a smaller, local hospital, and much to Mace, Sylvie, and David's happiness, she'd taken over David's physical therapy until he was back on the soccer field with his team. And he'd discovered what the other Keepers had been saying all along: it takes a special partner to become part of them, and she'd fit in perfectly with the other Keepers.

The sky was darkening, and it appeared a storm was approaching. Her hair whipped in the wind, but she appeared oblivious as she offered David a high-five. So intent on watching her, Bray missed the ball Babs sent his way.

"Geez, go over and kiss her if your mind isn't in the game!" Babs yelled, laughing as she ran past him.

Bray kept smiling as he nodded, then jogged toward the sideline. "Think I will!" Passing David on the way, he called out, "Take my place," gaining an excited whoop as David joined his dad and the other Keepers on the field.

Not stopping until he reached Marie, he hesitated, but she stepped closer and wrapped her arms around him, her face glowing as she smiled up at him. "Babe, I'm sweaty—"

Laughing, she squeezed him. "Since when have I shied away from sweat? Come on and kiss me."

Not one to turn down her invitation, he bent and took her lips. Soft, sweet, silky. Every kiss jolted him just like the first one they'd shared in the middle of a raging thunderstorm in the Canadian Rockies. Lifting his head before he forgot they had an audience, he let out a long breath. The wind had increased more, and he heard the others yell as the game began to break up. "Remind you of anything?"

"Our first kiss," she said, her green eyes not wavering from his gaze.

"Yeah—"

A clap on the back had him look over as Josh jogged past. "One of my bunker alarms went off, so I gotta get home. See you tomorrow!"

A fat drop of rain fell, and as the others ran for their cars, he and Marie hustled to her vehicle. "I'll catch a ride tomorrow with Josh." He took the keys from her hand, and once she was safely inside, he rounded the front and climbed inside.

It didn't take them long to make it home, and he headed to the shower. Coming out of the bedroom, he found her standing at the open back door, watching the storm unleash the rain as it pounded onto the deck. Thunder rolled across the sky as lightning zinged down from the clouds to the ocean in the distance.

She was quiet, her face pensive as he approached. Stepping behind her, he wrapped his arms around her, pulling her back to his front. He leaned to whisper in her ear, "What are you thinking?"

She didn't speak for a long moment, and just like the time she always gave him, he remained silent until she was ready. Finally, she sucked in a deep breath and let it out slowly. "Life is strange... the winding path that brings us to where we're supposed to be. If I'd never had an accident or become ill, my brother would never have been so protective. There would have been no train trip. No meeting you. No chance to see thunderstorms in a new light."

She leaned her head back against his chest, and he rested his chin on the top of her head. Her delicate scent was mingled with the fresh, salty air and smell of pines rushing inside. He reached inside his pocket and pulled out something he'd bought weeks ago.

Bringing his hand around to the front of her, he held out a diamond ring. "And if we'd never met, I'd never be able to give you this ring along with my heart."

She gasped, one hand covering her mouth as the other grasped his arm tighter. "Oh, Bray." She turned in his arms and tears shone in her eyes as he dropped to a knee.

"Marie, will you marry me?"

Nodding, she swiped at her tears. "Babe..."

He blinked, his brow lowering. "Um... is that a 'yes?'"

She laughed and slid the ring on her finger before bending to clutch his cheeks. Kissing the uncertainty from his face, she mumbled "Yes, yes," against his lips.

He stood, and with the storm's electricity filling the air twirled her around, their kiss sealing their vows.

Don't miss Josh's story... the next Lighthouse Security Investigation novel
Josh

Also, don't miss the Lighthouse Security Investigation crossover novel introducing John (part of The Long Road Home multi-author series)
Home to Stay

Lighthouse Security Investigation
Mace
Rank
Walker
Drew
Blake
Tate
Levi
Clay
Cobb
Bray
Josh

Rafe

Cael

Jaxon

Jayden

Asher

Zeke

Cas

Lighthouse Security Investigations

Mace

Rank

Walker

Drew

Blake

Tate

Levi

Clay

Cobb

Bray

Josh

Long Road Home

Military Romantic Suspense

Home to Stay (a Lighthouse Security Investigation crossover novel)

Hope City (romantic suspense series co-developed

with Kris Michaels

Brock book 1

Sean book 2

Carter book 3

Brody book 4

Kyle book 5

Ryker book 6

Rory book 7

Killian book 8

Torin book 9

Blayze book 10

Griffin book 11

Saints Protection & Investigations

(an elite group, assigned to the cases no one else wants…or can solve)

Serial Love

Healing Love

Revealing Love

Seeing Love

Honor Love

Sacrifice Love

Protecting Love

Remember Love

Discover Love

Surviving Love

Celebrating Love

Searching Love

Follow the exciting spin-off series:

Emma's Home

Laurie's Time

Carol's Image

Fireworks Over Fairfield

Please take the time to leave a review of this book. Feel free to contact me, especially if you enjoyed my book. I love to hear from readers!

Facebook

Email

Website

ABOUT THE AUTHOR

I am an avid reader of romance novels, often joking that I cut my teeth on the historical romances. I have been reading and reviewing for years. In 2013, I finally gave into the characters in my head, screaming for their story to be told. From these musings, my first novel, Emma's Home, The Fairfield Series was born.

I was a high school counselor having worked in education for thirty years. I live in Virginia, having also lived in four states and two foreign countries. I have been married to a wonderfully patient man for forty years. When writing, my dog or one of my four cats can generally be found in the same room if not on my lap.

Please take the time to leave a review of this book. Feel free to contact me, especially if you enjoyed my book. I love to hear from readers!

Facebook

Email

Website

f

Made in the USA
Coppell, TX
19 October 2022

84962777R00194